A

CANDLELIGHT REGENCY SPECIAL

CANDLELIGHT REGENCIES

216 A GIFT OF VIOLETS, Janette Radcliffe
221 THE RAVEN SISTERS, Dorothy Mack
225 THE SUBSTITUTE BRIDE, Dorothy Mack
227 A HEART TOO PROUD, Laura London
232 THE CAPTIVE BRIDE, Lucy Phillips Stewart
239 THE DANCING DOLL, Janet Louise Roberts
240 MY LADY MISCHIEF, Janet Louise Roberts
245 LA CASA DORADO, Janet Louise Roberts
246 THE GOLDEN THISTLE, Janet Louise Roberts
247 THE FIRST WALTZ, Janet Louise Roberts
248 THE CARDROSS LUCK, Janet Louise Roberts
250 THE LADY ROTHSCHILD, Samantha Lester
251 BRIDE OF CHANCE, Lucy Phillips Stewart
253 THE IMPOSSIBLE WARD, Dorothy Mack
255 THE BAD BARON'S DAUGHTER, Laura London
257 THE CHEVALIER'S LADY, Betty Hale Hyatt
263 MOONLIGHT MIST, Laura London
501 THE SCANDALOUS SEASON, Nina Pykare
505 THE BARTERED BRIDE, Anne Hillary
512 BRIDE OF TORQUAY, Lucy Phillips Stewart
515 MANNER OF A LADY, Cilla Whitmore
521 LOVE'S CAPTIVE, Samantha Lester
527 KITTY, Jennie Tremaine
530 BRIDE OF A STRANGER, Lucy Phillips Stewart
537 HIS LORDSHIP'S LANDLADY, Cilla Whitmore
542 DAISY, Jennie Tremaine
543 THE SLEEPING HEIRESS, Phyllis Taylor Pianka
548 LOVE IN DISGUISE, Nina Pykare
549 THE RUNAWAY HEIRESS, Lillian Cheatham
554 A MAN OF HER CHOOSING, Nina Pykare
555 PASSING FANCY, Mary Linn Roby

SENSIBLE CECILY

Margaret Summerville

A CANDLELIGHT REGENCY SPECIAL

Published by
Dell Publishing Co., Inc.
1 Dag Hammarskjold Plaza
New York, New York 10017

Dell ® TM 681510, Dell Publishing Co., Inc.

ISBN: 0-440-17908-4

Printed in the United States of America

First printing—May 1980

CHAPTER 1

"Prunella, aren't you up yet?" said Miss Cecily Camden as she briskly entered her cousin's room. She found Lady Prunella lying in bed, propped up by numerous pillows, her face rapt, deep in the pages of a romantic novel. Her two King Charles spaniels were lying on the bed in their usual position at their mistress's feet. Cecily's entrance had caused the dogs to lazily lift up their heads, but their interest was short-lived and they plopped their heads back down on the bed.

"Oh, Cecily," said Prunella crossly. "Don't interrupt me. Can't you see I'm busy?"

"I do beg your pardon, Cousin," said Miss Camden, who did not sound in the least contrite. "But it is nearly twelve o'clock and you really must have the final fitting of your gown for Lady Halberton's party next week."

Prunella sighed as she reluctantly pushed the book away from her. "Why do I have to have another fitting?" She sulked as she reached over a pillow and grabbed a chocolate from a nearly empty box.

"That's why!" said Cecily in an exasperated voice as she watched Prunella greedily pop the chocolate into her mouth. "Cousin, you must really try to cut down on chocolates. They are very bad for the figure."

Her plump cousin eyed her angrily as she chewed on the candy. "Mama says men admire a full-figured woman." She cast a smug look at Cecily. "You should take heed, Cousin. You are much too thin to find a husband!"

Cecily controlled an urge to laugh as Prunella cast a critical gaze at her. Prunella was eighteen, seven years younger than her cousin. Although she had only been out one season, Prunella had numerous suitors dangling after her, and she thought Cecily was well on her way to spinsterhood.

Cecily Camden had only recently come to live with her cousin and had found life with Prunella severely trying. Miss Camden's parents were both deceased, and Miss Camden had been living with her aged great-aunt Sophie for several years. As this well-beloved aunt had become increasingly infirm, it was decided that Aunt Sophie should go to live with a nephew near Manchester. Miss Camden was invited to come to London to live with Lady Throxton, her mother's sister.

At first Miss Camden had been reluctant to accept Lady Throxton's invitation, preferring to go with Aunt Sophie to Manchester. However, the worthy great-aunt had been certain that the Throckmorton household would be much more suitable for a lively young woman, especially since Miss Camden would have the added advantage of living with her young cousin and the opportunity to move in the best circles.

Cecily was not eager to join the glittering social scene, preferring the quieter life of the country. However, Miss Camden had very little choice in the matter, being without fortune and, therefore, wholly dependent upon the generosity of her relatives.

Lady Throxton had been happy to have Miss Camden join her household and, in fact, had been urging Aunt Sophie to allow her to do so for years. Lady Throxton saw in her niece a sensible young woman who would help restrain her daughter's more frivolous impulses. And being twenty-five years old and without fortune, Miss Camden was on the shelf and no competition for the plump Prunella.

Cecily Camden presented a great contrast to her cousin. While Miss Camden was tall and slim, Lady Prunella was short and inclined to chubbiness. Miss Camden's troublesome red hair plagued her constantly, while Prunella's smooth black tresses easily conformed to the latest mode. There was a slight resemblance in the cousins' faces, but Cecily's eyes were green, set upon a countenance sprinkled with unfashionable and unwelcome freckles, while her cousin's brown eyes highlighted a creamy complexion that was the envy of her friends.

In spite of her excessive plumpness, Lady Prunella made a claim to beauty. Her cousin made no such claim, realizing that figure and face, although presentable, were certainly not quite the thing.

"I know you dislike advice from someone who is on the shelf," said Cecily, a smile quivering on her lips, "but I am thinking of your own good. You know you've had that gown refitted three times already."

Prunella tilted her head in a haughty position. "It isn't my fault the dressmaker is so dreadfully incompetent. I don't know why Mama allows that woman to continue here."

Cecily stifled a giggle and decided to change the subject. "Pray what are you reading, Cousin?"

Lady Prunella's face suddenly lit up. "Oh, Cecily, it is the most exciting book! *The Mysterious Count.*" She shivered. "Parts of it have almost caused me to have a fainting fit!"

"But why do you read a book that has such an effect?"

"Oh, Cecily, you don't understand. It is so very thrilling and so romantic!" cried Prunella.

Cecily smiled at her cousin and shook her head. "Well, it is true that my tastes don't run toward the romantic."

"Alas, I'm afraid you're right," said Prunella in a mournful voice. Lady Prunella would have been surprised to learn that her cousin had already read *The Mysterious Count* and had felt no inclination whatsoever to collapse in a fainting fit. "Oh, I don't want to go to Lady Halberton's party," she said temperamentally. "Nothing exciting ever happens. The same people are always there."

"Why, Pru, I thought you enjoyed parties."

Prunella sighed. "None of the gentlemen I meet are the least bit like the Mysterious Count."

"I should hope not!" said Cecily in mock horror. She looked at her cousin closely. "I thought you liked Lord Higglesby-Smythe. He seems like a very nice gentleman and very well-mannered."

"Nice! Nice is not romantic," Prunella said dejectedly.

"Perhaps, but it often makes for a better marriage. But if you are not interested in someone nice there is always Sir Chesterfield Willoughby."

"Cecily," gasped Lady Prunella, "what a thing to say! But I am tired of you all trying to marry me off to Gerald. I will marry whom I choose!"

"I'm sure you will," said Cecily dryly. "Come now, Cousin, maybe there will be a more romantic character at the party next week."

"Well, perhaps," said Prunella as she reluctantly climbed out of bed. She reached for one of her dogs and patted it affectionately on the head.

"Tutti," she said with exaggerated sweetness, "your aunt Prunella says it's time to get up." The dog lifted its head, irritated at being disturbed. After sniffing the air in a regal manner, it sunk its head back on the bed.

"Oh, my Tutti is being naughty today," chided Prunella. She reached for a chocolate and held it enticingly before the dog's nose. Tutti's mouth snapped open and the dog quickly grabbed the candy and gulped it down.

Prunella squeaked in delight as Cecily looked on disapprovingly. "Prunella, you shouldn't spoil your dogs so much. They are so fat they can hardly even waddle around anymore. They need some exercise."

"Cecily, I know how to take care of my dogs!" snapped Prunella, offended. "Don't I know how to take care of you?" she murmured as she gave both dogs a hug.

CHAPTER 2

Mr. Reginald Stonecipher stretched languidly upon waking. His valet, Hacker, had drawn the blinds and the sunlight streamed in upon Reginald's recumbent form.

"God, Hacker," said Reginald, yawning. "Must you wake me so damned early?"

"It's eleven o'clock, sir," replied Hacker, "and Mr. Crimpson said I was to wake you."

"Blast Jeeters!" cried Reginald harshly.

"Ah ha!" cried a voice from the outer hall, and a dapper young man strode into the room. "Did I hear my name called?"

"Blast you, Jeeters. How can you be so damned cheerful so early?"

"Come, come, old man," laughed the young gentleman. "You can't expect to stay abed all day. Get up and get dressed and quit lying about like some sluggard."

"Oh, dash it, Jeeters," said Reginald Stonecipher, flinging a pillow at his companion's head. Jeeters deftly dodged this soft missile, which hit Hacker squarely in the face.

"Oh God!" cried Jeeters, laughing hysterically.

"Oh, awfully sorry, old fellow," said Reginald, attempting to hold back his own laughter.

Hacker gave his young masters a long-suffering look. He

made no reply, but approached Reginald and handed him a letter on a salver.

"A letter arrived today, sir," he said.

"So I see," said Reginald, taking the letter and examining the seal. "It's from my mother. Well, you may go, Hacker. I'll call you when I need you."

"Very good, sir," replied Hacker and stepped quietly from the room.

"Nothing serious, I hope," said Jeeters as he watched his friend read the letter.

"My mama," said Reginald as he threw down the letter, "will fly into fits over the merest trifle. Listen to this. 'You are urgently needed at home. I must see you about a matter of the gravest importance.' "

"Sounds serious, old boy," said Mr. Crimpson.

"Oh, I doubt that. You know how my mother is. She will get upset over the silliest things."

"Oh, so you take after your mother, Reggie," said Jeeters with a schoolboy giggle.

"Why, Jeeters, when have you ever seen me in a rage?" asked Reginald in mock innocence.

"Well, it was a pretty piece of a tantrum that you threw at Hacker yesterday."

"He deserved it, blast him!" shouted Reginald, remembering his earlier anger. "The man was about to send me into the street without a proper shine to my boots!" Jeeters shook his head at the valet's shocking laxity. The pair of them were dandies of the top order and agreed nothing could be worse than creating a shabby appearance in public.

Drawing Reginald's attention away from the dreadful memory of his boots, Jeeters asked, "Maybe your mama's heard some nasty rumors about her darling boy."

"Lord, no!" said Reginald, highly amused. "Mama never believes any ugly tattle about me. She knows I'm a paragon and can do no wrong."

"Reg, you are a regular rounder!" chortled Jeeters.

The rounder proceeded to put his mother's message at

the back of his mind and would have forgotten it altogether if he hadn't lost every farthing he had the next day in a game of cards. When he realized his allowance would not be forthcoming for another week, Reginald decided it was indeed an opportune time to go home. He would soothe his mother and then put the touch on her for a hefty advance on his allowance.

"I fear I may have to return to the country," said Reginald to Mr. Crimpson upon his return from his ill-fated game of cards.

"Reggie!" exclaimed his friend. "You can't go off now."

"It's not as if I want to, you know," Reginald replied, "but I can't see how to avoid it. I've lost so damned much lately that I have to go back and replenish the old stores. Lucky for me that my mama can never resist her darling boy. Of course, I hope I can avoid my father, but perhaps the old boy will be at his blasted factory and I won't have to endure him this visit. But in any case, I will have to return home."

"Rough business, old chap," said Jeeters sympathetically, "but buck up. You'll be back in no time, and what larks we'll have with Lady Arabella's kind generosity."

Reginald smiled in return and called for Hacker.

"What a dead bore it is to visit the old homestead!" muttered Reginald Stonecipher as he sat contemplating the familiar landscape passing by the coach's window. It was a long, tedious journey, and the sight of his childhood home always depressed him. Most would have found the Stonecipher mansion impressive, but to Reginald it was vastly inferior to the ancient houses of the titled aristocracy, which were filled with family history.

Reginald alighted from the coach and was met by the ever civil Littlejohn. "How was your journey, sir?" said the butler. "I hope it was not too tedious." His voice and face showed no expression at all as he mechanically mouthed the words. Indeed Littlejohn prided himself on keeping his cool formality in the face of such trying obstacles as Master Reginald.

"Not too tedious," mimicked Reginald in the butler's monotone. "Let me tell you, Little J, it was damned tedious."

"How unfortunate, sir," replied the stone-faced butler. He paused for an appropriate moment and then announced, "Lady Arabella is quite anxious to see you, Master Reginald, and is waiting in the downstairs parlor."

"Yes, yes," mumbled Reginald as he abruptly turned his back on the butler and went into the house.

After examining himself carefully in a hallway mirror and making a minor adjustment to his extravagantly arranged neckcloth, Reginald made his way to the parlor. "Mama!" he cried as he gave her a quick embrace. "Your letter had me quite concerned."

"Yes, you were so concerned you waited two days to come," said his mother, curling her lip in what she had always considered an attractive pout. "But I am so glad that you are here."

"Why, Mama," said Reginald in deeply offended tones, "I came as soon as I could manage it." He stuck out his lip in a pout that rivaled even his mother's.

"Oh, Reginald, darling, I didn't mean to be a scold. I know you care about your mama." She looked at him appreciatively and lovingly patted his cheek. "I see you are as handsome as ever."

Although she observed him with the prejudiced eye of a mother, Lady Arabella did, in fact, have a remarkably handsome son. Reginald inherited her fair skin and delicate features. His mischievous blue eyes were offset by curly blond hair carefully styled in the latest Corinthian mode. Many women found his classical appearance quite dashing. Reginald himself thought he rather resembled Apollo, the only redeeming thing he had learned in his ghastly Greek studies at school. *I do cut quite a figure,* he thought every time he glanced in a mirror, which happened to be quite often.

"Now, Mama," he cooed as he propelled her to the nearest chair, "tell me what all this bother is about." He sat down opposite her and waited for what he imagined would be an outpouring of stupid trivialities.

"I don't know how to tell you, Reginald," his mother said, choking back a sob. "It's so horrid!" She sniffed and searched for her handkerchief.

What the deuce could be the matter? thought Reginald impatiently. But remembering his allowance, he controlled his temper and said sweetly, "Mama, you know you can tell me anything. Come now, what's putting you in such a spin?"

Still sniffing, she looked up at him and took a quick breath for support. "You are such a wonderful son," she said, dabbing her eyes, "and I've been such a . . . wet goose of a mother!"

Fearing she was about to go off into hysterics, Reginald grasped her hands and reassured her she was a dashed fine mother.

"Oh, fiddle!" cried Lady Arabella. "And I fear I've been a terrible failure as a wife, too."

"Good heavens, Mama!" exclaimed Reginald. "Surely you and Father haven't been quarreling. Why, you two get on so famously. The last time you had it out was when I left Eton. Of course, Father can be so damned unreasonable at times. But you know how he dotes on you."

Her ladyship shook her head sadly. "It wasn't always easy for Albert and me, you know. After my family acted so stupidly, your father has always felt that I missed my former position."

"And well he should, Mama," said Reginald severely. "For it must have been an awful letdown for you after spending your girlhood among the nobs, being the daughter of a marquis and all, and to then be stuck out here among Father's relatives. I don't know how you bear it."

Lady Arabella frowned at her son. "I won't have you talk that way. I won't listen to your father's nonsense and then hear his son repeat it."

"So that's it," said Reginald, somewhat relieved. "Father's been giving you his old story about how he's caused you to live a life of degradation. I have to admit, Mama, that he's been good about supplying you with everything. I mean he's kept you in the style of a duchess. Although I ain't sure that's enough compensation for forcing you to live out here removed from civilization.

"Of course, he's never too eager to supply his only son and heir with the necessary funds. And I don't know why he shouldn't, him being as rich as Croesus."

"But that's just it, Reginald," said his mother in a tight voice. "I'm afraid we may not be rich for long. It appears we will soon be sunk into the depths of poverty. And Albert would not even tell me. He could not even confide in me. I had to learn it from your aunt Maggie."

"What? Come now, Mama, this is no time for gammoning me."

"I wish I were," she replied sadly.

"What in God's name happened?" he sputtered, his face growing pale. "What could Aunt Maggie have possibly said?"

His mother sighed. "It's your father's business. He never did like to talk to me about it, you know. Or perhaps," she said thoughtfully, "he did talk about it until I told him that I found it all such a bore. Oh, but that doesn't signify. Maggie called on me last week and said that the blacking business was going under."

"Good God, Mama," interrupted Reginald. "And you would believe Aunt Maggie? I surely thought better of you."

"Maggie Skruggs has never been one to make up tales, my dear," said her ladyship. "She hasn't the wit and she heard this from Mr. Skruggs, who should know, I daresay."

"But Mama," said Reginald, "that blacking factory has always cut a capital profit. Been one of Papa's best."

"Yes, but that was before Beau Brummell came into the picture."

With that startling revelation, Reginald let loose a hysterical shriek of laughter. "Mr. Brummell getting his fingers dirtied in the bootblacking business? That's a ripe one! Aunt Maggie must have gotten her gossip mixed up. You can't believe that of Brummell!"

Lady Arabella was unamused by her son's remarks. She replied crossly, "I never said Brummell was getting into the blacking business."

Reginald sat back, puzzled. "But you said he was involved. And I don't think he would be caught dead within sight of that blasted factory."

"It wasn't exactly Mr. Brummell's doing," she explained. "Actually, it was all the fault of his dreadful valet."

Reginald looked at his mother incredulously.

"You see," she continued, "his valet made a claim in some disgusting advertisement in *Town Tattle* that Mr. Brummell refused to use any brand but Bingham's Blacking.

"Bingham's," said Reginald slowly. "By God, Bingham's Blacking!" he repeated loudly, beginning to feel the fog clearing in his brain.

"Yes. After that advertisement appeared, everyone of the least consequence deserted Stonecipher's for Bingham's," said his mother dejectedly. "And your father has been losing an alarming amount of money."

Reginald looked down at his own boots. He remembered seeing the advertisement with the famous man's valet himself. In fact he had instructed Hacker to order him a case of Bingham's immediately. "What is to be done?" Reginald shouted in a distraught tone.

"I don't know, dearest," replied his mother. "But we must not allow your father to find out that I am aware of his financial distress. And you must not plague him with anymore of your debts."

"But Mama," cried Reginald, "I've got some debts that I've got to settle. Some of these merchants are getting damned impudent. What will I do? Oh God. I am on the road to the poorhouse." Reginald hung his head in misery.

"Well, don't this make a sight!" exclaimed a gruff, familiar voice. Reginald glanced up at his father, who had suddenly appeared at the doorway. "Such a pair of sad faces. Whatever is the matter?"

Anyone seeing the two of them together would never have guessed they were father and son. Albert Stonecipher was dark and stocky, with gray peppering his thinning hair. His rugged features contrasted sharply with his son's delicate looks.

"Father," said Reginald coldly. "It is good to see you, sir."

"Yes, I am sure it is," replied his father stiffly. "From the expression on your face, I can see that you are in more trouble."

"Albert!" cried Lady Arabella. "Must you always think the worst of your son?"

"I fear, ma'am, that I have got into that habit."

"Well, you are wrong, Albert, for Reginald is here to see his family."

"Yes sir," replied Reginald. "I suppose you will have a hard time believing it but I do like to see my family once in a while. And I also want to apologize for losing so much money."

"Oh? I have heard that tale before. How many times have you repented of your foolish ways and gone right back to London and spent even more?"

"I'm sure I will not continue to do that," said Reginald.

"But I suppose you are going to ask me for money anyway," continued Mr. Stonecipher.

"No sir, I am not," replied his son bitterly, "for I know it would do me no good. I shall sell my watch and my grandfather's ring and live like one of those poor devils who work in your damned factory."

"Reginald!" cried Lady Arabella, noting with alarm that her husband's face was purpling with rage.

"I must continue, Mama," cried Reginald in his most dramatic fashion. "I am doomed to live in poverty, but I would rather do that than ask you for one farthing! I will leave your house, sir, and never bother you again." Reginald started to walk hotly from the room but turned and said, "I hope you will permit me to write to my mother once in a while."

"Oh, Albert!" cried her ladyship, clutching her husband's arm as her son left the room. "Stop him. Please stop him."

"By God, Arabella," said Mr. Stonecipher, "he's acting like such a fool."

"But you can't let him go. I shall never speak to you again if you do."

"Oh, damn," cried Mr. Stonecipher, extricating himself from his wife's grip and following after his son. He would even try and placate his impossible son for the sake of his wife, whom he loved deeply. After all, she had given up so much to marry him, a man far below her in social station.

"Reginald!" shouted Mr. Stonecipher at his son's retreating form.

Reginald stopped, hoping that his tantrum had served its purpose and that his father would be more reasonable. "Yes, Father."

"Come back to the drawing room. I will not have you walk out on your mother. She is quite upset."

"I'm sorry," said Reginald, realizing that some compromise at this point would be to his advantage.

"And so am I," said his father without much conviction. "And you may have the money, as much as you need, but I warn you, my boy. Do not think that I will continue to throw my hard-earned money at you."

"No sir," replied Reginald, relieved that at least there would be some money coming to him before his father was plunged into ruin.

"Now you go back to your mother," said Mr. Stonecipher. "I have some business I must attend to at the factory." Reginald watched him go and returned to the drawing room.

"Never fear, Mama," he said. "Papa and I have patched things up. All is well between us."

"Thank heaven!" said Lady Arabella.

"But whatever are we to do to avoid ruin?"

"Well, perhaps there is a way," said his mother thoughtfully.

"Good God, Mama," exclaimed Reginald, "don't tell me you have a scheme?"

"Perhaps I do, and it involves you."

"Me?"

"Yes, and it also involves Lady Prunella Throckmorton."

"Prunella Throckmorton!" exclaimed Reginald.

"You know, the daughter of the Earl of Throxton. The Throckmortons are extremely wealthy."

"I am familiar with the Throckmorton name," said Reginald, "but I can't see where I figure in. What role does Lady Prunella play in your scheme?"

His mother smiled. "Reginald, don't be such a ninny! You must marry the girl!"

"What?" shouted Reginald. "For one thing, Mama, although I've never met her, I've heard Prunella is bird-witted. Besides, how would I ever contrive to meet her, let alone marry her? I'm not exactly running in the Throckmortons' circle, if you get my meaning."

"It doesn't signify what the girl is like," said his mother with a shrug. "Once you are married you won't have to see very much of her." A frown creased her forehead. "Getting into society is a problem, but I have considered that and have decided the only way is through my brother."

"Your brother, the Marquis of Ashford?" asked Reginald in amazement.

"That's the only brother I have," she replied. "I know I swore I'd never go crawling back to my family, but circumstances being what they are . . ."

"But Mama, didn't you try to make peace one time with your sister and she—"

"She snubbed me royally!" said Lady Arabella Stonecipher, her face turning an angry red. "Isabelle always was a horrible person. Imagine refusing to receive my call after so many years. My only consolation is that she married that detestable Sir Richard Willoughby. They certainly were well suited for each other, I must say," she added spitefully.

"But forget about that. As I was saying, I think my brother may be of assistance to you. I've heard he is quite a tulip of the ton."

"Lord, yes!" replied her son, well aware of his uncle's standing. "What makes you think he would help his black sheep nephew?"

"Oh, I can't be sure, of course," she said. "When I eloped with your father, my brother was still a schoolboy. No doubt he has few memories of me. Perhaps he would help you if his mind hasn't been poisoned against me by the rest of the family. All he would have to do is introduce you into society. Certainly my brother can do that much for me," she said bitterly.

"Once you are in society you can contrive to meet Prunella Throckmorton. I know you could sweep her off her feet in no time with all your charm."

"From what I've heard of Prunella Throckmorton," said Reginald, "it would take a couple of strong men to sweep her off her feet!"

"Now, Reginald," chuckled his mother. "Don't be making remarks like that about your future bride."

Reginald stood up and walked over to a small mirror above the mantel. After carefully examining his neckcloth, he turned around and faced his mother. "Mama, I will take your advice and go see my uncle, although I shouldn't be surprised if his lordship will have me tossed from his doorstep. But I'll be dashed if I'll marry Prunella Throckmorton! I'd rather be a penniless beggar!"

"Reginald," countered his mother, "would you rather see your parents reduced to poverty?"

"Oh, of course not, Mama," said Reginald, placing his arm around his mother. "If I can contrive it, I will even marry the fair Prunella. After all, I can't think that I have much choice."

CHAPTER
3

Jeeters arrived back at his room at a late hour after spending an amusing evening at the card table. He was met at the door by Hacker, looking more persecuted than usual. Cheerfully tossing his hat and gloves to the valet, he asked, "Why so glum, Hacker?"

The valet grimaced but replied that nothing was amiss. In the next breath he announced that Mr. Stonecipher had returned from the country. "Ah, so that's it, Hacker!" laughed Jeeters, hurrying to the drawing room in search of his friend.

"You scoundrel!" he shouted as he stepped through the doorway. "It's about time you got back here!" Jeeters stopped abruptly as he observed Reginald lying on the couch in a tragic pose.

"Oh, it's you, Jeeters," said Reginald halfheartedly. He flicked his hand across his brow and sighed dramatically. Jeeters stared at his friend and wondered what could have put him in such a state. He was used to Reginald flying off into tantrums, but this seizure of melancholy was something new.

"What's wrong, Reg?" asked Jeeters, studying his friend with a puzzled but sympathetic look.

Reginald moaned and whispered hoarsely, "I'm ruined . . . completely ruined, Jeeters!"

"What!" exclaimed Jeeters in amazement.

"Yes, it's true!" muttered Reginald bitterly. "My papa's business is up the chimney and I'm on the road to the poorhouse. Or even worse," he shuddered, "the army!"

"But what happened?" asked the shocked Jeeters.

Reginald shut his eyes as if it were painful to have them open. "My papa's getting cut out of the bootblack market. The competition from Bingham's is too stiff, especially with Beau Brummell coming out and singing its praises."

"Singing its praises? Brummell?" repeated Jeeters.

"You see," Reginald continued, "Brummell's valet made a claim for an advertisement in *Town Tattle* that Brummell refused to use any other brand. Now absolutely no one is buying Stonecipher's."

"Why, dash it, Reggie, surely a little advertisement wouldn't put your papa's business under!"

Reginald shook his head. "You know Brummell's word is law. What person of any consequence would be caught wearing an inferior brand of bootblack? Would you?"

Jeeters looked down at his own boots. He glanced sheepishly at Reginald. "Well, to tell you the truth, old boy, I did see that advertisement and . . . well, I told Hacker to order me a case of Bingham's." To his surprise Reginald burst out laughing.

"Then we have two cases of the blasted stuff! I told Hacker to order me one, too." The two friends looked at each other and began giggling. However, it wasn't long before Reginald's face turned grim again.

"Oh, Jeeters, what can I do?" he cried in a distracted voice as he began pacing the room with an agitated stride. He stopped suddenly. "You know what my mama suggested? She said I should contrive to marry Prunella Throckmorton. What a notion!" he said disgustedly.

"Prunella Throckmorton," mumbled Jeeters. "Of course, the daughter of the Earl of Throxton. Why Reggie, their fortune is tremendous! What's more, the Thröckmortons are in the uppermost circles."

"I know, I know," said Reginald impatiently. "But there is nothing that would induce me to marry Prunella. I've heard she is bird-witted! No, thank you, I don't wish to be shackled to her for the rest of my days. I'd rather join the infantry!"

"Now don't be unreasonable, Reg," said Jeeters, patting his friend on the shoulder. "Let's consider the advantages Prunella has to offer over getting shot up by one of Napoleon's yokels."

Reginald stuck out his lip in a pout but said nothing.

"Just imagine, Reggie," said Jeeters, "you would be married to an earl's daughter. Why, you'd be a leader of the ton in no time, hobnobbing with Brummell, even the Prince Regent himself!" Although Reginald remained silent, Jeeters noticed his pout was departing and was being replaced by a dreamy look of contemplation.

"Think of it," Jeeters continued enthusiastically, "all that property. Throxton has no male heirs I know of and I've heard the Earl has the finest stables in England. Why, the man is absolutely mad about his horses. And what hunts they have at Throxton Hall!"

Jeeters could tell that Reginald was thawing considerably. "Yes, that's a very pretty picture you paint," Reginald said with a sly smile, "but I notice you are leaving Prunella off the canvas."

"The girl can't be all that bad," chuckled Jeeters. "She probably has a score of good qualities."

Jeeters began mumbling to himself. "Now the problem is, how do you meet the eligible Prunella?" His face took on such a strained expression that Reginald laughed.

"Don't worry your head about that, Jeeters. Mama has the strategy all planned."

"Oh, really?" said Jeeters, much relieved. "Pray, what is it?"

Reginald sat down and stretched out his legs in front of him. "Meeting Prunella would be simple," he said matter-of-factly. "All I would have to do is get invitations to the parties and other social events she attends."

"Oh yes," mocked Jeeters, "that would be dreadfully simple!"

"Of course, I would need a sponsor who would introduce me into society. Someone like my uncle Geoffrey."

"Your uncle Geoffrey?" exclaimed Jeeters. "You don't mean the Marquis of Ashford?"

"Exactly," said Reginald with a grin.

"But I thought you had nothing to do with your mama's relations," said Jeeters. "Or rather," he added wryly, "they would have nothing to do with you!"

"Quite true, quite true," said Reginald, unconcerned. "However, my mama thinks I may be able to soften my uncle. He was quite a young chap when she flew off, you know. I could play up to his sentimental nature, tell him what fond memories of him Mama cherishes."

"Ashford sentimental? That's a good one! Why, I think you'd have better luck trying a different tactic, like blackmail for instance."

"Blackmail?" said Reginald, his eyes widening in interest.

"Yes," said Jeeters, trying to keep back a smile. "You could tell your uncle if he doesn't introduce you into society you'll put him in an advertisement for Stonecipher's blacking!"

This idea started them both giggling again. "Famous, Jeeters," said Reginald, regaining control with some effort. "But if I did I'm afraid my uncle would boot me right out of his house. Imagine trying to blackmail Lord Ashford with bootblacking!"

"Yes," replied Jeeters regretfully. "I suppose it just wouldn't be the thing. From what I hear your uncle is a capital boxer. You certainly wouldn't want to tangle with him."

"No, certainly not," said Reginald, becoming serious.

"But it wouldn't hurt to go see him," said Jeeters encouragingly. "Maybe your mama is right and he would help you. God, if you had Ashford's support, every door in London would be open to you. It's worth a try, old man. After all, what use is it to have highborn relations if you can't take advantage of them?"

"Well, actually I did think I might give my uncle a try. But Prunella . . ." moaned Reginald.

Jeeters laughed. "I tell you she can't be all that bad. Besides, once you marry her you won't have to see that much of her."

"I swear you are in league with my mama!" said Reginald in an exasperated voice.

"Face it, Reggie, we're only thinking of your future. I really can't see that you'd be happy as a penniless soldier, getting blisters and dodging bullets."

"I suppose you're right," sighed Reginald. He appeared to be resolved to a fate that included Prunella Throckmorton.

Now it was Jeeters's turn to pace the room. "I must find out all I can about Prunella. My cousin Sally knows about her. Said she's mad about dogs for one thing. Yes, that's right, owns some wretched little curs. I'll go see Sally and find out more. In the meantime, Reggie, you must go see your uncle."

"Yes," replied Reginald with a slight smile, "perhaps I will still receive the honor of having my uncle throw me out of his house!"

A few days later Lord Ashford did have the inclination to throw his nephew out of his house. However, it wasn't Reginald who was responsible for Ashford's rare display of temper but his other nephew and heir, Sir Chesterfield Willoughby. The uncle and nephew had never been on good terms. Ashford thought Chesterfield a spoiled, willful brat who spent his time gaming and chasing after women. Besides cards and women he also had a passion for horses, and in fact it was this passion that had caused the latest rift with his uncle.

Chesterfield had taken his uncle's best curricle and

matchless grays without permission. Due to his alarming ineptness he had had an accident that nearly lamed one of Ashford's prize horses. His lordship was understandably furious and had reprimanded his nephew severely. Chesterfield had replied insolently, but had wisely retreated before he infuriated his uncle even more.

The day following this mishap, Ashford was preparing to leave for his club when his butler approached him. "My lord, your nephew is here to see you," he said with a faint glimmer of amusement in his eyes.

"What the deuce did he come back here for?" shouted Ashford. "I can't believe his impudence! And what do you find so damned amusing about it, Smithson?" he added crossly.

"It is not your nephew Sir Chesterfield who's here to see your lordship. This young gentleman says he is your nephew Mr. Reginald Stonecipher."

"Reginald?" cried Ashford. "Oh God. You don't mean my sister Arabella's brat?"

"Yes, my lord. I mean," corrected the butler primly, "the young gentleman claims to be Lady Arabella's son."

"What the devil has he come here for?" muttered Ashford. "Well, send him in, Smithson, I'm sure we're both anxious to find out what this business is about."

Smithson appeared offended and quickly exited the room. He soon returned and icily announced Reginald to his uncle.

Lord Ashford stood by the fireplace and lifted his quizzing glass at his nephew. His critical observation did not appear to ruffle Reginald in the least.

"How do you do, sir? I hope you do not think it too much of an impertinence of me to call on you."

What is this young coxcomb up to? thought Ashford as he took in Reginald's clothes. To his amusement he noted that Reginald was the exact opposite of his other nephew. While Chesterfield couldn't care a fig how he looked, Reginald was the ultimate dandy. He wore his neckcloth in an elaborate style that must have taken him half the day to arrange. His hair was carefully brushed in the latest Corinthian mode, and he wore a dazzling blue waistcoat and enough fobs and rings for ten men.

Ashford finally put down his quizzing glass and said with cold civility, "I must admit I am surprised to see you here. What has caused you to seek out an uncle who is a complete stranger to you?"

"Oh, not a complete stranger!" exclaimed Reginald.

"Indeed?" said Lord Ashford, lifting his eyebrows in surprise.

"Well, I mean, sir, that although circumstances have prevented us from knowing each other, my mama has often spoken of you in the warmest terms."

"She has?" questioned Ashford, his lips beginning to twitch in amusement.

"Oh, yes," Reginald replied enthusiastically. "She has many fond memories of you as a little boy."

"How charming," murmured Ashford, remembering how his sister Arabella had always referred to him as a "beastly little toad."

"Of course, my lord," Reginald continued, oblivious to the sarcasm in his uncle's voice, "you are quite well known on your own accord. I . . . I have always admired you very much," he added shyly.

The boy is really a dreadful actor, thought Ashford. "Well, sit down, Nephew, and tell me what brings you here," he said with exaggerated politeness.

Reginald gave him a grateful look and promptly sat down. "Actually, sir, the only purpose for my visit was to meet you. I hope you don't think it too ill-mannered of me. I know of the scandal my mother caused and I am much obliged that your lordship has condescended to see me. Not that my mother don't have her side of it, of course. But I've wanted to meet you, sir. I mean, a man of your standing. I've admired you for the longest time and have just now worked up my courage to call on you."

Ashford gave his nephew a cynical smile. *It can't be money he's after,* he thought. *Stonecipher has earned a considerable fortune with his factories. Unless, of course, he threw the young rascal out.* He sat back and watched Reginald as the youth continued to flatter him with every utterance he made.

"It must be exciting to be in the thick of things," Reginald finally sighed.

"The thick of what?" muttered Ashford, who was rapidly growing bored with his nephew's chatter.

"The ton, of course!" said Reginald. "I mean it must be wonderful to meet all the nobs and fine ladies."

"Indeed," said his lordship, suddenly interested.

"Oh yes, my lord," continued Reginald in his most ingratiating manner. "To meet all the important people and be on the first terms with Lord Alvanley, Mr. Brummell, the Prince Regent, and the Earl of Throxton."

Lord Ashford's lips curled in a faint smile. "Especially Lord Throxton," he said sardonically, thinking how the wealthy Earl was one of the greatest bores, and how Beau Brummell would cringe to hear Throxton named as one of the pink of the ton.

"Oh yes," answered Reginald, "I am especially interested in meeting Lord Throxton and his family."

"His family?" said Ashford. "You mean the Countess and their daughter Prunella?"

Reginald flushed slightly and agreed he'd like to meet them very much.

So that's what this is about, thought Ashford. *The rogue wants into society and the Throckmorton family.* He was just about to get rid of his nephew with a rude remark, when an idea suddenly occurred to him. He smiled benevolently at Reginald, but there was a calculating gleam in his eyes.

"Perhaps, Nephew, you'd care to join me at a party tomorrow night at Lady Halberton's? I'm sure there will be many people there you'd like to meet, including the Throckmortons."

Reginald stared at his uncle in disbelief. He couldn't believe he had accomplished his goal so quickly. It was apparent his uncle was as easily fooled as his mother.

"Oh, really, sir, could I?" cried Reginald. He decided to push his luck. "I wonder, Uncle, would you mind if my friend, Jeet . . er . . James Crimpson, came along. We share rooms here and he is really a decent chap."

"I'm sure he is," murmured Ashford in an ironic voice.

"Oh, capital!" exclaimed Reginald.

Ashford stood up. "Well, then I shall see you and your friend here tomorrow night."

Reginald jumped up to take his leave. "Thank you, Uncle," he said as he warmly grasped Ashford's hand. He paused a moment, hoping he had not stepped over the bounds of propriety. "I do hope I may call you Uncle, my lord."

"Do so by all means," replied his uncle, smiling.

Reginald was escorted out of the room by Smithson, who was having a difficult time hiding his amazement at seeing his employer on such friendly terms with Mr. Reginald Stonecipher. He could only wonder what his lordship was up to. On the other hand, Reginald did not have the slightest doubt about his uncle's motives. He was sure his appearance and charm had won his uncle's approval, and hurried back to tell Jeeters of his success.

That evening Lord Ashford experienced second thoughts about escorting his nephew to Lady Halberton's party. He had made the offer to Reginald on impulse, imagining how angry it would make his sister Isabelle to see him introducing Arabella's brat into society. But on reflection Ashford wondered whether enraging his sister was worth getting saddled with a dandified cub like Reginald.

This unpleasant thought was interrupted by Smithson, who announced that Mr. Stonecipher and a Mr. Crimpson had arrived. "Yes, all right, Smithson. I'll be right down." Expecting to spend a tedious evening, Ashford slowly descended the stairs and hoped that his young charges would do nothing to embarrass him.

However, upon entering the drawing room Ashford feared that his worst suspicions were confirmed. There stood the Messrs. Stonecipher and Crimpson in all their magnificence. Ashford was too well-bred to display the scorn that he felt. He contented himself with peering at them disdainfully through his quizzing glass.

Reginald, not to be outdone by his uncle, quickly pulled out his own quizzing glass and leveled it at Ashford. At first he was startled by his nephew's action, but then his lordship became amused under Reginald's critical gaze. *No doubt the young peacock thinks I'm not quite up to snuff,* he thought to himself.

Indeed, Reginald was thinking precisely along that line. As he studied Ashford's restrained elegance, he wondered why his uncle was considered such a man of fashion. *Why, he ain't got but one fob,* Reginald noted incredulously. *There's nothing that would make him stand out in a crowd.*

While Reginald was pondering his uncle's appearance, Ashford advanced toward him, holding out his hand in a friendly greeting. "Well, Nephew, I see you plan to outshine your uncle at Lady Halberton's tonight."

Reginald turned red and stammered in embarrassment at Ashford's putting into words his very thoughts. "Oh no, Uncle Geoffrey! I could never hold a candle to you." Jeeters, who had been watching the scene a trifle impatiently, cleared his throat.

Remembering his friend, Reginald made a hasty introduction.

"Ah, so you are Mr. Crimpson," observed Ashford in a polite voice.

"Yes, my lord. James Crimpson. Actually, all the fellows call me Jeeters. A dashed silly nickname and I can't remember how I got stuck with it. But I suppose we all get tagged with some ridiculous nickname." He looked at Ashford but received no confirmation of this from his lordship.

Undaunted, Jeeters continued chattering away, saying how smashing it was of Lord Ashford to invite him and Reginald to the party. He then proceeded into a sentimental discourse on his friendship with Reginald and their days at Eton. Reginald gave his friend a threatening look. He had no desire to have his uncle learn the details of his disastrous career at Eton, which had concluded abruptly with his expulsion. However, his worry was unwarranted, since Ashford had been paying little mind to what Jeeters was saying. His lordship was already weary of the young man's conversation and was thinking what an interminable evening it would be. His only satisfaction was that Isabelle would be at the party, but as he looked at Mr. Crimpson, he wondered if that would be sufficient.

CHAPTER 4

The arrival of the Marquis of Ashford and the Messrs. Stonecipher and Crimpson at Lady Halberton's party caused a considerable amount of talk and speculation.

One elderly gentleman was heard to exclaim, "Good God, who are those jessamies Ashford has saddled himself with? I never thought I'd see the day when Ashford would keep such company."

The three gentlemen did make an impressive entrance, and Ashford's tasteful appearance clashed so sharply with his young companions' that the spectacle afforded much amusement to Ashford's modish friends.

The Marquis of Ashford ignored the looks of amusement on his friends' faces. He graciously introduced his young charges to Lady Halberton and then to a number of other guests. Very soon most of the assembly were well aware of the identity of Ashford's dandies.

The Countess of Throxton had watched Ashford's entrance with a puzzled look. "Dear me," she said to her niece and daughter. "Whoever are those two young men who arrived with Ashford? It is surely odd to see him chaperoning some young sparks."

Miss Cecily Camden looked across the room at Lord Ashford. She had seen him once before but had never been introduced. His elegant evening dress suited him perfectly, marking him a man of fashion. He was neither tall nor particularly handsome, but had a kind of commanding presence that was certainly attractive.

"Perhaps they are some type of relatives," suggested Miss Camden.

"I suppose you are right," replied her aunt. "I imagine we will soon have the pleasure of meeting them. Of course, Ashford has never made much of our acquaintance, although his father was an intimate friend of Lord Throxton's."

"His young friends appear to be quite handsome," said Lady Prunella, gazing eagerly in their direction. "Especially the gentleman with the divine blond curls. He is so elegant. Oh, who could he be?"

The lady's curiosity was very soon satisfied, for a short while later Lord Ashford, with his two young friends close on his heels, approached Lady Throxton.

"My dear Lady Throxton," began his lordship with one of his most charming smiles. "I would like to introduce you to two young gentlemen of recent acquaintance."

Lady Throxton peered curiously at Ashford and offered him her hand. "I am quite eager to make their acquaintance, I am sure, but first I must introduce you to my niece, Miss Camden."

"Charmed, ma'am," replied Ashford, graciously taking Miss Camden's hand.

"Miss Camden is the daughter of my late sister," explained Lady Throxton. "Her father was Sir Giles Camden. Poor man, killed during the Peninsular War. But we are so happy to have Cecily living with us now. She is such a dear girl." Cecily, already somewhat disconcerted by Lord Ashford's gaze, blushed at her aunt's words. "And of course, you remember my daughter, Lady Prunella," continued Lady Throxton.

Ashford nodded. "And now, Lady Throxton and ladies," he said, "may I present my nephew Reginald Stonecipher and his friend Mr. Crimpson?"

Reginald and Jeeters accepted the introductions with gracious bows and endeavored to engage the young ladies in small talk while Ashford listened politely to Lady Throxton.

"My dear Ashford," said her ladyship, "I see so little of you." Lord Ashford murmured how much this unfortunate circumstance distressed him.

"Of course, I do see your dear sister Isabelle quite often. She is, as you know, one of my dearest friends. I do hope Isabelle has had the pleasure of meeting her nephew. He is quite a charming young man."

"Yes, he is," smiled Ashford. "Isabelle has not yet met her nephew, but shall soon have that pleasure."

"That is wonderful," replied Lady Throxton, somewhat puzzled at the lack of any family enmity. Lady Throxton knew the story of Arabella Stonecipher well and wondered if Reginald's appearance meant that Arabella had been forgiven.

"And I do wish you would endeavor to see more of us."

"I shall indeed do so, ma'am," replied his lordship. "And how is Lord Throxton? I do not see him in attendance."

"Alas, Ashford," said her ladyship, "my dear husband's gout has been plaguing him."

"I am so sorry."

"But he would so love to see you."

"Then I shall be sure to call on him shortly."

Lady Throxton looked at Ashford in some surprise. "That would be very good of you, sir." She hesitated for a moment and then continued, "Perhaps you might wish to come up to Throxton Hall during the hunting season. We are planning some famous hunts, although I find it difficult to get excited over the hounds myself. More to the young folks' entertainment, I always say."

"That would be delightful," replied Lord Ashford.

Lady Throxton was again puzzled, for Ashford had not been in the habit of accepting her invitations to the country.

"Your sister Isabelle would be there, of course," continued Lady Throxton, "and, of course, her dear son Sir Chesterfield."

Lord Ashford's face remained a mask of charming civility but inside he cursed himself for agreeing to spend time at Throxton Hall in the company of his sister and abominable nephew Chesterfield. Suddenly a thought struck him that removed part of this gloom.

"Could I be so bold, ma'am," he said, "to ask if my nephew Reginald and his friend might be included in your kind invitation? I know it is an impertinence but I have the responsibility of showing them about town for the next few months."

"Dear me, yes," exclaimed her ladyship. "It is always good to have a few extra gentlemen about. They are most certainly welcome."

While Lord Ashford was engaged in conversation with Lady Throxton, his two young charges were engaging in a lively discussion with the young ladies.

"It is a lovely party," began Mr. Crimpson, and Reginald and the two ladies nodded in ready assent. "But I fear I had a frightful time cajoling Mr. Stonecipher into coming."

Lady Prunella cast a startled look at Reginald. "And why pray is that, sir?"

Reginald cast an angry look at his friend and replied, "I'm sure I don't know what you could be referring to."

"Oh dear," said Jeeters Crimpson, undeterred, "I am afraid Mr. Stonecipher won't want me to say it but Reginald did not want to leave his darling spaniel at home tonight. The little fellow was feeling poorly." Reginald looked at his friend in amazement as Mr. Crimpson continued. "And don't look at me that way, Reg. I know the ladies will understand your concern over the dog's health. He's so attached to it, you know."

Reginald had flushed red with embarrassment and could have cheerfully strangled his childhood friend.

Lady Prunella cried, "Oh, Mr. Stonecipher, you must be the kindest man. I can well understand your concern. I have two darling puppies myself and if they were sick I should be absolutely beside myself."

Miss Camden listened to this conversation with considerable amusement and found it hard to refrain from laughing.

"And what type of dog do you own?" asked Prunella.

Jeeters chimed in with the answer. "The little fellow is a King Charles spaniel, is he not, Reginald?"

"Why, yes," stammered Reginald.

"Oh, this is marvelous," gushed Prunella. "My darlings Tutti and Frufru are of the very same breed."

"Wonderful dogs," said Reginald unsteadily.

"Marvelous," agreed Prunella excitedly. "And what is the name of your little darling?"

The two friends replied simultaneously, "Spot." "Blackie."

Prunella looked at them in bewilderment. "Does your dog have two names?"

"Oh no, Lady Prunella," answered Jeeters quickly. "His name is Black Spot actually, and I call him Spot while Reg calls him Blackie."

"It must be rather confusing," contributed Miss Camden, who was still finding it difficult to keep from laughing.

"Oh no, Miss Camden," replied Reginald. "Blackie is a most intelligent animal."

"Oh, I would dearly love to see him," said Prunella.

"Well, perhaps you will, ma'am," said Jeeters. "Reginald and I often walk dear Spot in the park. Perhaps some happy chance may cause us to find you there some day."

"Why perhaps so," said Prunella eagerly. "I will be walking my little dears there Wednesday. Perhaps we may see you there."

"Perhaps so," answered Reginald.

There was one guest at Lady Halberton's party who had watched the entrance of Lord Ashford with great consternation. Young Lord Higglesby-Smythe had looked at the two young gentlemen in disbelief and had muttered an exasperated "Damn."

Good God, he thought in great distress. *It is Jeeters and Reginald. No doubt returning to plague me.* The Baron looked around the ballroom for a suitable hiding place. His memories of his years at Eton continually resurfaced, and each time he thought of his school days, Lord Higglesby-Smythe experienced a sharp pain in his stomach. Those days had been unbearable for his lordship, since his rotund figure and halting speech had made him the brunt of numerous jokes. The worst of his tormentors had been James Crimpson and Reginald Stonecipher, and one of his lordship's few happy moments at Eton had been when Reginald had been expelled.

Throughout the evening Lord Higglesby-Smythe tried to blend into Lady Halberton's wall, but to his great dismay a familiar, mocking voice called his name.

"I say," cried the voice, "aren't you Lord Higglesby-Smythe? It is famous to meet an old friend."

Lord Higglesby-Smythe's face grew rather gray as he readied himself for the worst.

"It is Crimpson, isn't it?" said his lordship timidly as redheaded Jeeters approached him.

"It's good of you to remember, eh, Reg? And of course you remember Reginald Stonecipher."

Reginald looked at Lord Higglesby-Smythe and smiled, noticing his lordship's discomfiture with some satisfaction.

"I daresay, Higglesby-Smythe," said Reginald, "I am sure you have no trouble remembering us. We had some famous times at school, didn't we?"

"Yes, I'm sure you did," replied Lord Higglesby-Smythe.

Jeeters laughed. "Oh, that's a good one, Higglesby-Smythe, but I'm sure you will forgive those schoolboy pranks."

Higglesby-Smythe hesitated for a moment and then lied. "Oh, dear me, Crimpson. I never give such foolishness a thought."

"That's awfully good of you, Higglesby-Smythe," said Reginald, shaking his hand and smiling. "I hope we can be friends."

Higglesby-Smythe looked at him dubiously but answered politely.

"I certainly hope so. I see you are with Lord Ashford. A wonderful man, I am sure."

"A dashed fine one," said Jeeters. "And Reginald's uncle as a matter of fact."

"Oh," replied Higglesby-Smythe. "I did not know that. You are fortunate to have an uncle like that."

"Oh yes," answered Reginald, preparing to move on, "and it is so great to see you again. Brings back the old school days."

"Yes," answered Lord Higglesby-Smythe, who had often tried unsuccessfully to erase those days from his memory. Lord Higglesby-Smythe sighed in relief as the Messrs. Crimpson and Stonecipher moved on.

The Marquis of Ashford was having an enjoyable time at Lady Halberton's party and he realized this with some surprise. He enjoyed watching his nephew and his red-haired friend and the reactions of various people to them. They were actually a great success, and Ashford's fears that they would disgrace him were entirely groundless.

What amused him most was the reaction of his sister Isabelle, Lady Willoughby, when she learned Reginald's identity. Lord Ashford noted with great satisfaction the expression of disbelief that had come to her face as she talked to Lady Throxton and the look of outrage that replaced the disbelief as she approached her brother.

"And what is this I hear, Geoffrey?" demanded Lady Willoughby. "Have you indeed brought Arabella's son to this affair?"

"I have indeed," answered her brother smugly. "You will enjoy meeting your nephew, Isabelle. He is quite charming and a change from your own Chesterfield."

"I don't know what you could have against my son Chesterfield. You have always disliked him. And now to try and make a fool of him by ignoring him and fussing over Arabella's brat. It's shameful."

"My dear Isabelle," said Lord Ashford, "Chesterfield needs no help from me to appear the fool. He has succeeded extremely well at that object."

Lady Willoughby looked at her brother with an outraged expression, turned abruptly, and stalked off to find more agreeable company.

Miss Cecily Camden had witnessed this unfortunate family scene in spite of her attempts to discreetly retire from the vicinity. Miss Camden had been having a less than enjoyable evening. While her cousin had been besieged by handsome young gentlemen asking her to dance, Miss Camden was scarcely noticed.

To have been completely ignored would have been unfortunate, but Miss Camden could have reconciled herself to it. However, there was one gentleman who seemed fascinated by Miss Camden's charms. That discerning gentleman was James Crimpson.

Mr. Crimpson had been delighted with Miss Camden's appearance and deportment, and had made great efforts to talk to her at every possible opportunity. To Miss Camden's chagrin, Mr. Crimpson did his best to charm her. At first she had been amused but later began to find his attention annoying.

To escape this young gentleman Miss Camden had vanished behind a strategically placed Corinthian column, hoping to remain there until she saw Mr. Crimpson safely engaged elsewhere.

Unfortunately Lord Ashford and his sister had chosen this same pillar as the site for their unfriendly discussion. It was, therefore, impossible for Miss Camden to leave her hiding place without appearing to be some frightful eavesdropper.

After the voices had stopped, Miss Camden felt more secure and moved quietly out from behind the column. Thinking no one had seen her make her move, Miss Camden gave a sigh of relief.

However, her relief was soon checked by a stern voice

behind her. "Really, ma'am," said Lord Ashford icily. "I did not know you were engaged in espionage."

"Oh dear," exclaimed Miss Camden, blushing as red as her hair. "My Lord Ashford, it's not as it appears."

"Indeed?" said his lordship.

"I was not listening to you," began Miss Camden in some confusion. "And well, if I did listen, it was only because I could not help it."

His lordship looked at Miss Camden and for the first time his eyes showed some sign of amusement.

"Do you mean, dear lady, that you cannot help yourself and are somehow compelled to hide yourself and overhear other people's conversations? I am sure it is an unfortunate malady."

Miss Camden was now quite flustered and had difficulty in speaking. "I had no intention of spying on you, my lord," she said finally. "Why, I hardly know you. It is just that I was behind the pillar and you came up and began talking and I couldn't appear without seeming an awful goose and I waited for you to leave and you caught me and I have made an awful mess of it to be sure."

Lord Ashford listened to this confession with increasing humor. "But dear Miss Camden. It is Miss Camden, is it not?" Miss Camden nodded reluctantly. "Why on earth were you located in this curious position?"

"You will think me ridiculous."

"I prefer to think you ridiculous than dishonorable."

"Dishonorable? By my word, sir, there is nothing dishonorable about it! If you must know, I was hiding from a young gentleman who has been plaguing me throughout the evening. And it is all your fault, my lord, for if I am not mistaken it is you who brought Mr. Crimpson to this gathering."

"Yes," replied his lordship, now thoroughly amused. "I am guilty of that. And I can well understand your reason for finding safety behind this pillar. Pray forgive me."

The look of mock dismay on his lordship's face caused Miss Camden to laugh. "I am ridiculous," she said.

"Indeed you are not," returned Lord Ashford, "for I think it very sensible for a young lady to hide from a fellow like Crimpson. You can tell from the color of his hair that he's a dangerous one."

Miss Camden found herself laughing again, for Mr. Crimpson's bright red locks very nearly matched her own.

"Alas, my lord," said Miss Camden, "I fear Mr. Crimpson and I are both equally cursed. I suppose that's why I so fear to be seen with him."

His lordship smiled broadly, but before he could reply he glimpsed a shadowy form behind another column across the ballroom.

"Good God, ma'am," said his lordship, motioning toward the column. "It seems as though someone else is hiding. I had no idea Lady Halberton's establishment contained so many fearful personages. This is absolutely famous. It is so seldom one gets involved in exciting intrigues."

As Miss Camden and Lord Ashford watched, Lord Higglesby-Smythe appeared from the shadows.

"Why, it's Lord Higglesby-Smythe," said Miss Camden. "I had been wondering where he was all evening."

"I had seen that young gentleman talking to my nephew and the fearsome Mr. Crimpson a few moments ago," replied Lord Ashford. "I am sure a conversation with those two formidable gentlemen would unnerve anyone."

Miss Camden laughed. "But my lord," she said, "Lord Higglesby-Smythe is rather shy and never appears to best advantage in large gatherings. If you will excuse me, sir, I will go and talk to him. He looks rather forlorn."

"An admirable thought," cried his lordship, "but please allow me to accompany you." Lord Ashford extended his arm and escorted Miss Camden toward Higglesby-Smythe.

Lord Higglesby-Smythe had had some difficulty in recovering from talking to his old tormentors. His knees had felt rather weak and it had been with great effort that he had conversed with Messrs. Stonecipher and Crimpson. He had been surprised at Mr. Stonecipher's apology but wondered bitterly if Reginald had been using an act of sincerity to put him off guard.

Lord Higglesby-Smythe's thoughts were thus engaged when he saw Miss Camden approaching on the arm of the Marquis of Ashford.

"Lord Higglesby-Smythe," began Miss Camden, noting the bashful look on his lordship's face. "May I present the Marquis of Ashford?"

Higglesby-Smythe looked shyly at Lord Ashford. "It is an honor to meet you, sir," said Lord Higglesby-Smythe with some difficulty.

Noting the young man's discomfort, Lord Ashford shook his hand warmly and said, "I've been wanting to meet you, Higglesby-Smythe. Your father was well acquainted with mine, I know. And I have heard good things of you."

Higglesby-Smythe looked at Ashford in amazement. That such a leader of the ton had condescended to talk to him was remarkable, but to suggest that he heard good things of him?

"I can hardly believe that, sir," stammered Lord Higglesby-Smythe.

"Oh, don't be modest, sir," replied Ashford with his usual charm. "I have heard my nephew Chesterfield tell of your scholarship at Oxford."

It was quite true that Chesterfield had informed his uncle of Higglesby-Smythe's academic accomplishments. However, the subject had come up whenever Chesterfield wished to deride scholarly pursuits as bookish and suited for soft-headed ninnies.

Higglesby-Smythe accepted Lord Ashford's praise although he was somewhat skeptical that Sir Chesterfield Willoughby had been the source of the compliment. Even so Higglesby-Smythe glowed with pride and as he took his leave of Ashford, his confidence was nearly restored and he was able to propel himself into the main group of guests.

Miss Camden looked at the Marquis in admiration. "I have never seen Lord Higglesby-Smythe so pleased. That was very kind of you to compliment him."

"Really, Miss Camden," said his lordship, "I am never kind. In fact I am woefully lacking in virtue."

Miss Camden's eyes sparkled with amusement. "If you would have me believe that, sir, I will not dispute with you. But I fear I have been monopolizing your time. In fact I have seen several worthy matrons glancing in our direction."

"Why, Miss Camden," replied Lord Ashford, "are you ashamed to be seen in my company?"

"Good heavens, sir," replied Miss Camden with a smile. "Being seen here with you has undoubtedly raised my standing immeasurably. It is your standing I am worried about."

"Perhaps you are right," nodded his lordship, glancing around the room. "If I am seen with you I will sink so low that I will be forced to hide behind a column and stay out of sight of polite society."

Miss Camden laughed and looked at him entreatingly. "Pray, sir, do not make me laugh so."

"Forgive me, ma'am," returned Ashford with his usual charming smile. "I do not want to inject levity into this solemn occasion."

"Indeed not, sir," laughed Cecily, who then noticed that her aunt was looking in her direction. "Pray excuse me, sir," she said. "I must rejoin my aunt." She turned and walked toward a group of ladies.

A nice girl, that, thought Ashford as he turned and joined a group of fashionable gentlemen.

The Throckmortons returned home very late from Lady Halberton's party. The young ladies were ushered quickly to bed and Lady Throxton went quietly to her husband's room to see if he was resting comfortably.

Lord Throxton was not yet in bed. He sat in a large chair near the fire, his gouty leg propped up on numerous pillows. Her ladyship was surprised to see her lord still awake and greeted him disapprovingly.

"Heavens, Robert," she said, "you should be sleeping. You need your rest."

"Fiddle!" returned his lordship with a grin. "I ain't an infant." He held out his hand to his wife, who clasped it firmly and leaned over to kiss him on the cheek.

"I worry about you, sir," said her ladyship. "And you do need your rest. Where is Hayes? Why has he allowed you to stay up?"

"By Jove, ma'am," cried his lordship. "I don't have servants telling me when to go to bed. And will you quit this nonsense about me. I want to hear of the party."

"Oh, Robert," said her ladyship, sitting down in a nearby chair. "It was marvelous. Prunella was positively brilliant. She was surrounded by the most charming young gentlemen and was an amazing success."

"That's my girl," said his lordship with great satisfaction. "So Pru had a good time, I'd reckon."

"A wonderful time. I know she'll talk about it for weeks. There were so many eligible young men. It will be difficult for us to choose."

"For us to choose?" repeated his lordship. "Don't forget, dearest Elizabeth, that Prunella ain't one to meekly accept a husband that she don't want."

"Yes," said her ladyship, "and that could well be a problem. I shall have to tread carefully or Prunella may ignore our wishes altogether. In fact, she seemed rather taken with the young Stonecipher."

"Stonecipher?" asked his lordship.

"Reginald Stonecipher. He is Arabella Billington's son. You remember, dearest. She ran off with some person who was engaged in trade or something."

"By Jove!" cried Lord Throxton. "Don't tell me Arabella Billington is back? Is she reconciled with Isabelle? By God, I never thought I'd see those two on speaking terms."

"Goodness no, my dear," replied her ladyship. "Arabella is not back. It is her son and he was with Ashford. I say, it was most peculiar."

"With Ashford? Then has Ashford been reconciled with his sister?"

"It must be so," said Lady Throxton, "but I never thought Ashford the type to take unknown relatives under his wing. But he brought young Stonecipher as well as another young man of undistinguished family. I forget his name but he had the most shocking red hair."

"I must say," ventured his lordship cautiously, "Ashford's showing up with a couple of young 'ens is a bit odd."

"Indeed it is," agreed Lady Throxton. "Especially Arabella's son. And I hope Prunella don't grow too fond of him."

"I don't know," answered Lord Throxton. "If I recall it, that Stonecipher chap was damned rich. Some sort of factories. The boy should have mighty good prospects. No reason to suppose him a fortune hunter."

"That could be," said her ladyship coldly, "but whatever his financial state, his father is a tradesman and he undoubtedly has a score of vulgar relatives. I only hope Prunella will have some sense about her and not discourage dear Gerald."

"I don't know, Liza dear," said his lordship, dubious. "I don't think we ought to rely on Prunella's sense, seeing as she never had much. And after all, Higglesby-Smythe ain't exactly a prince charming."

"That may be, but he is surely the man for Prunella."

"But aren't you forgetting Isabelle's son?" said Lord Throxton. "I thought you'd been considering him."

"Oh, good lord, sir," cried her ladyship. "I only humor Isabelle, for I know how she would love to see that match. But Chesterfield Willoughby. Oh no!" Lady Throxton let out a whoop of laughter.

"Really, Liza," said his lordship disapprovingly. "I know he ain't much but he is the son of your dearest friend."

"That may be," returned Lady Throxton, "but he certainly wouldn't be a brilliant match. Why, his father gambled away most of their fortune. And although he is Ashford's heir, that don't signify because Ashford is not past thirty and bound to have a nursery filled with hearty children."

"Yes, that is true. And did you speak to Ashford? I fear that young fellow ain't at all like his father."

"Yes, I spoke to him and he was perfectly charming. Indeed, he agreed to come to Throxton Hall for the hunts."

"By Jove!" exclaimed Lord Throxton. "That is capital! What hunts we'll have with a man of Ashford's cut. Oh God, will the hunt master be glad to hear it. I must tell Sir Harold." Lord Throxton seemed lost for a moment in his thoughts.

"But he is also bringing Stonecipher and that redheaded boy."

"Eh?" said his lordship, coming out of his reverie. "Stonecipher coming, too?"

"Yes, Arabella's son."

"That is good. Indeed I am eager to get a look at the cub. Oh, we'll have a famous time in the country, I know. I can't imagine why Ashford would agree to come, but perhaps he is finally coming around to his senses."

"That must be it," said her ladyship, nodding. "And now, dearest, you must get to bed. I shall call Hayes and I insist you obey him." Her ladyship did not wait for a reply but swept out of the room.

Although she had gotten to bed at a late hour and had been thoroughly exhausted, Cecily Camden had a great deal of difficulty falling asleep. Try as she would, she could not shake the party from her mind and found herself thinking continually of Geoffrey Billington, Marquis of Ashford.

Her inability to remove his lordship from her thoughts exasperated her. It was ridiculous. She was twenty-five years old and far from being a silly schoolgirl. Yet here she was lying awake at night thinking of a man she had just met.

Good heavens, thought Miss Camden, burying her head in her pillow. *I must be an incredible ninny. To fall victim to Lord Ashford's fatal charm.* She smiled. *To become one of the vast horde of females that is undoubtedly mooning over the dashing Marquis. It is so unbearably absurd.*

After some time Miss Camden was able to fall asleep, but early in the morning she was awakened by a soft whisper.

"Cecily."

"What," cried Miss Camden in confusion.

"It's me, Prunella," came a voice.

"Oh Lord, Pru," cried Cecily, wiping the sleep from her eyes. "What are you doing up? It's not much past dawn."

"Forgive me, Cecily," said Prunella, coming over to her cousin and sitting down on the edge of the bed, "but I have to talk to you."

"Oh, gracious, Prunella," exclaimed Miss Camden, irritated at having her sleep interrupted. "Can't it wait for a while?" Miss Camden yawned. "I am so tired."

"I am sorry, but I really must talk to you."

"All right, Pru," said Miss Camden. "I suppose I must listen, and it is something to see you up this early. I thought you'd sleep until dinner time."

"Oh, Cecily," cried her cousin. "I cannot sleep. I am in love!"

"Oh no," exclaimed Miss Camden. "And who is the object of this devoted attention?"

"Oh, he is the most romantic gentleman I have ever met. He is everything a girl could wish for. Why, he is very much like the Mysterious Count."

"The Mysterious Count?" cried Cecily in alarm, remembering her reading of that all too lurid melodrama. "You can't mean Lord Ashford?"

"Ashford?" replied Lady Prunella in astonishment. "Of course not. How could you think that? Why, Ashford is so old, for one thing. Mama has told me he is nine and twenty! And he is not at all romantic. Oh, perhaps some silly schoolgirls would think he is quite dashing and I suppose he was quite the thing in his younger days."

Cecily looked at her cousin with a mixture of amusement and embarrassment. To have immediately suggested

Ashford's name as soon as Cecily mentioned *The Mysterious Count* was horribly indiscreet. However, last night in her tangled thoughts she had somehow associated Ashford with the fictional Count. Fortunately for Miss Camden, Prunella was too caught up in her own thoughts to pay too much attention to her cousin's response. She continued rapidly. "It is Mr. Reginald Stonecipher I am talking about. He is the most wonderful man. Handsome and kind, and he loves animals. He is so handsome," Prunella paused and added, "like the Mysterious Count."

Cecily struggled to keep from bursting into laughter. It was all too absurd. To compare Reginald Stonecipher's delicate blondness to the fictional count's dark, brooding countenance was ludicrous at best.

"I know he doesn't look like the Count, being blond and all." She hesitated a moment. "Perhaps Ashford is more like the Count in physical appearance, but that don't signify. After all it is the romantic nature that is most important."

"But Pru," cried Miss Camden, still trying to restrain her giggles, "you find Mr. Stonecipher so romantic?"

"Indeed, and did you know that his mother, Lady Arabella Billington, eloped with his father and she was disowned? I heard the story from Cook, who was once in service to the old Marquis."

"Prunella," cried Cecily, "you have been gossiping with the servants? Really, Cousin, that will never do."

"Oh, Cecily, don't be an old stick. It's horribly romantic. I mean, poor Reginald. His mother banished from her family, exiled to some dreadful part of the country.

"At least providence has intervened and made Lord Ashford see the wickedness of his treatment of his sister and nephew. Do you know he had not spoken to his sister in twenty years? What a dreadful man to hold such grudges."

Cecily heard her cousin's comments with great irritation. "Prunella," she said, "I do not feel you are in a position to judge Lord Ashford or his family. You really know so little about it."

"But I do know that I love Mr. Stonecipher," replied Prunella stubbornly, "and that is all I need to know. And I hoped you would understand."

"Oh, Pru," said Cecily, "I don't mean to sound so severe, but I wish you would think things over. You barely know Mr. Stonecipher."

"Oh, Cecily," claimed Prunella, "you are hopeless. You do not understand." Prunella gave her cousin a frustrated look and got up and left the room.

Cecily smiled ruefully. *Silly Pru and her infatuations. But I shall have to be more understanding. After all, I fear I am developing my own silly infatuations.*

CHAPTER 5

"Damn it, Hacker!" cried Reginald Stonecipher, looking at his watch. "Where is that blasted Jeeters?"

Hacker, the long-suffering valet, entered the room reluctantly. "Mr. Crimpson is due to return shortly, sir," he said.

"God, he'd better," said Mr. Stonecipher, irritably tucking his watch into his pocket. Reginald sat down disgustedly and folded his arms.

Fortunately Mr. Stonecipher did not have to remain in this posture long, for his waiting was soon interrupted by Mr. Crimpson's arrival.

"Where have you been, Jeeters?" cried his friend as Mr. Crimpson appeared at the doorway. "Have you forgotten that we were to walk in the park?"

"Indeed, old man, I haven't forgotten," replied Jeeters with a grin. "I am sorry for being late but my errand proved more difficult than I expected."

"What errand?"

"You'll see, Reg," said Jeeters, turning toward the hallway. "Hacker," he called, "you may bring him in now."

"What—" began Reginald with a puzzled look, but before he could continue, Hacker entered the room leading a rather reluctant four-legged creature.

"Oh God!" cried Mr. Stonecipher. "Not a dog!"

"Indeed, a dog," returned Jeeters, taking the leash from Hacker. "A wonderful animal and a worthy representative of its breed."

Reginald stared at the small dog dubiously. "And what breed could that be, Jeeters? That's the sorriest looking animal I have ever seen."

The dog seemed to understand this tactless remark, for it snarled dangerously.

"You must be mad," cried Reginald. "That's nothing but a bloody cur!"

"Really, Reginald," cried Jeeters with a hurt expression. "It is not easy to procure prime specimens on short notice, but I was assured that this is a King Charles spaniel and although of indifferent breeding, a passable animal. And remember, Reginald, how are you to meet Lady Prunella today without your beloved pet?"

"Surely you don't think we can pass this mangy cur as my beloved pet? Why, Prunella Throckmorton will think me a proper gudgeon. I think we had better get rid of this flea-ridden mongrel." He looked scornfully at the little dog. "I don't even know how you can call this creature a dog. More like a spotted rat, I think."

The little dog needed no further provocation but lunged forward and tried to sink his teeth into Reginald's boot.

"God!" cried Reginald, shoving the dog aside with the toe of his boot. "Nasty little brat!"

"Good heavens, Reginald," laughed his friend, picking up the dog. "You must make friends with him. Good old Blackie, or whatever his name is."

"Good lord," cried Reginald, bursting into laughter. "Jeeters, you are the damnedest scoundrel. I could murder you for getting me into this fix. You and your absurd tale of me and my devoted pet. As if I would have something like that hanging about me. And the creature hates me. How do I explain it when my devoted pet attempts to sink its fangs into the ankle of its beloved master?"

"Come on now, old man," said Mr. Crimpson, patting

the little dog soothingly. "Old Blackie just ain't used to you yet. But I'm sure he'll take to you. Come on now, Reg, we've got to be off."

Reginald Stonecipher continued to shake his head as he followed his friend out of their rooms. Midway down the street Jeeters relinquished the dog's leash to his friend, and with some difficulty Reginald was able to propel the temperamental canine toward the park.

"You see, Reginald?" said Mr. Crimpson. "He ain't a bad little dog. Just give him a bit of time. Come on, Blackie."

Reginald looked distastefully at Blackie, who was now walking by his side. Pet and master had developed a mutual dislike for each other and the little dog was behaving sulkily. Suddenly Blackie stopped and sat down on the pavement. "Come on, you little bastard," said Reginald, pulling his leash.

Blackie began to yap noisily and rushed back and forth around Reginald's leg. "What the . . .?" cried Reginald in dismay as the leash became entangled around his feet.

"Oh Lord," cried Jeeters in delight as his friend struggled to disentangle himself. "This is famous!"

"For God's sake, Jeeters. Help me," cried Reginald.

At this unfortunate moment a phaeton came alongside the two gentlemen and Reginald looked up to see the smiling face of his uncle, Lord Ashford.

"Oh no!" muttered Reginald pitifully.

Mr. Crimpson noted his lordship's arrival with nearly as much embarrassment as his friend. "Oh no," gulped Jeeters, kneeling down and grasping the little dog firmly. He disentangled the leash and stood up quickly.

"I am grateful to you, Mr. Crimpson," said his lordship affably, "for rescuing my nephew."

Mr. Crimpson grinned in reply. "It was nothing, my lord," he said. "Blackie has always been a rough one to handle."

Reginald looked blackly at his friend but turned to his uncle. Lord Ashford surveyed the two young gentlemen and their obstinate pet with considerable levity. Noting his nephew's embarrassment, he said graciously, "Yes indeed, those little fellows can be most difficult. But wherever did you get such a beast? Don't tell me it is a new fashion. If so I don't think I care to follow the new mode."

"It's not that, my lord," answered Jeeters mischievously. "But Reginald has been quite devoted to old Blackie since his school days. He refuses to leave him in the country. But perhaps his lordship can convince you that Blackie would be happier amid the rolling meadows."

If Mr. Stonecipher had had a pistol in his hand there would have been a good chance that Mr. Crimpson would not survive the afternoon. However, Mr. Crimpson seemed oblivious to his friend's threatening looks and continued blithely, "Yes, indeed, my lord, your nephew dotes on the dear little fellow."

Lord Ashford noted how the "dear little fellow" growled menacingly at Reginald and wondered what the two dandies were up to. The mystery was quickly cleared up at the approach of two young ladies, one of whom was leading two energetic spaniels.

So that's it, thought his lordship as the ladies approached. *Prunella Throckmorton.*

As Lady Prunella and her cousin neared the gentlemen, Lady Prunella waved eagerly.

"Oh Lord," muttered Reginald.

As the ladies neared, Lord Ashford handed the reins of his phaeton to his groom. "Robbins," he said, "take them around a bit. I don't like to have them standing."

"Yes, my lord," answered the groom as Ashford deftly leaped from the vehicle. The phaeton continued on its way as the two ladies joined the three gentlemen.

Upon seeing Lady Prunella's dogs, Blackie began to bark excitedly and squirm in Mr. Crimpson's arms. Jeeters put him down and he approached Lady Prunella's dogs. For a moment Reginald feared Blackie would attempt to attack one of them, but to his relief the three little animals sniffed each other in an agreeable manner.

"Why, gentlemen," said Lady Prunella. "What a surprise. And Lord Ashford. It is so nice to see you again. And Mr. Stonecipher and Mr. Crimpson."

Each of the gentlemen acknowledged her greeting. After the amenities had been dispensed with, Prunella knelt down and patted Blackie enthusiastically. "Oh, Mr. Stonecipher, he is such a darling. And how my dear girls seem to like him."

Jeeters looked triumphantly at his friend. Mr. Stonecipher looked rather uncomfortable but managed to express his delight with Prunella's charming little pets.

"Oh yes," squealed Prunella, "they are such sweet little things. I am sure that you, Mr. Stonecipher, can well understand my feelings."

Reginald nodded solemnly in assent while Miss Camden watched the conversation with great amusement. Her eyes met Lord Ashford's and the look on his face nearly caused Miss Camden to break out in laughter.

"And which of these delightful creatures," said his lordship to Miss Camden, "belongs to you?"

"Oh, I am afraid to say, my lord," replied Miss Camden with mock seriousness, "that I can claim neither. Lady Prunella is the fortunate mistress of both of the dear animals."

"I have always known that Lady Prunella was a fortunate lady," said his lordship.

"Miss Camden," said Mr. Crimpson, gazing at her devotedly, "I am so glad to see you again."

"Oh, thank you, sir," replied Miss Camden evenly. "I hope you and Mr. Stonecipher are enjoying your walk with Spot."

"Yes indeed, ma'am," beamed Jeeters. But at that moment a large gray tomcat appeared from behind a bush and Blackie lunged suddenly after him, causing Mr. Crimpson to release his leash. Blackie ran after the cat, and Tutti and Frufru, Lady Prunella's dogs, joined in the pursuit. Their sudden action jerked their leashes from their mistress's hand and Prunella's two little darlings sped off down the street.

"Oh no!" cried Prunella in alarm. "They will be killed." Lady Prunella gasped, collapsing in a faint, and Lord Ashford and Miss Camden were barely able to support her. Reginald stared at Prunella in dismay and Ashford shouted brusquely, "Go after the dogs!" Jeeters had already started after the animals and Reginald joined him, cursing his fate and the abominable Blackie.

The two gentlemen and the dogs disappeared around the corner, and Miss Camden tried vainly to bring Prunella out of her fainting fit. Luckily Ashford's phaeton appeared again and Ashford, with his groom's assistance, was able to lift Prunella into the phaeton.

"Come now, Pru," said Miss Camden, patting her cousin's hand. "Please, Prunella, you must come round."

Prunella finally opened her eyes and placed her hand over her eyes. "Oh dear," she moaned.

Lord Ashford looked at Miss Camden sympathetically, thinking how unbearable it must be to live with such a goose. Miss Camden seemed to sense his thoughts and said, "You see, my lord, she is terribly attached to those dogs." He shook his head in disgust.

"I admire your patience, ma'am," he said. "I imagine that it would be best to get Lady Prunella home. I will drive you and Robbins will wait here until my nephew returns."

However, before he could put this admirable plan into action, Reginald Stonecipher appeared at the corner with Prunella's two dogs in tow.

"Pru," cried Miss Camden. "Mr. Stonecipher has retrieved your dogs."

At this information Lady Prunella recovered herself and cried joyfully, "Oh, my little dears!" Aided by Ashford, she hurriedly got down from the phaeton and ran toward Reginald.

Lord Ashford looked up at Miss Camden, who was regarding him with an amused expression.

"Miss Camden," said his lordship seriously, "I do not see how you can live in the same house with that creature and remain sane."

"Really, my lord," said Cecily, "Prunella does have some excellent qualities."

They both looked over at Prunella as she hugged her dogs and gushed uncontrollably at Reginald, who now appeared in her eyes as a gallant knight.

"Oh dear," said Miss Camden, "she does tend to overdo everything."

Lord Ashford looked at Miss Camden and they both began laughing.

"I am afraid, my lord, that Prunella will be unable to understand our levity at such a moment."

"And I am afraid, Miss Camden," returned his lordship, "that Lady Prunella is unable to understand much of anything."

"Really, sir," cried Miss Camden, laughing.

"I will say, ma'am," said his lordship, "that I have never before witnessed such ridiculous folly, and I am astonished that we two sensible people should be a party to it."

"But surely, sir," rejoined Miss Camden, "the rescue of Tutti and Frufru is an exciting event and I am so happy to have witnessed it. Why, I will be the envy of everyone to have been involved in such an adventure. But I do hope it does not end in tragedy." She looked closely at Lord Ashford. "If Mr. Crimpson does not recover dear Spot, Mr. Stonecipher will be inconsolable."

Lord Ashford laughed loudly at this and helped Miss Camden down from the phaeton. Fortunately for Mr. Stonecipher, his friend appeared, looking rather disheveled, with the troublesome Blackie in his arms.

Prunella's joy was then complete and she clapped her hands excitedly. Reginald was easily able to contain his joy and Lady Prunella accepted this as typical masculine restraint. "Oh, this is a happy ending," cried Lady Prunella.

"Yes," said Reginald with less enthusiasm. Jeeters looked down at his mud-spattered boots and pantaloons in disgust, and Reginald was able to obtain some satisfaction from his friend's appearance.

"Now," began his lordship and he and Miss Camden approached the two gentlemen and Lady Prunella, "I suggest that I take the ladies home in my phaeton. If that is agreeable to you gentlemen."

"Of course, sir," said Reginald.

"Then I will help you ladies up," said his lordship, escorting Miss Camden toward his vehicle.

"And dear Mr. Stonecipher," cooed Prunella, "I am eternally in your debt. And I certainly hope you will call on me."

"Certainly, ma'am," said Mr. Stonecipher, taking Prunella's hand and kissing it gallantly. "I would enjoy nothing more." Reginald helped Lady Prunella into his uncle's phaeton and then handed her darling dogs up to her.

"Thank you," said Prunella, gazing adoringly into his eyes. Lord Ashford watched this exchange with some curiosity, murmured a word of farewell to the young gentlemen, and instructed Robbins to drive to the Throckmortons'.

"Well, Jeeters," said Reginald as he watched his uncle's phaeton disappear down the street, "I don't believe I have ever spent a more miserable afternoon. Good God, man. You are a mess and you deserve it too for getting me into this. Lord, I have never met a bigger goose than Prunella. And that accursed dog. Why didn't you let it go? I am sure the most sensible thing to do would be to wring its miserable neck."

"Of all the damned ingratitude," said Jeeters in a rare fit of temper. "I rush all over town for the wretched creature and am spattered by a damned mail coach, nearly run over by some fool's carriage, pelted with stones by some idiot schoolboys, and catch up with the cur and you are the hero, and I have to put up with your ill humor and damned ingratitude. And that ridiculous Prunella is mad for you and not a word of thanks I get." Jeeters glared hotly at his friend. "And I will take your dog, sir, and try to keep him out of your way." Mr. Crimpson turned and started to walk off.

Alarmed, Reginald ran after him and grabbed his arm. "I'm sorry, old boy," cried Reginald. "I'm an ass." Jeeters looked at his friend and his anger left him quickly.

"I will even walk Spotty or whatever his name is home."

"Well, old boy," said Jeeters, handing him Blackie's leash, "I suppose that is punishment enough."

CHAPTER 6

Reginald Stonecipher was making final adjustments to his attire the next morning when Jeeters Crimpson entered his room. Reginald did not turn around but made a face at his friend in the mirror. Jeeters made such a ridiculous face in return that Reginald burst out laughing.

"Well, old boy," said Jeeters, grinning, "what are your plans for today?"

"My plans?" asked Reginald, eyeing his friend suspiciously.

Jeeters walked over to the mirror and fidgeted with his neckcloth. "You know what I mean, Reg. What course of action are you taking today to woo and win the lovely Lady Pru?"

"Blast it, Jeeters! Give me a day's rest, will you? I just saw her yesterday on that damned dog fiasco."

"I wouldn't call it a fiasco, dear boy," replied Mr. Crimpson, who was now concentrating on an unruly lock of hair. "It was quite a smashing success. Lady Pru was in raptures over you as if you were some knight in shining armor."

"Well, then?" said Reginald impatiently.

"Well, the thing is, Reggie, you can't sit back and relax

yet. There's still a lot of work to be done before you get Prunella to the altar."

Reginald groaned and sat down heavily on his bed. "I suppose you have some new plan. I hope to God it don't involve those pug-faced monsters again."

"Rest easy, old friend. Blackie ain't a part of this particular scheme."

His friend sighed and asked apprehensively, "Go ahead then. What is it?"

Mr. Crimpson smiled and said in smug satisfaction, "Almack's."

"Almack's?" replied his confused friend.

"Of course, Reggie. Why, getting an invitation to Almack's would prove you've been accepted into society. And I know the Throckmortons are always appearin' there. Why, it'd be another opportunity for you to see Prunella."

"But . . ." said Reginald hesitantly.

"Just think how impressed the Throckmortons will be when they see you chatting with all those nobs like you was in the pink of the ton."

"That's all very well, Jeeters, but how the devil am I going to get an invitation to Almack's?"

Jeeters Crimpson grinned. "Old Uncle Geoffrey, of course."

"Old Uncle . . . come now, Jeeters, ain't that pressin' it a bit?"

"Well, after all, Reggie, your uncle did invite us to that party the other night. I'll be dashed if I can explain it except that he's a might touched in the head."

"You really think he would get us into Almack's?"

"Oh, I am glad you said *us*," cried Jeeters excitedly.

"But I can't just go out and ask him," said Reginald.

"Certainly not, Reg, you have to be very devious and cunning."

"Hmmm . . . I think this task is more up your line," said his friend.

Jeeters smiled gratefully. "I suppose it is, Reg, but the

old master will give you some lessons. First you have to keep flattering your uncle and soften him up."

"Oh Lord, I can do that all right," muttered Reginald.

Jeeters chuckled and continued. "Then you just give him some hints. Nothing too obvious, you know."

"And what if he don't get the hint?"

"Don't worry about that," said Jeeters with overwhelming confidence. "I can tell his lordship has really taken to you. Actually he seems quite fond of me, too. Of course," he added, "that's no wonder."

Reginald got up and went back to the mirror. He smiled at his reflection. "You know, Jeeters, I think you're right. I'll go over and see Uncle Geoffrey right now. You want to come along?"

"All right, but I can only stay a short while. I have another engagement," he said, smiling mysteriously. The two friends were soon ready and started on their way over to Ashford's house.

Lord Ashford was in his library going over some bills when Smithson approached him and announced that a letter had just arrived. Ashford glanced up questioningly and the butler added, "I believe it is from Lady Throxton."

Ashford uttered an involuntary groan and picked up the small, gilt-trimmed envelope. He quickly read the note, hoping Lord Throxton's gout was still acting up and the hunting party would be called off. However, in the missive Lady Throxton informed him that her husband was in wonderful spirits and quite looking forward to having the son of his old friend at Throxton Hall. She concluded the invitation by saying how pleasant it would be to see Ashford, his charming nephew Reginald, and Mr. Crimpson again.

"Serves me right for wishing the old boy's gout was still plaguing him," muttered Ashford. He disdainfully tossed the invitation away from him. The thought of spending a fortnight at Throxton Hall was a horrible prospect. Ashford remembered his last visit there and what a dreadful bore it had been. Lord Throxton had spent entire evenings raving about the capital hunts he had been on and reminiscing about his days in the military. The old gentleman also had a talent for drawing together people who were as dull as he was.

But the countryside is magnificent for hunts, and I have been wanting to try out my new hunter, thought Ashford, finding a shred of consolation. *Of course, I will have to endure Isabelle and her darling Chesterfield.* However, he decided they would no doubt find the company at Throxton Hall more intolerable than he. *And wait until Isabelle sees what lovesick glances Prunella will be throwing in Reginald's direction,* smiled Ashford, imagining his sister's fury. He shook his head as he considered Prunella's many suitors. Ashford found Prunella dreadfully spoiled, a silly goose of a girl, and he reflected that Miss Camden was very different from her cousin.

Ashford thought Miss Camden an intelligent, sensible young woman with a ready wit. Unlike the score of giggling young maidens and designing mamas he had encountered over the years, Miss Camden was frank and unpretentious. Although she could not be considered a beauty, Lord Ashford could find little fault with her appearance. She was a lady of quality, dressing simply but well.

Miss Camden would have been surprised to know that Lord Ashford found her green eyes and red hair charming. In fact she would have been surprised to learn that he had been thinking of her at all.

Ashford picked up the invitation again and said, "Well, at least Miss Camden will be at Throxton Hall. Perhaps it will not be so dull after all."

At that moment Smithson returned to the room and told his lordship that Messrs. Stonecipher and Crimpson had arrived to pay him a call. Ashford received them, the invitation still in his hand.

After an exchange of pleasantries, his lordship mentioned the invitation and asked if the two gentlemen would care to accompany him to Throxton Hall.

"Oh, famous!" exclaimed Jeeters. He directed a look of triumph at Reginald, who appeared surprised but not overly enthusiastic about the invitation.

"What an absolute lark!" continued Jeeters enthusiastically. "It will be so awfully exciting!"

"I'm certain of that," said Ashford dryly.

"It was capital of Lady Throxton to invite Reg and me," said Jeeters. "Perhaps Lady Prunella had something to do with it. Or," he added slyly, "Miss Camden."

"Miss Camden?" said Lord Ashford, his eyebrows arching in surprise.

Jeeters grinned broadly. "Well, you see, my lord, I think Miss Camden is a bit taken with me."

"Indeed?" said Ashford, staring at him incredulously.

"We do have so much in common, you know," explained Jeeters.

"Obviously," murmured Ashford. Although he knew Miss Camden had far from tender feelings for the young dandy, Ashford was surprised to find himself so provoked by Crimpson. He hoped Miss Camden gave the boastful cub a well deserved set-down.

Although excited about the hunting party invitation, Mr. Crimpson had not forgotten the purpose of their visit. "I say, Lord Ashford," he said in a voice filled with admiration, "that certainly is a dashed fine coat you're wearin'. Reggie always told me you was a leader of fashion. Yes, Reg has always held you in the highest esteem, my lord," said Jeeters, giving his friend a meaningful look.

Instead of taking the hint, Reginald stood in awkward silence. Jeeters, undeterred by his silent friend, continued to lavish praise on Ashford. The Marquis listened to the young man with a distasteful expression on his face. *What is the young rascal toadeating me for now?* he wondered.

As Jeeters chattered on, Reginald finally remembered his reason for visiting his uncle. He had been so preoccupied thinking about the hunting party to Throxton Hall, he had forgotten all about Almack's. Reginald looked guiltily at his friend, who he now perceived was eyeing him with an impatient look.

"Uncle," burst out Reginald suddenly, "that's a dashed fine coat you're wearin'."

Ashford studied his nephew with some surprise. "I believe, nephew," he answered dryly, "that Mr. Crimpson has already commented on my entire wardrobe."

"Yes, I am sorry," grinned Jeeters. "I'm afraid I monopolized the conversation. But I will leave you two now because I must be off to an engagement. A very important engagement," he added, winking.

Before Ashford or Reginald could utter a word, Jeeters retreated from the room.

"I'm sorry too," said Ashford, who felt he had endured both Crimpson and his nephew long enough, "but I also have an engagement at my club."

"Oh, I see," said a downcast Reginald. He was desperately thinking how he could accomplish his mission and blurted out, "Uncle, would it be possible for you to drive me to Hastings Street, since I believe you're going in that direction?"

Ashford answered in some annoyance, "Certainly, Nephew."

Reginald smiled gratefully. At least now he would have some opportunity to bring up the subject of Almack's.

As they set out in Ashford's phaeton, Reginald was quick to admire his uncle's skill with the team and the fine horses he had. He then launched abruptly into some broad hints about Almack's.

"You know, Uncle," he said enviously, "it must be wonderful at Almack's."

"Almack's?" questioned Ashford, glancing at his nephew with surprise. "How did my horses put you in mind of Almack's?"

"Oh, they didn't actually," replied Reginald. "Almack's just seemed to suddenly pop into my head."

"Ah, I see," replied his lordship, smiling. He was now

aware of Reginald's and Crimpson's ulterior motive for visiting him. He had no intention of taking the two dandies to Almack's and was anxious to dampen his nephew's enthusiasm.

"I've always heard so much about Almack's," said Reginald. "Of course," he added in his most pitiful voice, "I've never been there myself." To his dismay his uncle remained silent. "I suppose you go to Almack's quite often?"

"No," replied Ashford in a disinterested voice. "I usually find that assembly a dead bore."

"Oh, certainly not?" cried Reginald. "Why, all the nobs go there and . . . and . . . I would like to see Almack's for myself, Uncle."

"Well, perhaps you shall some day," replied Ashford noncommittally.

Reginald was about to make another remark when his uncle gave an exclamation. Reginald looked ahead and observed a curricle coming around the turn at breakneck speed. Due to its great speed the vehicle was unable to make the turn and, swinging far too wide, crashed into a lamppost.

"The idiot," Ashford muttered contemptuously as he pulled his phaeton over.

The driver of the curricle jumped off the wrecked vehicle and began to curse. "I should've guessed it," said Ashford wearily. "Chesterfield." He got down from his phaeton and ordered his groom to take the reins. Reginald got down and followed his uncle in some bewilderment.

As they approached the scene of the mishap, Reginald got a better glimpse of the driver. He was a burly youth with dark features. His large face was contorted in anger and he was screaming at an unfortunate fellow who appeared to be his groom. As Reginald studied the unkempt driver, he thought, *Lord, don't tell me my uncle knows such an uncouth character.*

"Why, Chesterfield, whatever has happened?" said Ashford, fishing out his quizzing glass and studying the damaged vehicle. At the honeyed voice Chesterfield started and glared maliciously at Ashford.

"Where did you come from?" he asked angrily.

Ashford turned the glass disdainfully toward him. "A more suitable question, Nephew, is where in the deuce were you going?"

Chesterfield scowled.

At the word *nephew* Reginald had gaped in shock. Surely this hulking, mud-splattered person couldn't be related to his uncle.

His lordship, noticing the deepening color in Chesterfield's face, decided it was an opportune time for an introduction.

"Chesterfield, I don't believe you've met your cousin Reginald yet." Reginald, still incredulous, flashed his most charming smile and stuck out his hand.

"How do you do, Cousin?" Chesterfield made no move toward him but merely stared at him with his mouth open. Reginald put down his hand and an angry flush appeared on his face.

"You must try to excuse Chesterfield," Ashford told him. "I'm afraid his manners are shockingly bad."

"My manners, damnation!" snorted Chesterfield, suddenly animated. He pointed a huge finger at Reginald. "I ain't related to that jessamy!"

"Thank God for that," sighed Reginald dramatically. Ashford burst into laughter.

"Come now, Nephew," he said, clapping Chesterfield on the shoulder. "I know you're upset about your little mishap here. Although," he added, "I'd think you'd be used to this sort of thing by now."

Chesterfield angrily shrugged his uncle's hand away from him. "I would be obliged, sir, if you and my . . . cousin left me alone. I am quite capable of handling this myself."

"Yes, I'm sure of that," replied Ashford sarcastically. "As capable as you were of turning that last corner."

Chesterfield glared at his uncle and then at Reginald. "I

can handle this," he said angrily. "As if you'd ever help me," he muttered under his breath.

Ashford answered coldly, "It seems, Chesterfield, you've forgotten how I kept that damned collector fellow from skinning you alive. In fact, I believe you've forgotten quite a few things."

Chesterfield temperamentally kicked his foot against the wrecked curricle. "I ain't forgot. You've always disliked me and now you're parading this coxcomb about trying to humiliate me."

"I doubt very seriously, Chesterfield, that anything could humiliate you."

His nephew grumbled and turned toward his curricle and groom. "Blast you, man, don't just stand there gaping, get some help!" The groom quickly hurried off.

"Come now, Chesterfield," said Ashford. "Despite what you think, I will help you with this."

"Don't bother, Uncle," growled Chesterfield. "I can see you are quite busy." As he said this he looked at Reginald. "I heard you was at Lady Halberton's, Cousin. No doubt I'll be seeing you at Almack's tonight." He smiled contemptuously at his cousin.

Reginald glared angrily at Chesterfield and made no reply. Ashford took his arm and directed him back to the curricle.

"I think we best be going, Reginald. I have no desire to referee a street brawl between my two nephews." As he and Reginald climbed back into the vehicle, Ashford looked back and saw Chesterfield watching him.

"You know, Nephew," he said, turning back to Reginald, "I think I shall go to Almack's tonight. Would you care to accompany me?"

Reginald's face immediately brightened. "Would I! Oh, but . . ."

"Yes?" asked Ashford, taking the ribbons from his groom.

"Well, could James go along too, Uncle?"

"James?" said Ashford, looking puzzled.

"Jeeters . . . Crimpson."

"Oh," said Ashford unenthusiastically. He suddenly smiled. "Certainly, bring Mr. Crimpson along. We wouldn't want to deprive Almack's of that young man's company."

While his friend was securing invitations to Almack's, James Crimpson was on a mission of his own. He was paying a call on the Throckmortons, hoping to further Reginald's cause with Lady Prunella. Mr. Crimpson was sure he could help secure Reginald in that lady's affections. However, he also hoped his visit would help secure himself in Miss Cecily Camden's affections.

When he arrived at the Throckmorton residence, Jeeters was ushered into a large parlor. "Lord, what a place," he said, whistling in admiration. "Old Boy Throxton certainly got left a tidy sum. And to think some day this will belong to Reggie."

As he stood examining an ornate silver vase, Lady Prunella and her mother entered the room. Mr. Crimpson was disappointed by Cecily's absence but smiled charmingly as he took Lady Throxton's hand.

"Mr. Crimpson, how nice it is to see you again," murmured Lady Throxton, studying him curiously. She was wondering why he had come without young Stonecipher. The horrible thought crossed her mind that perhaps the red-haired Crimpson was interested in her daughter. However, when Cecily entered the room, Lady Throxton observed the look that immediately appeared on Jeeters's face. She sighed in relief. *So it's my niece he's interested in.* Although Lady Throxton doubted him suitable for Cecily, she thought her niece could use some male attention.

"Miss Camden," said Mr. Crimpson, hurrying over to her. "How lovely you look."

"Thank you, sir," said Miss Camden, wishing she had gone riding. To her dismay Cecily found her aunt having a hushed conversation with Prunella, leaving her to cope with Mr. Crimpson.

"And how are you today, sir?" she inquired politely. "I hope you have not had to chase any more dogs about town."

"Oh no," grinned Jeeters. "Reggie and I are being careful to keep a firm hold on little Spot."

"I think that's a good idea," smiled Cecily. She looked over at her aunt and cousin and noticed they were now watching her and Mr. Crimpson with interest. "Mr. Crimpson," she said to him, "I think we should join my aunt and Prunella."

"Oh, I suppose so," said Mr. Crimpson, reluctantly following Cecily over to the two ladies.

Lady Throxton perceived the admiring look Mr. Crimpson was giving her niece. *Perhaps the young man wouldn't be unsuitable for Cecily after all,* thought Lady Throxton, determined to find out more about Mr. Crimpson. "Do be seated, sir," she said, motioning Jeeters to the sofa. She sat down next to him and regarded him with a calculating look.

"Well, Mr. Crimpson, for all your heroic efforts on my daughter's behalf I find I know little about you. That must be remedied."

Lady Throxton's declaration would have discomfited most young men in Mr. Crimpson's position, but he merely smiled at her in reply.

"Do you come from a large family, Mr. Crimpson?" inquired Lady Throxton.

"Tolerably large, my lady," replied Jeeters. "I have four sisters and one brother."

"An elder brother?"

"No, Jack's a mere whipster. Yes, Jack is the image of his big brother," said Mr. Crimpson proudly.

Heavens, thought Cecily, amused. *Imagine another James Crimpson loose in the world.*

"And your father?" inquired Lady Throxton curiously. "I don't believe I've ever met him."

"Oh no, ma'am, Papa detests the city. He much prefers

country life." Mr. Crimpson did not elaborate but Lady Throxton shook her head in acknowledgment.

"Just like my dear uncle Godfrey. He always hated London society and much preferred to stay on his country estate all year long. He was so much happier there."

"Yes," said Mr. Crimpson, "that is Papa, all right." He failed to include the information that his father, unlike Uncle Godfrey, was a country parson.

"It appears, Mr. Crimpson, that you do not take after your father," said Miss Camden.

Miss Camden's statement was common knowledge in the Reverend Crimpson's parish. Jeeters had been a constant trial to the devout Reverend Crimpson. While he was growing up, Jeeters was constantly pulling pranks and getting into mischief. His behavior had caused the Reverend Crimpson untold embarrassment, like the time he let a mouse loose among the choir. Although he gave his son numerous lectures, the Reverend Crimpson was not a disciplinarian. He and his wife were both too good-natured and easygoing to control their wayward son.

"I mean, Mr. Crimpson," continued Cecily, smiling at the look of surprise on Jeeters's face, "unlike your father you seem to enjoy city life."

"Oh yes, Miss Camden," replied Jeeters enthusiastically. "That's a fact. I like London awfully well. And I've liked it even better," he added, "since meeting you and your charming family."

"Thank you," replied Cecily sedately. "But I don't think we've heard enough about your charming family. Pray tell us more about them."

"Well, you may be interested in my great-uncle Alistair. He was quite an amazing fellow . . . handsome, charming . . . he was a military man, a hero. . . ."

"Really, Mr. Crimpson?" said Prunella, finally finding something to contribute. "Just like my uncle Giles, Cecily's poor father. He was a hero too, died on the Peninsula."

"I am sorry," said Jeeters. "Miss Camden's father and Uncle Alistair were probably very much alike." He then launched into a long discourse on his great-uncle's military exploits.

Cecily listened to Mr. Crimpson's stories with some amusement. Uncle Alistair indeed sounded like a remarkable man. During his military career he had saved the British empire an untold number of times with his dazzling feats.

"My word, sir," exclaimed Lady Throxton after listening to Mr. Crimpson's glorious accounts of his great-uncle, "you must be very proud of such a man. It is surprising, though," she said, "that I have never heard of him. I must ask Lord Throxton. I'm sure he is familiar with such an illustrious military man."

"Alas, Lady Throxton," said Mr. Crimpson sadly, "poor Uncle Alistair never achieved the fame that was deserved him. He was one of those 'unsung heroes.' "

"That is indeed unfortunate," said Lady Throxton gravely. Cecily suppressed a chuckle and wondered what work of fiction Uncle Alistair came from. *Perhaps he is Mr. Crimpson's original creation,* she thought, smiling. *If so, Mr. Crimpson should take up a writing career.*

"I'm afraid, dear ladies," said Mr. Crimpson, "that I really must be going and see how Mr. Stonecipher and Spot are getting along."

"Oh yes," cried Prunella, "and tell Mr. Stonecipher I am eternally grateful to him."

"Of course," said a beaming Jeeters as he took Prunella's hand.

Lady Throxton instructed Mr. Crimpson to visit them again and he readily agreed to do so. Turning to Cecily, he took her hand. "My dear Miss Camden," he said in a low voice, "I do hope to see you soon." Cecily managed a faint smile and Mr. Crimpson reluctantly left the room.

"He is a most charming young man," observed Lady Throxton, watching her niece.

"Yes, charming," murmured Cecily. "He must take after his great-uncle Alistair."

CHAPTER 7

The Marquis of Ashford detested Almack's and he was fast beginning to detest his nephew Reginald Stonecipher. As to Stonecipher's ever present companion James Crimpson, Lord Ashford had for some time felt a strong aversion to that gentleman. Therefore it was remarkable that his lordship did accompany the two young gentlemen to the exclusive assembly rooms.

Although Lord Ashford viewed a visit to Almack's with little enthusiasm, the Messrs. Stonecipher and Crimpson were greatly excited. To be accepted at Almack's was the key to social success. Admittance to this exclusive society was rigidly controlled by an elite group of its matrons, and no one could hope to succeed in the ton without their approval.

The Marquis of Ashford was, of course, always welcome at the most exclusive gatherings, and his appearance at Almack's was regarded with considerable interest by a number of worthy matrons. "Perhaps," suggested one elderly lady, "the Marquis is looking for a wife."

This suggestion generated a great amount of discussion among the ladies, who began to ponder their own daughters' prospects for ensnaring such a prize. Other ladies, not as optimistic, began to make inquiries as to the standing of the two fine-looking young gentlemen who accompanied Lord Ashford.

His lordship was greeted by several distinguished ladies, and then Ashford greeted his friend George Brummell. The Beau, that great leader of fashion, had been watching Ashford's progress with amusement.

"Geoffrey, old man," said Mr. Brummell, extending his hand. "You are certainly the sensation of the evening."

"Oh God," said his lordship, shaking his friend's hand. "I must have been mad to come here."

"I must say, Geoffrey, I am amazed to see you. You have not graced this elite assembly in ages."

"And I swear, George, I will not do so again. At least I am safe with you. No one would dare approach Mr. Brummell without leave."

"I should hope so," replied the Beau with a faint smile. "But tell me, my dear Geoffrey, are you, indeed, here looking for a wife?"

"Oh God," exclaimed Lord Ashford in horror, "is that what they're saying?"

"But of course. But it is only wishful thinking on their part. A rich, handsome marquis is not a bad connection for even the most discriminating of mamas."

"Oh, blast, George," said Ashford, smiling. "I thought they had given up on me. I shall be forced to retreat to the country to escape all these eligible young ladies and their scheming mamas, for I have as much intention of marrying now as you do."

"I don't know, Geoffrey. You had better marry, you know. Had I an heir like Sir Chesterfield Willoughby I should marry at the first opportunity. But I am told the other gentlemen who accompanied you are also relations, and although I have somehow managed to tolerate Sir Chesterfield, it will be exceedingly difficult to forgive you for introducing two such sparks as relations."

"Oh, please don't connect me with James Crimpson."

"Crimpson?"

"Yes, that one with the red hair. I am guilty of being the uncle of Reginald Stonecipher, the blond one who thinks himself Adonis, but I am happy to say I can claim no blood relationship with James Crimpson."

Mr. Brummell surveyed the two gentlemen through his quizzing glass. "They seem to be enjoying themselves. Isn't that Prunella Throckmorton your nephew is talking to? What a ninny that girl is. Met her last week. Couldn't help it. But who is the other young lady talking to Crimpson? Could be his sister with that red hair."

"Oh, heavens no," exclaimed his lordship, looking in Mr. Crimpson's direction. "Pray, don't thrust such a brother upon Miss Cecily Camden."

"Camden?"

"Yes, daughter of Sir Giles Camden. He was killed on the Peninsula. She's living with her aunt, Lady Throxton."

"The poor girl."

"Indeed, from what I've seen of her cousin, Lady Prunella. And now it appears that Miss Camden must also suffer the attentions of a fellow like Crimpson. Excuse me, George, I must be off to rescue Miss Camden. I feel responsible for Crimpson. After all, I have had the bad taste to foist him on society."

"As long as you do not attempt to foist him on me, Geoffrey," replied Mr. Brummell as Lord Ashford took his leave and hurried toward Miss Camden.

Jeeters Crimpson and Reginald Stonecipher had quickly left Ashford's chaperonage after arriving at Almack's. The Marquis of Ashford was relieved that they were not eager to hang about his coattails and hoped they would conduct themselves well.

Actually, their conduct at Lady Halberton's party had caused his lordship little concern, and Ashford was able to note with satisfaction that both his sister Isabelle and his nephew Chesterfield were in attendance that evening at Almack's. The Messrs. Stonecipher and Crimpson had met a number of well-connected people at Lady Halberton's and they were soon able to recognize a number of those acquaintances and greet them as old friends.

Mr. Crimpson had an extraordinary gift for remembering names and faces and, therefore, was able to charm a number of people. Reginald's good looks and easy manners were two more assets that endeared the pair to several excellent matrons.

While Reginald and Jeeters were hard at work ingratiating themselves in high society, Lord Higglesby-Smythe was doing his best to charm Lady Prunella Throckmorton. The young lady was quite indifferent to his lordship, but looked eagerly about the room for a sign of Reginald Stonecipher.

"I say, Prunella," said Higglesby-Smythe, "I hope you will dance with me tonight."

"Oh, for heaven's sake, Gerald," replied Lady Prunella. "You are always telling me how much you detest dancing."

Lord Higglesby-Smythe colored and looked at his feet. "I don't like it much to be sure, Pru, but I would like to dance with you."

Miss Cecily Camden, who was standing with them, gave her cousin a reproachful look. Prunella ignored her and replied, "Oh, I will dance with you, Gerald, but later. I don't feel like dancing at the moment. Oh, look, Cecily, there's Helena. Helena!" cried Lady Prunella, waving to a blond young lady in a fawn-colored dress.

Miss Helena Chatham approached them, smiling broadly. "Oh, Prunella! I am so glad to see you here, and you, too, Cecily. And how are you, Lord Higglesby-Smythe?"

Lord Higglesby-Smythe acknowledged his greeting without much enthusiasm. He had never liked Helena Chatham. She was Prunella's best friend and inclined to make jokes at Higglesby-Smythe's expense. His lordship suspected that Miss Chatham also discouraged Prunella from taking him seriously.

"Have you seen Mr. Stonecipher yet, Lord Higglesby-Smythe?" asked Miss Chatham.

His lordship looked at her in surprise and replied haltingly, "Stonecipher? Why, no, I haven't."

"I asked because I spoke to Mr. Stonecipher a few minutes ago and he told me that you were such famous friends."

"Were you?" asked Prunella, looking at Lord Higglesby-Smythe for the first time with interest. "Did you know Mr. Stonecipher very well?"

Miss Camden watched Lord Higglesby-Smythe sympathetically as he stammered, ". . . he was at Eton with me."

"Oh yes," chattered Helena. "He said that you were the best of friends. Mr. Crimpson said that the three of you were inseparable."

"But Gerald," protested Prunella, "why didn't you tell me? You never mentioned anyone from school except that tedious Edmond Thornridge. Oh, Helena, you must meet Edmond Thornridge. Such a queer, bookish young man."

Lord Higglesby-Smythe stared glumly at the polished ballroom floor, greatly resenting this reference to his closest friend. He was about to defend Mr. Thornridge when Helena Chatham cried, "Oh, look, Prunella. Here comes Mr. Stonecipher and Mr. Crimpson."

Cecily sighed softly as they approached. *I knew I should have to face them,* she thought as she studied the two young gentlemen.

"Good evening," said Mr. Crimpson with a gracious bow. "Lady Prunella, Miss Camden, and Miss Chatham. It is remarkable to find three such charming ladies in such close proximity."

Miss Chatham and Lady Prunella smiled appreciatively, but Miss Camden looked down at her fan, suppressing an urge to laugh.

"And of course, my dear friend Higglesby-Smythe. How do, old fellow?"

Mr. Crimpson took his lordship's hand and pumped it vigorously. "Oh yes," said Reginald Stonecipher, smiling in a most charming manner and looking exceedingly handsome. "What a joy it is to see you ladies. And, if I may be so bold, you are the three most beautiful ladies in the entire assembly."

Prunella and Helena giggled and Cecily managed a gracious smile.

"And dear Higglesby-Smythe," said Reginald, shaking his lordship's hand. "You are in top form, I see. But it will never do, sir, never do at all."

"What do you mean?" stammered Higglesby-Smythe.

"Why, monopolizing the attentions of these fair ladies, old man," replied Reginald with a mischievous look.

"Indeed, Higglesby-Smythe," added Jeeters, "but then you always were one to interest the ladies."

Higglesby-Smythe reddened in embarrassment and Prunella looked at him in surprise.

"Gerald? Surely, Mr. Crimpson, you are jesting."

"No, indeed, Lady Prunella, but I know you ladies often take to a scholar of his lordship's caliber."

Helena Chatham laughed and Lord Higglesby-Smythe desperately wished he had the power to disappear.

"Gerald," said Prunella, "it seems that I am learning some new facts about your character. I am amazed to find that you and Mr. Stonecipher and Mr. Crimpson were such fast friends."

"Well, not exactly . . ." began Lord Higglesby-Smythe, but Reginald interrupted him.

"We were indeed, Lady Prunella."

"And were you also a friend of Mr. Edmond Thornridge's?" asked Miss Camden, entering into the conversation.

"Thornridge? Oh yes, Miss Camden," replied Jeeters. "Thorny was a dashed fine fellow. A bit bookish, of course, but fine company. The four of us had some splendid times, eh, Higglesby-Smythe?"

His lordship made no reply, thinking how he and Edmond Thornridge had spent much of their time at Eton trying to avoid the Messrs. Stonecipher and Crimpson.

Miss Camden smiled as she attempted to picture the two

outspoken dandies as schoolboys spending time with Higglesby-Smythe and the studious Mr. Thornridge. Realizing his lordship's great discomfort, Cecily kindly changed the topic of discussion. "I hope you gentlemen are enjoying the wonderful weather we are having," she said.

"Oh, indeed," said Jeeters Crimpson. "Today Mr. Stonecipher and I were out riding in the park and Reginald said to me, 'The winsome white clouds, flying so high, are dancing merrily in the azure blue sky.' Poetical, is it not?"

"Oh, Mr. Stonecipher," said Prunella, "are you a poet, too?"

Before he could reply, Mr. Crimpson answered, "He is so modest, but my friend Reginald is a fine poet."

Mr. Stonecipher made what he hoped was a suitably modest acknowledgment of the compliment, and silently hoped his friend would keep his mouth shut.

"Were the clouds waltzing, Mr. Stonecipher?" asked Cecily, gallantly trying to prevent a smile from appearing on her face. Lord Higglesby-Smythe smiled for the first time, but Lady Prunella and Helena waited seriously for Mr. Stonecipher's answer.

Reginald looked at Cecily. "More of a country gig, actually," replied Reginald.

"I shall have to watch the clouds more carefully," murmured Prunella.

"Oh, it was grand though today," continued Jeeters. "The park was filled with flowers and I was riding my prancing stallion."

"Do you ride much, Mr. Crimpson?" asked Helena Chatham, whose main interest in life was her horses.

"All the time," replied Jeeters.

"And do you keep this prancing stallion in town?" asked Miss Camden.

"Yes, of course. Fine horse too. A real beauty."

"I should like to see him, sir," replied Cecily.

"And I would too," said Lady Prunella. "We shall all go riding. That's it. We must all go riding."

"Oh yes," cried Miss Helena Chatham. "Why don't we go tomorrow?"

Miss Camden noticed that Reginald Stonecipher was giving his friend a warning look and Cecily suspected this had something to do with Mr. Crimpson's prancing stallion. But Mr. Crimpson replied, undaunted, "That would be wonderful. It would be such fun. And I'd love you ladies to see Jeremy. That's my horse. He's a rare one, he is."

"He is indeed a rare one," replied Reginald, eyeing his friend strangely.

"Then we shall meet tomorrow and all go riding," said Prunella eagerly. "And Gerald, I suppose you may come too."

Lord Higglesby-Smythe received this invitation less than enthusiastically and was about to beg another engagement when Jeeters Crimpson spoke quickly, "Oh, Higglesby-Smythe, you must come. For old times' sake. I cannot bear to have you refuse. I insist you come."

His lordship, unable to think of a suitable refusal, nodded that he would come.

"And Miss Camden," said Jeeters, "I am sure you are an excellent rider."

"Oh, she is," remarked Helena Chatham. "I fear she puts the rest of us to shame."

"Dear Miss Chatham," exclaimed Jeeters. "No one could put a lady such as yourself to shame."

Miss Chatham blushed happily at this gallant remark. The orchestra began to strike up the opening chords of a country dance, and Mr. Stonecipher asked Lady Prunella if she would grant him the honor of the dance. Lady Prunella accepted eagerly.

Helena Chatham looked expectantly at the two remaining gentlemen and when Mr. Crimpson made no move, Lord Higglesby-Smythe reluctantly asked her to dance. Although Miss Chatham was somewhat disappointed at this, she smiled gamely and accompanied his lordship.

Mr. Crimpson was then left with Miss Camden. He smiled ardently at her. "Miss Camden," he said, impulsively taking her hand. "I do hope you will do me the honor of this dance."

"Heavens, Mr. Crimpson," replied Cecily, snatching her hand from his grasp. "I beg you to restrain yourself."

"But Miss Camden—Cecily—you mustn't refuse me. My heart would break."

The melodramatic expression on Mr. Crimpson's face made Cecily smile in spite of herself. "Mr. Crimpson, you are surely exaggerating."

"I am not, Miss Camden, and you mustn't refuse me."

Miss Camden thought desperately for some way to refuse the young gentleman, but was unable to think of anything. But just as she was about to reluctantly accept Mr. Crimpson's proffered arm, another gentleman appeared beside them.

"Ah, Miss Camden," he said. "I hope you have not forgotten that you had promised me this dance."

"Lord Ashford," replied Miss Camden in great relief. "No, my lord, I had not forgotten. I was just going to explain to Mr. Crimpson that I had another commitment."

"Oh dear," said his lordship with a smile. "Sorry, Crimpson, but I have the prior claim to this lady's hand."

"Of course, my lord," replied Mr. Crimpson with a hurt expression. "I shall have the honor of Miss Camden's hand for another dance."

Before Miss Camden could reply, Lord Ashford whisked her off and left Jeeters Crimpson standing there dejectedly.

"My lord," said Miss Camden. "I am indebted to you for rescuing me from Mr. Crimpson."

"That fellow is a damned nuisance and I feel that I am responsible for thrusting him upon unsuspecting society."

"Oh, I don't know, my lord," replied Cecily mischievously. "I have noticed that several young ladies seem to find him quite interesting."

"Then I am amazed that you do not find him interesting."

"Perhaps if he were not so young," said Cecily with a smile.

"Indeed, ma'am, and since you are in your dotage, you probably find his company far too exhausting."

Cecily laughed. "Well, I am not exactly in my first season, my lord."

"Yes," nodded Ashford gravely, "it seems that the two of us are fast approaching senility. Do you think that we might manage this dance?"

"Perhaps it would be unwise to attempt it," said Cecily in a serious tone, "but I do think we might try. After all, we have so little time left that we must use it to best advantage."

Ashford laughed and took Cecily's hand to begin the dance. As she had expected, Cecily found Lord Ashford to be a fine dancer, and Ashford was pleased to find that Miss Camden was also an accomplished dancer who moved with skill and grace.

As they completed the intricate steps of the country dance, Ashford said in mock surprise, "Miss Camden, I am sure that we are astonishing this assembly. I do believe we are making quite a creditable showing in spite of our advanced years."

"We shall cause a great deal of talk."

"I fear that is unavoidable."

Cecily smiled but then turned serious. "Really, my lord," she said. "I want to thank you. It's terribly kind of you to dance with me."

"Oh, Miss Camden. Pray don't be ridiculous. You are undoubtedly the best dancer here and a welcome change from those vapid females that I always find myself surrounded by."

"Is it as bad as that?" asked Cecily. "I have noticed that there are scores of beautiful and charming young ladies hanging about this room hoping to catch your eye. How they must hate me at this moment. Indeed, my lord, I think that for the first time in my life I have been the object of envy. I am sure none of my friends will ever speak to me again."

"If they are envious of you, my dear Miss Camden, it is

because you are such a fine dancer or because you have captured the heart of that pillar of the ton, James Crimpson. And such a conquest, for I see him scowling in this direction." Cecily looked over and saw Crimpson watching them intently.

The dance ended and as his lordship began to take his leave of Miss Camden, Mr. Crimpson began to approach.

"Oh dear," said Cecily. "Here he comes. I must find a place to hide."

Lord Ashford glanced about the room. "No convenient Corinthian columns like those at Lady Halberton's, but there are some potted plants that might suffice."

Cecily laughed. "Oh, you are terrible, my lord. I fear I shall just have to face him."

"No, wait, come with me."

Ashford led Cecily away from the dancers and toward another group of people.

"There is one place of safety. In the company of the illustrious George Brummell."

"Mr. Brummell?" said Cecily in surprise. "Oh, I have never met him."

"Then it is time for you to do so. He is second only to Mr. Crimpson as a leader of society."

Cecily giggled. "I fear that I will never be able to control myself if you say such things."

"But you must control yourself if you are to be presented to the great Mr. Brummell."

"Oh, please, my lord, I am nervous enough as it is. To meet the great Mr. Brummell. Prunella will be furious. She was terribly smug about being the only one to have met him."

"Then we must hasten to have you introduced."

Cecily laughed again and replied with mock gravity, "Please, my lord, to meet such a great and formidable personage as Mr. Brummell is no frivolous affair. I was once introduced to the Prince Regent, but the importance of that occasion is far overshadowed by this one. I must approach it with the proper amount of decorum."

"Certainly," replied his lordship, adopting a stern expression. "Let us approach the great man."

The great man was sitting with a rather bored expression, talking to a distinguished-looking gentleman of advanced years. The elderly gentleman rose and departed just as Ashford and Cecily approached.

"Oh, Geoffrey," said Mr. Brummell. "At last some agreeable company."

"Come now, George," replied his lordship. "If Sir Thomas Chillingworth is not agreeable company, I am sure you will find us much worse. I have never had any exciting military adventures."

"And I am properly thankful for that."

Ashford smiled, but quickly returned an expression of great gravity to his face. "Miss Camden," he said, "I wish to present Mr. George Brummell to you. And Miss Camden appreciates the honor of meeting you, George. She has told me so."

Cecily looked at Ashford threateningly and then extended her hand to Mr. Brummell.

"I am happy to meet you, sir," she said, "and I hope his lordship will restrain himself from embarrassing me further."

Mr. Brummell took her hand warmly. "Miss Camden, I fear his lordship never hesitates to embarrass people."

"Oh, come now, George, I am always gracious."

Mr. Brummell wisely ignored this comment and addressed Miss Camden. "I am told that your father was Sir Giles Camden. A fine man."

"Thank you."

"And now you are living with your aunt, Lady Throxton. I am not well acquainted with her ladyship, but I do know Lord Throxton."

"I am amazed, sir, that you should know so much about me," said Cecily.

"Actually, Miss Camden," said the Beau with a curious look at Ashford, "my dear friend Geoffrey had given me that information earlier this evening."

"Indeed?" asked Cecily in some surprise, looking at the Marquis.

"Goodness, George," replied Lord Ashford. "You're making me sound like a gossip. Mr. Brummell had inquired whether you were somehow related to Mr. Crimpson and I hastened to assure him that you were no such thing."

"And I am grateful for that, my lord," said Cecily, smiling, "I am in no way related to that gentleman, I assure you."

"And have no desire to be related to him, Miss Camden?" asked Ashford. "If you did I am sure he would be eager to arrange it."

"Lord Ashford, you are insufferable," cried Cecily.

"I am afraid, Miss Camden," said Mr. Brummell, "that his lordship, finding himself plagued with relations, hopes everyone else will be similarly plagued."

"George! I will not permit you to speak so of my family. I have some delightful relations. Oh, God, it appears that one of them is heading this way."

Ashford noted with irritation that Sir Chesterfield Willoughby was approaching them. However, as he inspected his nephew more closely, his irritation changed to amusement, for Sir Chesterfield had abandoned his usual careless attire for an extravagant suit of clothes that made the other young dandies seem bland by comparison.

He wore a cranberry-colored velvet coat cut in a very eccentric style. His thick neck was covered by a massive neckcloth inexpertly tied in an intricate series of knots. A huge quizzing glass hung from his neck and numerous fobs and seals hung from his waist, clinking noisily as he moved.

His curly black hair was pomaded into a peculiar hair style, giving his head an odd, triangular appearance. His thick fingers were covered with rings and as he crossed the room, he munched noisily on a piece of bread and butter.

"Geoffrey," gasped Mr. Brummell, catching sight of Chesterfield's remarkable appearance. "Can that offensive sight be your nephew? Oh God! He was bad enough before but I cannot bear this. Surely you cannot expect me to talk civilly to such a person."

"Certainly not," replied Ashford with a grin. "Do not be civil. In fact, if you are civil, I shall never speak to you again."

At that point Sir Chesterfield arrived. "How do," he said, his mouth still filled with bread and butter. Mr. Brummell blanched at the sight.

"Nephew," said Ashford coldly.

"Sir Chesterfield," said Miss Camden, stifling a chuckle.

"Yes," said Mr. Brummell weakly, looking at Sir Chesterfield with an expression of horror.

"And, of course, Brummell," said Sir Chesterfield, heartily grasping the Beau's hand and slapping him on the shoulder with a hand still greasy from the bread and butter.

Mr. Brummell looked down at his shoulder and noted a stain on his impeccable coat. He stared at Chesterfield with an icy look that would have silenced most people. Yet Chesterfield continued eagerly. "I am glad to see you, Miss Camden. I hope Lady Prunella is well today. I should like to talk to her."

"My cousin is very well, thank you," replied Cecily, who had watched Brummell's reaction to Chesterfield with amusement.

"Well, Brummell," said Chesterfield, turning again to that leader of fashion. "What do you think of my coat? Had it made by Jenkins of Haversham's."

"I think that drawing and quartering would not be punishment enough for Jenkins of Haversham's," said Mr. Brummell, still looking at the buttery stain on his shoulder, "and if it were not for the love I bear your uncle and Miss Camden's presence, I would shoot you here and now."

Sir Chesterfield gaped at him in astonishment.

"Pray, do not let our friendship deter you, George," said Lord Ashford, "and Miss Camden will not mind either, I daresay."

"What the devil?" exclaimed Chesterfield in bewilderment.

"Excuse me, Miss Camden, Lord Ashford," said Mr. Brummell, bowing and hurriedly turning and walking off. The entire assembly turned and watched his exit with great interest.

"Why, the impudent fellow!" exclaimed Sir Chesterfield. "How can he insult me like this? He's an odd one. I ought to call him out."

"Your boorishness never fails to amaze me," replied Lord Ashford, shaking his head. "Only you would smear butter all over Brummell's coat. And what do you expect him to do? God, he will never speak to me again, and you are lucky that he didn't kill you. He's a damned good shot."

Sir Chesterfield shrugged. "I ain't a bad shot myself, I'll have you know, and how was I to know I stained his damned coat? Lord, what a fop he is."

"I'll thank you to speak better of my friends, Chesterfield, or I shall thrash you within an inch of your life."

"Well, if you are going to be so difficult, I shall leave. Good evening." Sir Chesterfield retreated hastily, noticing the angry color that was coming to his uncle's face.

"Miss Camden," said Lord Ashford. "I shall be forced to kill that young idiot."

"I hope not," remarked Cecily, "for everyone has enough to talk about already. This episode will keep any number of parties entertained. But I fear poor Chesterfield's social standing may be irreparably damaged."

Ashford laughed. "I am sure that that is not worth worrying about. I am more worried about George's coat. Actually I suppose *my* social standing is irreparably damaged. I will be forever known as uncle to the infamous buttery fingered Sir Chesterfield. I shall be ostracized, and I am afraid, Miss Camden, you too may suffer."

"Indeed, my lord," replied Cecily with a grin. "My part in this affair will be long remembered. But I am sure it will work to my advantage, for I shall be in great demand. After all, I was witness to the whole episode and shall be able to tell it with great relish. I will have so many invitations. Why, my lord, this is a very lucky day for me. I really must thank you for all your kindness this evening. And especially for introducing me to Mr. Brummell. But please excuse me, my lord, for I must return to my aunt."

"Certainly, Miss Camden," said his lordship, bowing politely. "And I shall try to control my nephew's friend Crimpson in the future. But, considering that young gentleman, I can make no promises."

Cecily smiled, curtsied, and left the Marquis and returned to her aunt. Ashford watched her go and reluctantly turned to face a grim-looking dowager.

CHAPTER 8

The day following his triumph at Almack's, Jeeters Crimpson rose early and hastened to his friend Reginald's bedchamber. That gentleman was sleeping peacefully and, as usual, was not pleased when Mr. Crimpson awakened him.

"Oh God, Jeeters!" cried Mr. Stonecipher. "Why are you forever waking me up at some unheard-of hour? For heaven's sake, man, it's not much past dawn."

"Come on, Reggie," said Jeeters, "it ain't so early. Why, it's nearly eight o'clock and we've got work to do."

"Work?"

"To get ready for the ride in the park."

"That is your fault, Jeeters," said Reginald, turning over in bed with his back to his friend. "I am going back to sleep."

"But we have to get ready to go. And you have to wear your new riding boots."

"Oh," said Reginald, sitting up in bed. "Have they arrived?"

"Yes indeed, my boy, and a prettier pair you'll never see."

"Well, where are they, Jeeters?" said Reginald, getting out of bed eagerly and looking about the room in his nightshirt. "Blast it, where are they?"

"I'll get them," said Mr. Crimpson, leaving the room and returning with two gleaming black objects.

"Oh God!" cried Reginald, taking the boots from Jeeters. "They're so dashed beautiful. And these tassels. Right smart."

Jeeters enviously eyed the new Hessians with their brightly colored tassels.

"You'll cut a fine figure, Reggie. You'll outshine me by far."

"No one could outshine you with that head of hair of yours," chortled Reginald, and Jeeters laughed.

"And I'm not sure which of these waistcoats to wear. You've got to help me decide."

Reginald's good humor was now completely restored and he followed Jeeters into his bedchamber. Jeeters had arranged the assorted waistcoats carefully on the bed and the two friends studied them intently.

Reginald stood in his nightshirt with his arms folded and knit his brows in concentration.

"You see," said Mr. Crimpson, "I am going to wear this pair of nankeen pantaloons and this coat. I don't want to make a mess of it."

"What has Hacker said?"

"Damn him. He's gone off to visit some cousin."

"What?" cried Reginald in horror.

"Oh, don't get so upset. It's only until this evening. What could I do? The old boy begged me to let him go. Some nonsense about a dying cousin. Not that I believed it, mind you, but I let him go nevertheless."

"Oh God, Jeeters. What a day for Hacker to go off. And what am I to do about this damned neckcloth? I wanted it done in the Cascade, but if Hacker ain't here . . ."

"Never fear, my dear Reggie," said Jeeters, crossing to the large oak dresser that dominated the room. He took a white object out of a drawer and held it up to his friend.

"What the deuce?" exclaimed Reginald.

"It's the latest thing. Perfect for times like these." It was a beautifully tied neckcloth in the latest Cascade style.

"And what do I do with that?" asked Reginald.

"Watch this." Jeeters attached some small pieces of tape to the neckcloth and fastened it under his chin.

"How does it look?"

Reginald moved in for a closer inspection. "By heaven, if that ain't the best looking one I have ever seen. But won't it come off?"

"Guaranteed," said Jeeters, shaking himself briskly. The neckcloth remained in place.

"It's a marvel."

"And I've got one for you." Jeeters returned to the dresser and produced another elegantly tied neckcloth.

"This is famous," cried Reginald, gleefully taking the white object.

"But now you must help me," said Jeeters. "Which one?"

Reginald resumed his careful study of Mr. Crimpson's wardrobe. "This, I think," he said after contemplating the waistcoats for nearly fifteen minutes. He pointed to a pale blue one at the edge of the bed.

"Oh, I was hoping you'd pick that one," sighed Jeeters. "Thanks awfully."

"But one other thing, my dear friend," said Reginald. "Have you found your prancing stallion yet?"

"Oh yes, I have. I've arranged for us to hire two fine animals from Taylor's."

"Oh, don't be ridiculous. I've seen the wretched hacks Taylor hires out. Are you mad?"

"Don't worry, old man," laughed Jeeters. "Lady Pru ain't going to be looking at the horses."

When the Messrs. Stonecipher and Crimpson arrived at the park, the rest of the riding party had already assembled.

As Reginald and Jeeters approached, Miss Camden looked critically at their mounts. *Two sorrier hacks I have never seen,* thought Miss Camden with amusement.

Lady Prunella, however, was not very concerned with

horses. Her gaze fell upon Reginald's erect form and she found his equestrian post quite dashing.

"Good day to one and all," called Mr. Crimpson.

The other riders returned his greeting.

"And is this the prancing stallion we have heard so much about, Mr. Crimpson?" asked Cecily, looking at the curious horse that gentleman was riding. Its coat was a peculiar mottled yellow and it hung its head in a tired pose.

Mr. Stonecipher's horse was little better. It moved slowly and resentfully and gazed dimly at the other horses.

"Oh, I see you are joking," laughed Mr. Crimpson. "Miss Camden, your wit is only surpassed by your beauty."

Miss Camden tried to ignore this remark and Mr. Crimpson continued. "This sad creature is not my Jeremy. I am, of course, ashamed to appear with you thus mounted, but I had little choice. The miserable groom who was taking care of my Jeremy and Reginald's horse was terribly careless. I fear that he allowed the horses to catch cold. And, of course, Reginald would not think of riding horses that were not in the best of health. You know how Reginald dotes on animals."

Lady Prunella nodded sympathetically and was about to speak when Jeeters continued. "And Mr. Stonecipher was furious. That groom will never be careless again. I can promise you that."

"Oh, come now, James," said Reginald.

"Oh, Mr. Stonecipher," said Lady Prunella. "I know that one must take a firm stand against laxness among servants."

"How true," said Jeeters, nodding solemnly.

"Oh, it's a terrible shame that you should have to ride such horses," said Helena Chatham. "I am glad my father is not here to see them. He is master of the hounds, you know, and a very keen judge of horses."

"Then as much as I'd be honored to meet your father, Miss Chatham, I am also glad he is not present," said Reginald. "I am afraid these poor creatures are a dreadful sight."

"But you are not a dreadful sight," gushed Prunella impulsively, "in spite of the horses."

The two gentlemen beamed proudly, aware that their carefully groomed appearances overshadowed the inadequacy of their horses.

Higglesby-Smythe had an uncomfortable expression on his face and sat silently contemplating the reins in his hands.

"But Higglesby-Smythe, old man," said Jeeters. "You're awfully quiet. Fine horse you are riding there. Same lines as my own Jeremy."

"Thank you," muttered his lordship.

"I think we ought to be off," said Miss Camden.

"Right," said Jeeters and the group was off. Due to the narrowness of the path, the riding party was split into three groups. Prunella was elated to find herself paired with Reginald Stonecipher at the head of the group.

Lord Higglesby-Smythe was something less than elated to find himself beside Miss Helena Chatham, and Miss Camden was rather dismayed at being paired with Jeeters Crimpson and his odd yellow horse.

"I had a marvelous time last night," said Mr. Crimpson. "But I was so disappointed at not being able to dance with you. I do hope you will favor me with a dance sometime in the future."

"Yes, of course, sir," replied Cecily. Mr. Crimpson began to chatter in an animated fashion and Miss Camden found it difficult to concentrate on his conversation. After a while she heard him mention the name *Ashford*, and Cecily turned to look at him.

"Yes, the Marquis is a fine enough fellow. A bit on the stodgy side though, being so much older than ourselves."

"Really, sir," smiled Miss Camden. "Lord Ashford is considerably older than you but scarcely four years older than me."

This reference to the disparity in their ages made Mr. Crimpson stop for a moment.

"I do hope you do not hold my age against me," he said.

"No indeed, sir. I do not hold that against you."

Jeeters looked relieved. "Oh, look up ahead," he said. "Why, if it ain't Beau Brummell himself riding alone."

Cecily looked up and saw that the Beau was indeed riding across the park.

"Do you think he'll see us?" asked Jeeters hopefully, looking down at his own coat and boots.

"He may," replied Cecily, hoping herself to meet the charming Mr. Brummell again.

"Oh no," cried Jeeters, "I had forgotten. I can't meet him like this. Riding this decrepit old nag. What would he think of me?"

Cecily noted the look of consternation on his face with amusement. "Oh, there is nothing to fear," she said, watching Brummell. "He is not coming in our direction."

"I am glad," said Jeeters. "Of course, I dearly want to meet him but not on this creature."

"If only Jeremy had not been sick," said Miss Camden in a sympathetic voice.

"Yes indeed," said Jeeters wistfully. "But one day I shall meet Mr. Brummell."

"I have no doubt of that, Mr. Crimpson."

Jeeters smiled. "It must be terribly exciting to meet him."

"It is," said Cecily. "I met him last night."

"You did?"

"Yes, Lord Ashford was kind enough to introduce me. He was very charming."

"I hope his lordship will introduce Reginald and me. Do you think he will?"

"Perhaps," said Cecily, trying to sound noncommittal. "You shall have to ask him."

"Oh, I'm sure he will," said Jeeters. "I mean he's awfully fond of Reginald, you know. Favorite nephew. Of course, the Marquis don't have many relatives. Sir Chesterfield Willoughby and Reginald."

"But I am sure that Lord Ashford will marry," said Cecily, trying to act unconcerned.

"I know," answered Jeeters matter-of-factly. "I heard the talk at Almack's."

"What talk?" asked Cecily, dismayed in spite of herself.

"Oh, you know, last night everyone said that Lord Ashford was at Almack's to look over the eligible ladies."

"I do hope he found someone to his liking."

"I don't know," said Jeeters thoughtfully. "He didn't seem to be very much taken with anyone." Mr. Crimpson paused and looked suspiciously at Miss Camden. "In fact, I believe that you were the only one he danced with all evening."

Cecily laughed. "Mr. Crimpson, pray don't be silly. I'm sure his lordship danced many times. Surely you were not watching his every move. I should be amazed if you were, since if I am not mistaken, you were usually well occupied last night."

Jeeters smiled. "Well, I did have a jolly time, I must say, but it would have been perfect if you had danced even one dance with me." Mr. Crimpson looked at her with an expression of youthful ardor.

At that moment Miss Camden's horse threw its shoe and began to walk lamely. Miss Camden pulled the horse up immediately.

"What is it, Miss Camden?" asked Jeeters.

"I fear my horse has lost a shoe."

"What rotten luck." Mr. Crimpson dismounted and helped Cecily to get down from her horse. He then examined the horse's foot. "Yes, lost the shoe. I fear you'd best not ride him."

"No, of course not."

The other members of the group had by this time noticed that Cecily and Mr. Crimpson had fallen behind. They stopped and turned back to see what had happened.

"Whatever has happened?" asked Reginald of his friend.

"Miss Camden's horse has lost a shoe. I'm afraid we shall have to return," said Jeeters.

"Oh no!" cried Prunella, who seemed at the brink of tears. "But we were having such a wonderful ride."

"And I saw Agatha Grimthorpe and her brother Charles up ahead. . . ." said Miss Chatham. "I had hoped to see Aggie."

"But Miss Camden's horse can't continue," said Lord Higglesby-Smythe, relieved that the riding had come to a premature end.

"Now, I will not spoil everyone's time," said Miss Camden. "I will walk my horse back to the stable at the edge of the park and see if this shoe can be remedied. I shall wait for you there. I see no reason that the rest of you should suffer because I was inconsiderate enough to ride a horse that was inconsiderate enough to throw a shoe."

"But surely, Miss Camden, you don't expect us to allow you to go back to the stables alone," said Reginald.

"Yes, that would not do, Cecily," said Prunella sadly.

"But I shall accompany Miss Camden," said Jeeters eagerly.

"Oh, I should be honored to do so," suggested Lord Higglesby-Smythe.

"Oh, I think I could escort her by myself, Higglesby-Smythe, old man," said Mr. Crimpson. "And we shall get another horse and catch up to you."

"That sounds like a splendid idea," said Helena Chatham. "If Cecily doesn't mind."

Cecily assured her that the arrangement was quite satisfactory, although she was a bit reluctant to have Mr. Crimpson escort her.

"Then it's settled," said Lady Prunella. "You must get another horse and join us back here. Now we must be off, since Helena is anxious to talk to Aggie." With that Prunella turned her horse and rode off followed by Reginald, Helena, and Lord Higglesby-Smythe.

Jeeters was overjoyed at this turn of events. "I suppose we should walk them back," he said.

"Yes," said Cecily, starting to walk and leading her horse. "I'm glad I didn't spoil Prunella's ride."

"Oh yes," said Jeeters. "Lady Pru was having a marvelous time." Mr. Crimpson winked knowingly at Cecily. "I wouldn't be surprised if that ain't due to the presence of a certain young gentleman."

"Oh yes," said Cecily with an innocent look, "Lord Higglesby-Smythe is an old and dear friend."

Jeeters gave her a puzzled look. "I wasn't referring to his lordship," he said.

"Oh, then you mean Mr. Stonecipher."

"But, of course, Miss Camden. I think the two of them are getting along quite well."

Cecily tried to refrain from smiling. "Oh, do you think so?" she asked.

"Yes, of course."

Miss Camden made no comment and the two of them walked in silence for a time. Mr. Crimpson kept wondering whether Miss Camden was truly ignorant of Prunella's feelings. *No,* he concluded finally. *She is too much of a lady to reveal her cousin's thoughts. That's all.* Thus reassured, Mr. Crimpson turned again to Cecily to begin more conversation.

But just as he was about to speak, he heard riders coming up behind him. "We'd best move aside," he said, turning his head to see the approaching horsemen.

"Oh no!" he cried and Cecily turned to see the cause of this exclamation. There was the Marquis of Ashford astride a beautiful chestnut horse, accompanied by none other than George Brummell himself. Mr. Brummell was mounted on a stunning black horse, presenting his usual picture of sartorial perfection.

"Miss Camden," said Lord Ashford as his horse came even with her and Mr. Crimpson. "Is there something wrong?"

"Oh, good day, my lord," said Cecily, looking up at Ashford. "I fear my horse has thrown a shoe. I had been riding with my cousin Prunella, and Mr. Crimpson has been gracious enough to accompany me to the stables."

"Very kind of him, I am sure," said his lordship, looking at her curiously.

"But if I may," said Miss Camden, trying to ignore his

gaze, "I would like to present Mr. James Crimpson to Mr. Brummell."

"Charmed," said the Beau.

"Oh, Mr. Brummell," said Jeeters, walking over to Brummell and extending his hand to him. "This is such an honor, sir. An honor to be sure."

"And I am honored to make your acquaintance," said the Beau with his famous charm. "You are a friend of Lord Ashford's nephew, I believe."

"Oh yes, sir," replied Jeeters. "Reginald Stonecipher. We share rooms, in fact. We've been friends ever since school days at Eton."

"But I hope there is nothing seriously wrong with your horse, Miss Camden," said Ashford.

"No, not at all," replied Cecily.

"There does appear to be something seriously wrong with the other horse, though," said Mr. Brummell, peering curiously at Jeeter's hired horse. "That is a remarkable-looking animal."

Mr. Crimpson reddened with embarrassment, but explained, "Oh, it is an odd one, ain't it, sir? Not the type I'm accustomed to ride, of course, but I didn't bring any of my horses to town this year and it's hard to hire any decent sort of animal."

Cecily tactfully refrained from asking Mr. Crimpson why he did not mention his prancing stallion, and changed the subject. "A beautiful day, is it not, gentlemen?" The gentlemen readily assented.

"But I am amazed that your cousin and the rest of the party have abandoned you," said Ashford.

"I am hardly abandoned, my lord," replied Cecily with a smile. "For Mr. Crimpson is certainly more than capable of escorting me."

Jeeters beamed at this.

"But please, Miss Camden, allow Mr. Brummell and myself to accompany you. We were heading in that direction and shall be glad to walk with you."

Ashford and Brummell dismounted and walked with

them. Jeeters somehow managed to maneuver himself into a position next to Mr. Brummell. Cecily found herself between Ashford and Jeeters, with Mr. Brummell forced into the unfortunate position on the other side of Mr. Crimpson.

"Truly, my lord," said Cecily to Ashford, noting that Mr. Crimpson had begun to talk excitedly to Mr. Brummell while the famous gentleman took on a rather pained expression, "to be in the park with you and Mr. Brummell. I swear that my social standing will be jumping even higher."

"But you have failed to mention Mr. Crimpson."

Cecily looked at Ashford with a sad expression. "I fear that gentleman has forgotten my existence. I should be quite insulted were it not Mr. Brummell himself who had captured Mr. Crimpson's attention."

Ashford grinned and looked over at his friend. "Poor George. To subject him to Chesterfield Willoughby and then James Crimpson. I fear it is putting far too great a strain on the bonds of friendship."

"Oh, I am not so sure of that, sir," said Cecily. "I'm sure Mr. Crimpson's conversation is quite stimulating. I'm sure Mr. Brummell is charmed."

Mr. Brummell did not look in the least charmed but Jeeters continued to talk, unaware that the Beau was becoming dangerously bored.

"And I think that Harrods is the most bang-up place for a night of cards, don't you, sir?" asked Jeeters.

Mr. Brummell had not been listening very closely, but since Mr. Crimpson for once expected him to say something, answered, "I'm unfamiliar with that establishment but I shall undoubtedly inform His Royal Highness of your opinion."

"Really, sir. The Prince?"

"And I shall certainly mention your name."

This comment caused Mr. Crimpson to adopt a euphoric expression, but he was soon brought back to reality when Mr. Brummell informed him dryly, "Oh, Mr. Crimpson, I fear your neckcloth is hanging a bit precariously."

"What?" asked Jeeters in bewilderment. Looking down beneath his chin, he saw that the tape on his ready-made neckcloth had come unstuck and the tie dangled ludicrously, bobbing as he walked.

Jeeters looked over at Ashford and Cecily, but they were engrossed in their own conversation. "Dear me," said Jeeters, quite flustered. He pushed the offending neckcloth back into place.

"It was guaranteed," he said weakly.

"Guaranteed?" said the Beau with great interest.

"Yes, to stay in place."

"How remarkable," replied Mr. Brummell. "But what a clever idea. I mean, saves hours of work."

"Yes indeed," said Jeeters, brightening. "Perhaps His Royal Highness would be interested to hear about it."

"Yes, I shall tell him," said the Beau. In fact, the Beau kept this promise and later recounted the affair of Mr. Crimpson's neckcloth to a most appreciative Prince of Wales.

Mr. Brummell was quite glad when they finally reached the stable. Lord Ashford quickly arranged for Miss Camden to leave her horse there so its shoe could be replaced, and hired another horse so Miss Camden could rejoin her cousin.

"Thank you, my lord," said Cecily, shaking Ashford's hand.

"Yes, thank you, my lord," said Jeeters. "And Mr. Brummell, such an honor it was meeting you. I shall not forget this day."

"Nor shall I," replied the Beau with a gracious smile.

As Cecily and Jeeters rode off into the park, Mr. Brummell turned to his friend. "My dear Geoffrey," said Mr. Brummell, "you have the most remarkable set of relatives and acquaintances of anyone that I know, with the exception of HRH, of course."

"I do hope you enjoyed Mr. Crimpson's company. I must say he seemed to be having a delightful time."

"Yes, I am sure he will have a great time telling everyone he knows how he condescended to talk to me."

Ashford laughed. "And poor Cecily. She is forever saddled with that young idiot."

Mr. Brummell looked intently at his friend. "A fine lady, Miss Camden. I hope she isn't becoming interested in a fellow like Crimpson."

"George!" cried Ashford. "How could you think such a thing? I've never heard such nonsense! I hope that you were joking."

"Of course," said Mr. Brummell, surprised at the vehemence of Ashford's response. He smiled at the Marquis and thought, *But I fear that you are expressing more than the usual amount of interest in this lady, my friend.* He then said, "Have you forgotten that we are to meet Alvanley? Come on. We'd best hurry."

The two gentlemen mounted their horses and headed away from the park.

"I find it dreadful that you should have met Brummell today, while I spent the time with Prunella," said Reginald that evening after they had returned to their rooms.

"Oh, I say, Reggie," said Jeeters. "It is a shame that you were not there. Especially since you were wearing your new boots."

"Yes," said Reginald sadly.

"But don't be so glum, old man. There will be other opportunities and I can introduce you."

"Yes, I suppose you can," said Reginald.

"And don't forget, Reginald, I could never have met him if Ashford weren't your uncle," continued Jeeters in an attempt to soothe his friend.

"Yes, I suppose so," agreed Reginald.

"So buck up, old chap," said Jeeters gaily, slapping his friend on the back, "and let's be off to Harrods. A few lucky cards and you'll be a new man."

"All right," said Reginald, still somewhat depressed.

"Let's go." The two young gentlemen then departed for a night of gaming.

Although Harrods was not the most fashionable gaming house in London, it was a very popular one and was occasionally frequented by some of society's high steppers. Usually the clientele were more on the fringes of society, but Harrods was known for its liveliness and plentiful though indifferent wine.

When the Messrs. Stonecipher and Crimpson arrived at Harrods, it was already packed with numerous noisy men. Some of the men were accompanied by sometimes dazzling ladies who were, as Jeeters Crimpson put it, "not the sort you'd see at Almack's."

The two young gentlemen moved through this exciting crowd and were at first unable to get a place at a table. They stood watching the different players.

"Oh, look, Reggie," said Jeeters. "Over there. There's a rough-looking chap at the table near that ghastly painting. And look at that woman he's got with him. Now there's a sight, eh, Reg?"

Reginald looked where his friend had directed and saw the man Jeeters had been referring to. He laughed. "Oh God, Jeeters, I'll thank you to speak more kindly of my kinsman."

"What?" exclaimed Jeeters.

"Why, that's Sir Chesterfield Willoughby. My own cousin."

"The devil!" cried Jeeters.

"I thought I'd pointed him out to you at Almack's."

"You did but he looks different."

Although Sir Chesterfield Willoughby had made a notable attempt at improving his appearance when he went to Almack's, he had taken little trouble to prepare for his appearance at Harrods.

He was dressed in a rough coat and his neckcloth was in great disarray. He had evidently been drinking heavily and the other players at the table were eyeing him angrily and looking at each other. Sir Chesterfield's lady friend was standing behind him, one hand resting on his broad shoulder. She was lavishly dressed in a bright green dress and carried an enormous fan. Her ornate coiffure was adorned with bright green feathers and her rather attractive face was heavily rouged.

"That's not a bad one he's got himself attached to," said Jeeters with a grin. "Wonder how he keeps her. He ain't rich, is he?"

"From what I hear, he gets his blunt from Uncle Geoffrey. But I suspect my uncle won't be keeping him much longer. I know he hates him."

"Well, from the looks of that one, Ashford has good reason."

As the friends watched him, Chesterfield seemed to get very angry. He pounded his fist on the table and yelled loudly at one of his fellow cardplayers.

Reginald watched this scene with great interest, hoping that his cousin would be called out. Jeeters's thoughts were running in the same direction. *Sure would be convenient if that one were killed. Reggie would be Ashford's only nephew then.* But unfortunately Chesterfield rose bearlike and walked away, his lady in the green dress on his arm.

Disappointed, Jeeters turned to Reginald. "When are you going to introduce me to Sir Chesterfield?"

Reginald laughed. "Immediately, of course." They made their way through the crowd until they came upon Chesterfield.

"Oh, Cousin," said Reginald as they came close enough to Sir Chesterfield. "How do? What a joy to see you here."

Chesterfield looked at him stupidly.

"Cousin?" he repeated slowly. "Oh, Stonecipher." In spite of this unflattering form of recognition, Reginald pressed on.

"It is so good to see you. And I want to present my friend Mr. James Crimpson. Mr. Crimpson, Sir Chesterfield Willoughby."

Sir Chesterfield acknowledged the introduction with an uncivil grunt and the lady at his arm nudged him.

"Oh yes," he said. "This is Miss Hill."

"Oh, you gentlemen may call me Daisy," said Miss Hill.

Jeeters smiled and executed a graceful bow. "Charmed," he said.

"And you are Chesterfield's cousin?" said Miss Hill, noting Reginald's blond good looks. "You sure don't look like him."

"That is so," replied Reginald, silently thanking providence for this. "But cousins we are, our mothers being sisters."

"How wonderful," said Miss Hill.

"Yes, a most fortunate circumstance."

Miss Hill seemed quite charmed by the two young gentlemen and began to talk excitedly. Sir Chesterfield looked rather disgruntled and kept silent.

"I think it is naughty of Chesterfield to have kept you two fine gentlemen a secret from me. But that's just like him. He ain't much of a talker, are you, Chesterfield?"

"Damn it, Daisy," growled Sir Chesterfield, "quit that stupid prattle."

Miss Hill looked at him with a hurt expression, but made no reply.

"Well, it is awfully good to meet Reginald's cousin," said Jeeters, filling the lull in the conversation. "I saw that you were playing. I hope you have been lucky."

Chesterfield scowled. "I must go," he said brusquely. He grasped Miss Hill's elbow firmly and pushed her toward the exit.

"Oh God," laughed Jeeters. "What a cousin you have. I can certainly see the family resemblance."

"What a terrible insult," said Reginald.

"But did you see his face when I asked him if he had been lucky?" said Jeeters. "He looked like he would murder me."

"Well, I will be apt to murder you myself if you ever tell me I resemble my dear cousin again."

"I shall beware of that. And did you see him look at the lovely Daisy? I was sure that he would hit her."

"My cousin is far too much a gentleman for that," laughed Reginald. "He will wait until he gets her outside to hit her." The two friends howled with laughter.

After a few moments Jeeters spied some open places at one of the tables. "We're in, Reggie," said Jeeters and the two of them took their places at the table and began to play.

CHAPTER 9

Life at the Throckmortons' London house was becoming increasingly difficult for Cecily Camden. Lord Throxton's gout had been acting up, putting that gentleman in a very disagreeable temper. Lady Throxton was beginning to make preparations for moving to the country and was in a state of agitation over the merest trifles, and Prunella was forever extolling the virtues of Reginald Stonecipher and rereading *The Mysterious Count*.

Cecily herself was finding that she spent far too much time thinking about the Marquis of Ashford. Therefore Miss Camden was overjoyed to receive a letter from her great-aunt Sophie urging her to come to Manchester for a visit.

"Goodness, Cecily," Prunella had said, "Manchester is such a dull, dreary place and we shall soon be removing to Throxton Hall. I certainly don't think you should have to go all that way."

But Cecily was eager to leave and could not be dissuaded. Two days later she and her maid were on their way to Manchester, and Cecily found her spirits improving with every mile the post chaise traveled away from London.

The only thing that dampened Cecily's joy at getting away from the Throckmortons was her worry that her aunt

Sophie was in poor health. Happily, this worry vanished when Miss Camden was reunited in Manchester with her beloved aunt.

"Aunt Sophie," cried Cecily, eagerly embracing her aged relative and kissing her on the cheek, "you are looking well, I am so glad."

Aunt Sophie smiled and stepped back to get a good look at her grandniece.

"I daresay, Cecily," she said, "you are looking well. Staying with the Throckmortons must agree with you."

"I don't know about that, Aunt, but I have been riding and walking a great deal. But you are looking marvelous! Life in Manchester must be extraordinarily healthful."

The elderly lady smiled in reply. She was indeed looking well and much better than when they had parted. Her eyes sparkled with vitality and her white hair gleamed. "I don't know what it is," said Aunt Sophie, taking her niece's arm and leading her into the drawing room. "I was miserable at first. I missed you of course, my dear, and found Thomas a rather poor substitute for your company." Aunt Sophie pulled Cecily closer and spoke softly. "Poor Thomas. You shall meet him soon. They said I was getting too old to run my old household. Such nonsense! And I was sent to live with Thomas so he might take care of me. By all I hold dear, it is Thomas who needed the care, and I believe I have been so busy taking care of him that I have forgotten my age and infirmity."

Cecily laughed. "Oh, I am so glad to see you like this. And I am eager to meet Cousin Thomas. Where is he?"

"He shall be back presently. He was called to visit one of his tenants. He is a good man although a trifle empty-headed. I think that you will like him. But you have had a long and tedious journey. You must go to your room and rest."

Cecily was shown to her room, which was pleasant and well-furnished, with a delightful view of the gardens. Cecily was relieved and happy to see Aunt Sophie in such good health and it was a joy to be away from London. *I believe that this trip will be good for me,* decided Cecily as she changed her clothes. She looked at herself in the mirror and smiled. *Why, I haven't even thought about Ashford for nearly twenty minutes.*

When Cecily returned to her aunt, Thomas Warren-Brewster had arrived at his home. A rather stout gentleman of three and forty years, Cecily's cousin appeared to be a good-natured man. "Cousin Cecily," said Mr. Warren-Brewster, greeting her warmly with a hearty kiss on the cheek. "It is a joy to have you here, Cousin. And dashed if you ain't the prettiest cousin I have. A shame we have never met. I daresay, I'm glad you could come."

Cecily received this greeting with a smile and replied, "Cousin Thomas, I am so glad to meet you. You have done remarkable things for Aunt Sophie. I have never before seen her in such glowing health."

"Balderdash," said Aunt Sophie. "I won't have you flattering Tom, for he knows very well it is in spite of him, not because of him."

"Now Aunt," said Mr. Warren-Brewster with a hearty laugh. He turned to Cecily and winked. "Ain't it like a woman? She won't admit that living with a handsome gent like me has done wonders for her."

Cecily laughed and found herself liking Cousin Tom immediately.

"Enough of this nonsense, Tom," said Aunt Sophie with feigned annoyance. "Cecily don't want to hear it. And if you weren't so unfeeling you would escort us to the table before your poor cousin dies from lack of nourishment."

Cousin Thomas laughed again and gallantly escorted the ladies to the dinner table. The food was excellent and Cecily saw that her cousin was used to setting a good table. His stout figure attested to this.

"And tell us about London, Cousin Cecily," said Thomas. "Aunt Sophie says you have been having a bang-up time. I suppose you've been hanging about with all the nobs. Must be dashed exciting."

"Oh, it can be fun," replied Cecily, "but I am sure you have as much excitement in Manchester."

Thomas laughed. "I reckon we do at that, eh, Aunt Sophie?"

"Heavens, Tom, must you be so ridiculous? I'm sure you will find Manchester society quite dull compared to London."

Cecily smiled. "I cannot see how that can be, my dear aunt, for you and Cousin Tom are part of it."

Cousin Thomas laughed and thrust a piece of partridge into his cavernous mouth. "Cecily, you're a fine girl," he said.

"But how is dear Elizabeth and Throxton and that silly girl Prunella?" asked Aunt Sophie.

"They are all extremely well."

"I imagine Prunella will soon be engaged to Lord Higglesby-Smythe. I know Elizabeth was eager for that match. And it's a good connection, to be sure."

"At present, Aunt, there is no engagement. I fear Prunella has been discouraging Lord Higglesby-Smythe's suit."

"I knew she was a silly goose of a girl," snorted Aunt Sophie. "I met her once and that was enough. Of course, being an heiress I imagine she has many suitors. I imagine she has fallen for some unsuitable fellow."

"Not that unsuitable," said Cecily. "I mean she has developed a strong partiality to a certain young gentleman. His name is Reginald Stonecipher."

"Stonecipher," cried Cousin Thomas. "The devil! I knew that young cub was in London. Oh Lord, he's a bad one. The bane of his father's life since being tossed from Eton. A damned coxcomb he is and a gamester. Poor Albert, for he's a fine man and never did a thing to deserve such a son."

"You know Mr. Stonecipher, Cousin?" asked Cecily in surprise.

"Since he was a red-faced infant. Why, Albert, his father, is one of my dearest friends. The shrewdest man and the richest and married to Arabella Billington. Oh, she's a beauty. Had I found a woman like that who would have married a man like me I would have given up my bachelorhood ages ago. Arabella is a fine lady. Sister of one of the nobs. A marquis in fact. Yes, the Marquis of Ashford."

"Oh," said Cecily, hoping to sound disinterested.

"How you talk, Tom!" said Aunt Sophie.

"Come now, Aunt, I am simply telling the truth. But Lady Arabella is a fine lady. She ran off, you know. To marry Albert, and not that she regrets it, for Albert Stonecipher is about the richest man in this vicinity. Even if he did make his money in trade, for I don't hold that against any man."

"Have you met the Stoneciphers, Aunt Sophie?" asked Cecily.

"Oh yes, and I know you will soon be meeting them too, for we've had them here many times and they are often at affairs we attend."

"Yes, to be sure," added Cousin Thomas. "As a matter of fact, we did see them just last week, and Maggie Skruggs, too."

"Maggie Skruggs?"

"Aye!" laughed Thomas. "Wait till you meet Maggie. She's Albert Stonecipher's sister. A rare one she is."

"Oh, I shall then be quite eager to meet her," said Cecily dubiously.

Thomas laughed and Aunt Sophie looked at him with a disapproving stare. "I'm afraid you will find our local society quite different from London, but it ain't boring," said Tom. "Right, Aunt?"

"At least it seems to amuse you, Nephew," replied his aunt. She turned to Cecily. "Tell us about London. How was the season?"

"It was really quite exciting, I suppose," replied Cecily. "I went to many parties and balls and I've met some very interesting people."

"Did you meet Brummell?" asked Cousin Thomas, quite interested.

"Yes, I did," replied Cecily, "and he really is very charming."

"I saw him once," said Cousin Tom, "two years ago when I was in London, and quite a sight he was. He was with the Prince, and oh yes, Arabella's brother was there with him. Of course, I've never met him nor have I met the Marquis of Ashford. Of course, I don't want to meet that one after the way he's treated his sister. A mean one he is. A damned arrogant knave from what I've heard. Too proud to associate with his sister, and Albert Stonecipher is as fine a man as any marquis, finer if what I hear of them that's of the Carlton House set is true."

"Tom!" exclaimed Aunt Sophie. "I have never heard such wicked gossip. I see no reason for you to slander a gentleman whom you have never met."

Mr. Warren-Brewster looked hurt by this rebuke but continued stubbornly. "I don't care but it is a fact that the noble Lord Ashford has never once seen fit to call on his sister Arabella, and a finer lady has never been born."

"But Cousin Tom," said Cecily. "I have met Lord Ashford and I fear you are too harsh on him. He is a good man and not at all arrogant. He never abuses his position and is always courteous. And he has been very kind in introducing his nephew Reginald into society. That is, in fact, how I met Mr. Stonecipher. Lord Ashford introduced him to Lady Throxton, Prunella, and myself."

"The devil," exclaimed Thomas. "I had thought it odd that the Stonecipher boy had met your cousin Prunella, for I didn't think he had too many London connections."

"You mean that Ashford has been introducing Reginald Stonecipher into society?" asked Aunt Sophie.

"Yes indeed, ma'am. And that is why I am amazed that Cousin Tom should condemn Ashford so."

"It seems Ashford may be mending his ways, then. And it is about time. But I find it odd that we haven't heard of this. Not that Lady Arabella is one to spread her family business about, but I don't think Maggie Skruggs could keep such a secret. And if they don't know, Lord, what a choice bit of gossip it will be," said Thomas gleefully.

"You are incorrigible, Tom," cried Aunt Sophie, "and

you will refrain from spreading tales. Whatever will Cecily think of you?"

"Oh, all right," said Thomas reluctantly, returning to his dinner.

"I am afraid that we are all too interested in London gossip here, Cecily," said Aunt Sophie. "Not that there isn't enough local gossip to occupy us. But you will be a great sensation in Manchester to have actually met Mr. Brummell. But you must be exhausted. It is late and I am sure Thomas will excuse you. I want you to get your rest."

"Dear Aunt Sophie, you need not be concerned about me. But I am so glad to be here with you." She took her aunt's hand and squeezed it affectionately. "I think I will retire early. It was a fatiguing journey, and Cousin Tom, it is wonderful to be here. Good night."

Cecily left the dining hall and retired to bed. Her aunt and Cousin Thomas watched her go.

"Cousin Cecily is a fine girl," said Mr. Warren-Brewster. "Looks something like Cousin Giles. Always did admire Cousin Giles, being a soldier and all. Only hero in the family. But why isn't a girl like Cecily married? She's a good-looking girl, she is."

"Heavens, Tom," replied Aunt Sophie, "you are a mite too inquisitive. I don't think Cecily ever really cared to be married."

Thomas looked at her in surprise. "A female that don't care for marriage? That don't seem likely to me. Of course, I imagine since Cousin Giles didn't leave her much money . . ."

"Yes, that is true. Cecily did get an offer from the Reverend Carter three years ago but she was adamant. Not the sort to marry just to have a husband. And of course, Cecily spent a lot of time with me after Giles died and life with an old lady like me ain't the best way to find eligible gentlemen. And Cecily is the finest girl, too."

"Hmmmm . . ." replied Cousin Thomas thoughtfully, "she does seem to be a dashed fine young lady."

"I am glad you think so," replied Aunt Sophie. "And I

must myself be off to bed. I am not so young and need my rest." Thomas escorted his aunt from the room and retired to the parlor, where he sat thoughtfully contemplating the fire.

The first few days at Cousin Thomas's home in Manchester passed rapidly. Cecily talked to her aunt, went shopping in town, and rode a great deal. Although not extremely wealthy, Thomas Warren-Brewster was comfortably well off and his home just outside Manchester was greatly admired. It was a very comfortable house with well-kept grounds and pleasant gardens, and Cecily found that she was enjoying herself immensely.

One morning she was sitting in the garden when her cousin joined her. As usual he was in a very amiable mood and greeted her enthusiastically.

"Lovely day, Cecily," he said.

"Indeed, Tom, it is," returned Cecily. "You know, sir, you have a lovely garden."

"Oh, I don't suppose it's much compared to what Lord Throxton has at his country estate."

"I would not say that," answered Cecily, "for although the gardens at Throxton Hall may be large, they are no finer than yours."

Thomas grinned happily. "I am damned proud of that garden, of course," he said. "I've always been a man of the land. Planted much of this myself. I'm glad you like it."

"Oh, I really do."

"Then you ain't bored here, are you?"

"My dear cousin Tom," replied Cecily with an amused expression. "I am not in the least bored. I love the country. My happiest days were spent in a small country village when I was a girl. In fact, your home reminds me so much of that place. And Aunt Sophie is so happy here."

"Well, I am glad to have her," replied Thomas, "for although she is apt to bully me, which considering her age and gender is natural, she ain't a bad lady and I have grown quite fond of her. But I wanted to tell you, Cecily, that we are going to have dinner at the Stoneciphers' manor house on Wednesday. I know you will like them, and I know you'll be glad to go out and meet some of my neighbors. Good people but not exactly elegant, except, of course, Lady Arabella, who is elegant if anyone is."

"I'll be happy to meet them," said Cecily, quite eager to meet Ashford's sister, "after hearing so much about them."

"I am glad to hear it. So Wednesday it is then. And would you like to join me in a ride to the village?"

"No, thank you, Tom," said Cecily, noting with surprise the look of disappointment that appeared on her cousin's face. "I told Aunt Sophie I would be in to read to her, so I must stay, but perhaps another day."

"Certainly, Cecily. Maybe tomorrow. But let me escort you to the house." Cecily took her cousin's arm and the two of them walked back to the house. "I will return in time for dinner," said Thomas, leaving her, and Cecily went into the house to find her aunt.

That venerable lady was sitting in her sitting room busy at embroidery. "Good day, Aunt Sophie," said Cecily, kissing her aunt and sitting beside her on the sofa. "You do such beautiful needlework. I will never do such work."

"Heavens, Cecily," replied her Aunt Sophie, "do not worry about such things, for I know your needlework is as competent as it has to be. Now tell me, my dear, are you happy here?"

"Yes, of course," replied Cecily. "I have been quite happy during this visit. Seeing you and Cousin Tom and everything has been lovely."

"Then you are not eager to return to Throxton Hall?"

"Goodness, no, ma'am."

"Then you are unhappy under Throxton's care."

"No, it is not that," replied Cecily. "My aunt and Lord Throxton are very good to me. I have no complaint. And Prunella is at times difficult but she is not a bad girl."

"I wish you could stay here with me and Tom," replied her aunt, "and possibly you could."

"Oh, Aunt Sophie. You know I would like to stay with

you but I do not want to place another female dependent in this household. I do think that would be asking too much."

"But what if you were not just another female relative dependent on him?"

"I don't think I understand."

"What if you were Tom's wife?"

"Aunt Sophie!" cried Cecily in astonishment. "Such an idea. However did you think of such a thing?"

Her aunt smiled. "Do not be so shocked, dearest, for it is not such a dreadful idea once one gets used to it. And it was Tom who suggested it."

"Tom!"

"Yes, of course. He is quite fond of you, you know."

"But I have known him no more than a week."

"I do not feel that that is an unreasonably short time. For I had known your uncle Leo less than two hours before I decided he was the man for me."

"Surely Tom is not serious. He is past forty and a bachelor all of his years."

"He is finally developing some sense and he would love to give you a home. He is not the brightest or handsomest of men, but he is good-hearted and would make you a good husband."

Cecily looked at her aunt with a puzzled expression. "He has said nothing to me of this."

"But he will. He has told me that he intends to make an offer for you and I thought I should tell you of his intention."

"And I am grateful to you for that, Aunt, for this has taken me by surprise. I am completely at a loss for a reply. But I cannot imagine marrying Tom!"

"Do think about it, Cecily. I am concerned for you. It will not be easy for you. Since you are single and without independent means, you must rely on the beneficence of your family. As time goes on I am sure this will become most unsatisfactory."

"Yes indeed," answered Cecily thoughtfully.

"And perhaps a marriage to Tom would be better than

living with your aunt Elizabeth, unless you have some other prospects."

"No, Aunt Sophie, I fear I have none."

"Promise me you will think this matter over carefully."

"I will, ma'am."

"Dearest Cecily," said her aunt, "are you opposed to Thomas? You look so dejected."

"Oh, I have nothing against my cousin," replied Cecily. "Indeed, I do like Thomas. He is a good man, and perhaps marrying him would be better than living off the kindness of my uncle. I will think the matter over carefully."

Aunt Sophie studied her niece for a moment. "My dearest child, is there someone else? Do you love someone else?"

Cecily laughed awkwardly. "Yes, my dear Aunt, but it is so pathetic to confess it to you. I feel like a silly, ridiculous schoolgirl."

"Come now, Cecily. Even as a schoolgirl you were never silly."

"Well, I am then being silly and ridiculous for the first time. You see, Aunt Sophie, I am in love with the Marquis of Ashford. I think I loved him the first time I met him and each time I see him I love him more. It is absurd, isn't it?"

"Absurd? And why absurd?"

"He is a leader of the ton and scores of beautiful women have been setting their caps for him. And I feel so terribly foolish but can do nothing about it."

"And he has no feelings for you?"

"I don't know. I think that he likes me, but I fear he is only being polite. After all, I am so plain and I have no fortune."

"Cecily Camden, you are not plain. There is nothing in your face or figure to discourage any man and besides that, you are a Camden. I only wish you would realize that you have many admirable qualities and if this Marquis has an ounce of sense, he would see them."

"I fear, dear Aunt," said Cecily with a smile, "that you are a trifle prejudiced in my favor. I do not intend to pine away over my fatal attachment to the Marquis, but I fear it will take some time for me to rid myself of these romantic notions."

"And that is why you do not want to consider your cousin's offer of marriage?"

"Yes, ma'am. I know it is silly, but I never did feel that one should marry simply to overcome the inconvenience of being a spinster. And I am not sure whether Cousin Thomas is ready to marry either."

"Perhaps you are right, Cecily," said her aunt, "but you will have some time to think this matter over. But do not be blind to your own worth."

Cecily smiled and, in spite of the depression that settled upon her as a result of this conversation, changed the topic and began to discuss the latest millinery fashions.

Wednesday afternoon was an overcast, somewhat threatening day and Cousin Thomas suggested that they delay their visit to the Stoneciphers' manor.

"Nonsense," Aunt Sophie replied in her usual authoritative tone. "I am not so delicate that I could not withstand a few drops of rain." And so the two ladies and Mr. Warren-Brewster set out in their carriage to call on Mr. Stonecipher and Lady Arabella.

As they drove through the great gate that marked the entrance to the Stonecipher property, Cecily caught her first glimpse of the Stonecipher manor.

"Good heavens," said Cecily, "it is a palace. Throxton Hall is dwarfed in comparison. Mr. Stonecipher must be frightfully rich."

Aunt Sophie nodded. "Yes indeed. There is money in bootblacking and this other frightful factory nonsense. But we must not hold that against him, as Thomas always says."

"Indeed not," said Thomas with a serious look. "Those not born with our advantages of birth must try and become rich. It's only natural. And I don't grudge Stonecipher any of this, for he's worked damned hard, although I'm not sure I hold with all these factories."

"I am sure I do not hold with these factories," said Aunt Sophie, "but I hold my tongue so I will not embarrass Thomas." The elderly lady sighed. "I suppose we must endure factories. I am told they are quite necessary."

"At least they are necessary for Stonecipher to become rich," laughed Thomas, and Cecily smiled too. She looked out the carriage window and surveyed the vast acreage that surrounded the great Stonecipher house. It was beautiful, Cecily decided, and the house appeared very grand indeed. It was a new structure of elegant design and quite attractive.

As Cecily gazed at the great house, she wondered again at Reginald Stonecipher's great interest in her cousin Prunella. *It is most curious*, thought Cecily, *for Reginald and Prunella are dreadfully unsuited. And I always get the impression that he really cannot abide her*. It was indeed odd, for the usual explanation would be that Reginald Stonecipher was a fortune hunter. Cecily knit her brows in concentration. *But Reginald Stonecipher is heir to this property. Surely the Stonecipher wealth far exceeds that of my uncle.*

Her thoughts were interrupted as the carriage arrived in front of the great house. A number of liveried servants awaited them, and the newly arrived guests were escorted into the house in grand style.

I feel like a duchess, thought Cecily. She smiled. *No, a princess at least.*

They entered the house and Cecily was awed at the grand staircase and the vast entry hall with its elegant furnishing. Cousin Tom leaned over and whispered to Cecily, "Anything to compare with this in London?"

"No," answered Cecily with a smile, "but I am told the Palace of Versailles would be nearly as grand as this."

Her cousin chortled loudly at this but was quickly silenced by his aunt's stern look. The guests were shown into the drawing room and again Cecily was impressed by the richness and elegance of it.

"My dear friends," said an attractive lady rising from a chair in the drawing room. "I am so glad that you could come."

Cecily studied this lady, whom she knew immediately to be Lady Arabella Stonecipher. Cecily saw that Lady Arabella was very much like her son Reginald. She had his blond good looks and charming smile. There was little about her that resembled her brother Geoffrey. *Perhaps a slight resemblance in the eyes,* noted Cecily to herself, *but they are quite dissimilar.*

Lady Arabella, although nearly forty years of age, retained a youthful beauty that was quite stunning.

"Dear Lady Warren," said Lady Arabella to Aunt Sophie, "you are looking so well."

"You are very kind, Lady Arabella," replied Aunt Sophie. "And I want to introduce my grandniece to you. This is Miss Cecily Camden."

"Miss Camden," said Lady Arabella, taking Cecily's hand and pressing it warmly. "I am so glad to meet you. Your aunt has told me so many nice things about you."

"And they were all true," chimed in Thomas as Cecily blushed.

"Oh, Mr. Warren-Brewster, what a pleasure to see you. Albert will be so pleased. He should be here any moment."

As if on cue, that gentleman appeared in the doorway and greeted the guests heartily and was duly introduced to Miss Camden.

"Such a pleasure to have you people over here. Please do be seated."

They were all seated comfortably and Lady Arabella began the conversation.

"I hear, Miss Camden, that you have been in London for the season. You must tell us all the news. Has anything exciting happened? I do hope you have some exciting gossip."

Before Cecily could speak her cousin answered, "Oh, Cecily has some dashed exciting news, haven't you, Cousin? About meeting Reginald, I mean."

Aunt Sophie gave her nephew another stern look and Lady Arabella looked curiously at Cecily. "Have you indeed seen Reginald, Miss Camden? He is, of course, in London, but we hear so little from him."

"Yes, ma'am, I have met your son on several occasions."

"Indeed?"

"Yes, I first met him at a party given by Lady Halberton."

Arabella tried to maintain an expression of unconcern but she was quite astonished to hear that her son had appeared at the home of Lady Halberton. That lady had been one of Arabella's former acquaintances who had joined the rest of society in ostracizing her.

"And what's more," said Cousin Thomas, "Reginald was with none other than the Marquis of Ashford, his uncle and your brother."

Lady Arabella now abandoned all attempt to hide her astonishment and stared incredulously at Thomas. "You mean Reginald was with my brother Geoffrey?"

Lady Arabella turned to Miss Camden and Cecily replied, "Yes, ma'am. Lord Ashford introduced Mr. Stonecipher to everyone. And did so again at Almack's."

"Almack's!" cried Lady Arabella with a delighted smile. "How marvelous. My brother must be changing. You see, Miss Camden, my brother and I have not been on the best of terms."

"Humph," snorted Albert Stonecipher. "Dash it, Arabella, that brother of yours has been so high and mighty that he hasn't associated with you since you married me."

"But he was just a boy. And away at school. I really hardly knew him. And Isabelle poisoned him against me, you can be quite certain of that."

"Even so," said Mr. Stonecipher, "I find it dashed queer that Ashford would befriend my son Reginald. But you have seen this yourself, Miss Camden?"

"Yes, I have, sir," replied Cecily with an amused expression.

"And is it not true, Miss Camden," said Lady Arabella, "that you have been living in London with Lord and Lady Throxton?"

"Yes, indeed, ma'am," said Cecily. "Lady Throxton is my aunt."

"And you have a cousin Prunella?"

"Yes, I do."

Lady Arabella looked at Cecily with a triumphant expression and thought that her son was certainly accomplishing his mission.

"I still think it dashed queer of Ashford. What sort of man is he?" asked Mr. Stonecipher.

Cecily flushed slightly, noting that her aunt was watching her intently. "I have not known the Marquis for very long," she said, "but I believe he is a good man and a gentleman. And of course, he is very charming and a leader of fashion."

"Well, I am gratified to see that my brother has decided to aid my dear son. Reginald is a dear boy. I do hope you like him."

"Oh, he is very charming," replied Miss Camden, "and very attentive to my cousin and me. And his love of animals is very endearing," she added mischievously.

"Animals?" asked Stonecipher. "He's fond of horses but that's due to his interest in gaming. Fast and expensive is how he likes his horses."

"Albert!" cried Lady Arabella. "Reginald has always had a fondness for horses."

"I was referring to his pet dog," continued Cecily gravely. "The one that he brought from the country."

Albert Stonecipher started to reply but his wife's stern look silenced him. "He did always like dogs," she said uncertainly.

"That's a new one to me," said Cousin Tom with a puzzled look, "for I remember when Reginald was a boy. He was the only young one that old Hector could not abide.

Old Hector was a dear one. No better dog for herding cattle, and a good-tempered animal. But as soon as he'd see young Reginald old Hector would bark and growl. Never could understand it. Good old Hector," said Tom wistfully. "I miss the old thing. Lived to be nigh on twenty years."

Everyone listened to this information with polite attention and Lady Arabella found it an appropriate time to change the subject. "And how do you like Manchester, Miss Camden?"

"Quite well, thank you, my lady. It is wonderful to be here with my aunt and cousin."

"And it is a joy to have her here," said Aunt Sophie. "I'm selfish enough to wish she could stay permanently."

"Aye, would be a fine thing," said Cousin Tom with an enthusiasm that Arabella noted with interest.

At that moment the butler entered the room and announced to Lady Arabella that Mrs. Skruggs and her daughters had arrived. Cecily noted the pained expression that appeared on Albert Stonecipher's face and the gleeful look that appeared on her cousin Tom's face.

"Oh good, Cecily," said Thomas. "I had hoped that you would get to meet Maggie."

Mr. Stonecipher said nothing but the expression on his face nearly caused Cecily to burst out in laughter. Soon the cause of Mr. Stonecipher's obvious discomfiture entered the room, followed closely by two young ladies.

As she entered, Maggie surveyed the company and exclaimed with pleasure, "Oh, how marvelous. If it ain't Tom Warren-Brewster and his dear aunt." Maggie then saw Cecily and exclaimed, "And how do, young lady. I imagine you are some relation to Lady Warren."

Lady Arabella quickly introduced her sister-in-law to Cecily and Miss Camden studied Mrs. Skruggs's attire with amusement. Maggie Skruggs was dressed in a remarkable style in a flamboyant dress of pink and gold that fitted her plump figure tightly. Cecily wondered what Mr. Brummell would make of Maggie Skruggs and then looked at her two daughters. The two Misses Skruggs, in contrast to their mother, were wearing simple, flattering dresses. They were quite young, neither of them much over fifteen, and they stood quietly and respectfully.

The three arrivals were soon seated and Maggie Skruggs began to talk rapidly to Cecily. "My dear Miss Camden, I am so glad to meet you. I am so fond of your dear aunt and she has only been with us for a few short months. Manchester was indeed lucky to have Lady Warren come to stay."

"You are awfully kind, Maggie," said Aunt Sophie with a smile. "I am very glad to be here."

"And I hope Miss Camden is to be with us for a while."

"I am afraid I will be returning shortly to my aunt's, Lady Throxton's, country home. They expect me."

"Oh, dash it, Cecily," said Cousin Tom. "I hope you'll stay a good long time. It's quite a change for an old bachelor like me to have two lovely ladies in my household."

"And you are too long a bachelor, Thomas," said Maggie Skruggs. "You ought to marry. It ain't right for an eligible gentleman like you to deprive some fortunate lady of a husband. Is that not true, Albert?"

Mr. Stonecipher looked at Thomas and nodded somewhat unenthusiastically.

"Well, who knows, Maggie," said Thomas, "perhaps I will marry. And had William Skruggs not been quicker than I, I should have been married long ago."

Maggie laughed loudly. "Thomas Warren-Brewster. You say the most foolish things."

"But Maggie," continued Thomas, "you must hear about Reginald. Cecily has been telling us that she has seen him in London and he's quite a success among the nobs. Intimate friend of Brummell's."

Maggie Skruggs looked at Cecily. "What news is this?" she said expectantly.

"My cousin is exaggerating, of course, ma'am, but I was simply telling Lady Arabella and Mr. Stonecipher that I had made the acquaintance of Mr. Reginald Stonecipher in London."

"How wonderful!" exclaimed Maggie. "He is the sweetest boy. And so handsome. Miss Camden, you shall have to tell me everything."

Cecily proceeded to repeat her story of meeting Reginald, and Mrs. Skruggs asked her numerous questions. Maggie had an insatiable curiosity about London society and Cecily found herself telling tale after tale about various members of the ton.

Actually Cecily was surprised to realize that she was enjoying herself, and the time passed swiftly. Soon it grew late and Cecily, her aunt, and her cousin took their leave and returned to her cousin's carriage.

"Isn't Maggie a rare one, Cecily?" asked Cousin Tom on the way home in the carriage. "I knew you'd like her."

"But that Maggie," said Aunt Sophie, shaking her head. "The way that woman talks and all those questions she asked about London. I am sure she cannot wait until tomorrow when she shall travel all over the countryside repeating those stories to anyone who will listen."

"And old Albert was so surprised to hear that Reginald has been taking up with Ashford. I must meet that man, for it seems damned odd that anyone should befriend Reginald Stonecipher."

"Thomas," said Cecily, "Mr. Stonecipher is not as bad as that, is he?"

"I reckon not, Cousin, but he ain't the sort I'd care to call a friend. But he's young and perhaps he's changing."

Cecily smiled and sat in thoughtful silence. It was indeed strange that Ashford would associate with his nephew. *But,* thought Cecily, *perhaps he is desirous of making amends with his sister. I am sure Isabelle did prevent him from seeking to do so earlier.*

Cecily sat back and watched the landscape dim as dusk settled on the countryside. *And I had vowed to stop thinking of Ashford. I do not believe Manchester is very conducive to that end.* She smiled as the carriage rounded the bend in the road and approached her cousin's house.

* * *

After her guests had left, Lady Arabella turned joyfully to her husband.

"Albert," she cried, "this is utterly marvelous. I am so happy. Our Reginald is moving in the best circles."

"Damned odd," muttered her husband. "Odd that your brother would take up with Reginald. Not that he shouldn't show some consideration to his nephew after ignoring him and you, but I never thought anyone could much take to Reginald."

"Albert," cried Lady Arabella, "how can you say these things about your son?"

"Sorry, my dear," replied Mr. Stonecipher, "but I am glad that the Marquis is coming to his senses. I always hoped that one day you'd get back with your family, for I always hated to be the cause of them deserting you."

"Oh, my dear Albert," said her ladyship with a laugh, "I don't care one bit to see my family but I'm glad Reginald is such a success. And Prunella Throckmorton would be such an admirable connection."

"Well, I imagine if that girl is like her cousin I wouldn't object. That Miss Camden seemed to be a nice girl. No airs about her. I liked her, I did."

"Hmmm," replied Lady Arabella with a thoughtful expression. "Miss Camden is a fine young lady. And I feel we shall be seeing more of her if I am not mistaken."

"What's that?" asked Mr. Stonecipher. "Is she staying with Tom, then?"

"Oh heavens, Albert," replied Lady Arabella in an exasperated tone. "You men are not in the least perceptive. Didn't you see how Tom looked at her? I'd wager that Mr. Warren-Brewster's days of bachelorhood are numbered, and a good thing it is too."

"Tom marry?" said Mr. Stonecipher in a surprised tone. "Now that would be something to see. But I hope you're right, for I myself know that married life is a dashed agreeable state." He looked affectionately at his wife, who smiled in return.

"But I must be going, my dear," said Mr. Stonecipher.

"Have to see Thomson and go over some of the accounts. Excuse me, Arabella. I'll be back soon." He kissed his wife and left the room, leaving Lady Arabella in an elated mood.

Her ladyship sat down on the sofa and smiled. *Things are going well,* she thought. *Albert has been quite happy. I am sure business will be taking a turn for the better, in spite of the way Maggie carries on about it every time I see her. And my darling Reginald! He is doing so well. I knew he could charm his uncle, and soon he will be wedding Prunella Throckmorton and I shall have no more worry about his future.*

Lady Arabella got up from the sofa. "I shall write him," she said out loud. "Yes, a letter to Reginald would be in order." Her ladyship then retired to her sitting room to compose a happy letter to her son.

Mr. Albert Stonecipher did not share his wife's joy at the news of his son. "Damned odd," he kept muttering while seated in his carriage on the way to the factory. "Damned odd. All these years the Marquis has ignored my wife and now he introduces my son all over society. And it would not be as odd if Reginald weren't such a dashed bounder. Can't see a man like Ashford having a thing to do with him, unless . . ." Albert Stonecipher had a sudden idea. ". . . unless he feels a connection with Reginald would work to his advantage."

Stonecipher frowned cynically. His vast wealth made him the target of numerous schemers, and he wondered if his brother-in-law, the noble Marquis of Ashford, was as rich as had been rumored.

He is one of the nobs, thought Mr. Stonecipher, *and those gentlemen are prone to acquiring large and embarrassing debts.* Mr. Stonecipher shifted his weight in the carriage. *I think I had best investigate this matter,* he concluded gravely as he arrived at the factory. *It bears looking into.* He left the carriage and entered the immense structure with a thoughtful expression on his face.

* * *

The Marquis of Ashford had been rather bored during the past month. The season had virtually ended and there were few parties to attend. Most of his friends had left for the country and Ashford sat in his London house in a melancholy mood.

Of course, he thought with a smile, *I shall soon be off for Throxton Hall. Such a fine time I will have, I am sure.* He winced as he thought about the dull time he would be having there. *At least Miss Camden will be there,* he thought. He had been thinking of Miss Camden frequently during the past few weeks and was looking forward to seeing her again.

"My lord," said a voice. It was Ashford's butler, with the usual emotionless expression on his face. "Your nephew Mr. Reginald Stonecipher is here to see you, my lord."

Ashford groaned. "Oh God. Tell him I am indisposed. No wait, bring him up here. I will see him after all. But is he alone or is that fellow Crimpson with him?"

"He is alone, my lord."

"Then send him up." The butler disappeared and Ashford waited for his nephew's appearance with mild irritation. "As long as Crimpson isn't coming I suppose I can bear to be civil," he said. "After all I did decide to be friendly to him."

Reginald Stonecipher appeared at the door of Ashford's sitting room attired as usual in his dandified style. Ashford looked at him glumly.

"Good day, Uncle," said Reginald with a jovial expression that made Ashford feel like tossing him out the door. "I have come to ask you about going to Throxton Hall next week. I know this is terribly bold, but might Jeeters and I accompany you in your carriage?"

"Of course, Nephew," replied Ashford. "I thought that was to be the arrangement."

"Yes indeed, sir, but I thought it might be best to ask you."

"Well, my man will inform you of the details. I shall have him write you."

"You are terribly kind, Uncle," said Reginald, "and I wanted to convey my mother's greetings to you."

"Indeed?"

"Yes, my mother has heard of your kindness to me and she wanted me to tell you that she is quite grateful."

"I hope she is well," said Ashford.

"Yes indeed, Uncle. She wrote me a long letter about life in Manchester. I was interested to hear that Miss Cecily Camden is there now."

"Miss Camden in Manchester?" asked Ashford, becoming interested. "I thought she was with Throxton."

"Oh, she is visiting her aunt Lady Warren, who is living at the house of Thomas Warren-Brewster. What a coincidence it is, sir, that Miss Camden is cousin to old Thomas."

"You are acquainted with her cousin?"

"Good Lord, Uncle, I have known Thomas since I was a boy and I never liked him much. Not at all like Miss Camden. A damned slow top he is. And what is funny is that my mama writes and tells me she thinks Miss Camden might marry her cousin. Oh, Mama must be in an odd mood to think up that one."

Ashford heard this with great irritation, and his nephew continued. "I don't hold with this news. I can't see Miss Camden marrying someone like old Tom. He is as old as my father. Of course I don't expect Miss Camden has many offers. She's a dashed fine lady but no prospects. I haven't told Jeeters about this, him being so fond of Miss Camden and all and, of course, Uncle, I think Mama has got the wrong story this time."

Although the Marquis could not explain it, his nephew's words enraged him. He controlled himself with difficulty.

"I pray you will forgive me, Nephew," he said, "but I have another engagement so I must ask you to excuse me."

"Certainly, Uncle," said Reginald with a smile. "I shall see you next week."

Ashford said nothing but watched Reginald go. "That young spark," he said. "And he comes here to tell me that Cecily is to marry some doddering fool of a cousin and I shall be at Throxton Hall without one intelligent person to talk to. Blast!" Ashford paced the room impatiently.

"Twilling," he called at last, and his valet hurried to obey his summons. "I am leaving immediately. Follow me with my luggage and have Perkins accompany you. I shall meet you at the King's Arms."

Ashford left his house, leaving his valet to reflect on his master's impulsive nature and then begin to pack his bags.

CHAPTER 10

Cecily walked about the grounds of her cousin's house reflecting how pleasant it was there in the country away from her cousin Prunella. The fall weather was brisk and excellent for walking and Cecily took a long stroll down a pleasant wooded lane.

"Cousin," cried a voice and Cecily turned to see Thomas walking toward her. He was slightly out of breath when he reached her.

"Good heavens, Cecily," said Mr. Warren-Brewster. "I had a devil of a time finding you. You are certainly one for exercise."

Cecily laughed. "Cousin, I have not gone that far. You must walk more yourself."

"I suppose you are right, Cecily," agreed her cousin, "but I fear I prefer to have a horse do my walking for me."

Cecily smiled and he continued. "But this is serious, Cousin, for Aunt Sophie has said you are to return to your aunt."

"Yes, I am leaving soon. My aunt and Cousin Prunella expect me and I fear I must leave. And I have been here nearly three weeks although it hardly seems a week. I have enjoyed it here."

"But I thought you would stay longer," said Thomas. "I didn't think you'd leave so soon."

"But I shall return and visit you in the spring, Thomas, and I shall miss you."

Thomas looked awkwardly at his feet. "But I thought maybe you could stay permanently. Dash it, Cecily, what I mean is I thought you might consent to marry me. I know it's a surprise and I don't say things like this very well. Not like those polished London gentlemen. And I know I ain't much to look at and I am a bit older than you, but I thought you might overlook that since I know you like it in Manchester."

"Cousin Tom," said Cecily, "you are terribly kind. I know you want to give me a home but I am not so sure you are ready to abandon your bachelor life."

"But dash it, Cecily, I am fond of you."

"And I am fond of you, Tom, but I am not sure that we are suited. I must refuse you, Thomas, but I do not do so lightly. You see, I am not ready to marry right now."

Cecily was surprised at the look of disappointment that appeared on her cousin's face.

"You are sure?" he asked.

"Yes, I am."

"But if you change your mind you will tell me."

"Yes, of course."

"Well, I guess we should be getting back to the house; it's nearly time for dinner and I'm dashed hungry."

Cecily laughed and took her cousin's arm and the two of them walked back to the house.

Leaving her aunt Sophie and cousin Tom had been very difficult for Cecily, and the prospect of returning to the Throxton household did little to dull the pain of leaving. Cecily and her maid sat quietly throughout the journey and Cecily thought mainly about Cousin Tom.

He is a dear man, she thought with a smile. *Perhaps I was wrong after all.*

"Miss," said her maid, "looks to be rain ahead." Cecily

looked out the vehicle's window and saw that the southern sky was filled with menacing clouds. They had not gone very far when the rain began in a steady downpour and the coach soon pulled up alongside an inn.

"I'm afraid, miss," said the driver through the window, "we are going to have to wait here for a while. The road is getting hard to see and the man here informs me that the bridge up ahead ain't safe."

"Oh dear," said Cecily. "Is this an inn we have come to?"

"Yes, miss, the King's Arms and not a bad place. I'll escort you ladies inside." The man led them through the pouring rain into the inn and Cecily was glad to be inside in a warm and dry place.

"Good day, ladies," said a voice and Cecily looked up to see an oddly dressed gentleman addressing them.

"Seems like you ladies is a bit wet and cold. Let Al Landen take care of you. Come and sit by the fire."

"Thank you, sir," said Cecily warily, "but we will be all right."

"But come over here," said the persistent Mr. Landen, taking Cecily's arm.

"I think the lady said she did not want to join you, sir," said a voice and Cecily turned around to see the Marquis of Ashford.

"Good day, then," said Mr. Landen, taking in Ashford's appearance and deciding he did not want to argue with him. He quickly retreated to his old place by the fire.

Cecily was so amazed to see Ashford that she found herself staring at him in stunned silence.

"My dear Miss Camden," said his lordship with a smile, "you don't look happy to see me. I think you were happier to see Mr. Landen."

Cecily burst into laughter. "Lord Ashford, I am glad to see you but forgive me, I am so astonished to find you here. But I suppose I should not be so surprised, for you are always rescuing me. The fates have decreed that each time I find myself in some ridiculous situation, you should appear. But I thank you, sir, truly."

As Cecily finished speaking there was a loud sneeze from behind her, and Cecily turned to see that her maid was wiping a very red nose with her handkerchief.

"Beg your pardon, miss," she said apologetically.

"Becky!" cried Cecily. "You look dreadful. And you are soaking wet. You shall catch your death. I shall have to see to you immediately."

"Allow me," said Ashford, motioning toward the landlord, who hastened to obey his lordship's summons and approached with an obsequious bow.

"And what may I do to serve your lordship?" he asked.

"You must see to the lady's servant. The girl is not well."

"At once, m'lord," answered the innkeeper. "My wife will see to 'er, never fear, m'lord. We'll take good care of 'er to be sure."

"I should appreciate that," said Ashford.

The landlord bowed again and led the sniffling Becky from the room.

Cecily smiled at the Marquis. "Thank you again, sir. I should have noticed before that Becky had caught a chill."

"I'm sure she will be fine," said Ashford, "but what about you? I hope you have not caught a chill."

"I am fine, sir. I think I will stand by the fire though."

"Of course."

Ashford led Cecily across the room to the fire. "That dampness," said Cecily, warming her hands, "it was terribly chilling. This fire is wonderful."

"But I fear you have gotten wet from the rain," said Ashford with concern.

Cecily looked down at her pelisse and found it to be damp and mud spattered. "I fear I did get a bit damp and I look a sight. I am glad Mr. Brummell is not here to see me."

Ashford laughed. "You look wonderful. I think Manchester must have agreed with you."

Cecily blushed. "I do not look wonderful in the least."

"Do not argue with me, ma'am," said Ashford with a smile. "But I will have that rascally innkeeper show you to a room and have one of these fellows bring in your baggage, for I fear you shall travel no further today."

"Oh dear," said Cecily with a concerned expression. "I thought I should be at Throxton Hall tonight."

"Are you that eager to arrive at Throxton Hall, Miss Camden?" asked Ashford with a smile. "I fear I have misjudged you."

Cecily laughed again. "Lord Ashford, you are dreadful. But I have not yet asked you what brings you to this rustic establishment." Cecily surveyed the inn with an amused look. It was a small, untidy place and the only people taking advantage of its questionable hospitality were themselves, the friendly Mr. Landen, and a balding middle-aged gentleman who was sleeping peacefully in a chair.

"I daresay, sir," continued Cecily, "it is hardly the sort of place one would expect to find the Marquis of Ashford."

"Indeed? I will have you know that this is an admirable place and I have been keeping it a secret so hordes of fashionable people from London will not descend upon it. I do detest crowds."

"Then you are fortunate, my lord, for I doubt whether we shall be too crowded here."

Ashford laughed. "Certainly not. Since the bridge to the south is now impassable we shall probably have few additions to this company. And I must admit, Miss Camden, that it is that despicable bridge that has forced me here without bag or baggage or even valet."

"You are alone?" asked Cecily in surprise.

"You see, I was in a devil of a mood today. I decided to visit Wingate and left on horseback, instructing my man to follow. And this damnable weather came up and here I am. But seeing you has certainly cheered me. But Miss Camden, do go to your room and rest for a while." His lordship motioned to the innkeeper and said in an imperious tone, "Show this lady to your best room and have her bags brought up. Oh good God, Miss Camden. I forgot that your girl is sick."

"Never mind that, sir," said Cecily. "I shall manage by myself. Excuse me, for I would like to retire to my room for a while."

Cecily turned and followed the innkeeper to the room. Fortunately she found it to be relatively clean and quite adequate. A well-worn chair and a large bed with a heavy oaken bedstead were the main features of the room. A wide window looked out to the north and Cecily could see the rain still falling in torrents. Flashes of lightning illuminated the landscape for brief periods and Cecily shivered as she peered out across the dark countryside.

A sullen country lad brought up her bag, and Cecily sat down on the bed and stared thoughtfully at the flickering candles that the innkeeper had left in the room.

To think that I should find myself in this wretched inn with Ashford, Cecily thought with a smile. *I spend a month trying to rid myself of my schoolgirl infatuation only to find him here. It is quite ludicrous.* She then thought of Mr. Landen. *But I am glad of it, for I do not think that gentleman would be good company. I shall simply have to refrain from sighing and staring longingly at his lordship. I'm sure it would be quite rude. I shall steel myself against his charm.* She laughed softly to herself and got up from the bed and opened her packing case to find another dress.

Lord Ashford sat restlessly at the wooden table. The fire burned vigorously and the middle-aged gentleman who was sleeping in the chair began to snore noisily. Ashford watched as Mr. Landen gave the man an impatient nudge and he awoke with a startled expression. The two men exchanged a few angry words and Mr. Landen loudly announced that he would not stay a moment longer in the same room with the balding man, who was evidently an acquaintance. Mr. Landen then left the room, leaving the older man to settle once again into a noisy sleep.

Ashford got up from the table and paced across the

room. *Why is Cecily taking so long?* he wondered; then he decided that it was only that time was moving so slowly. *Stuck in this accursed place,* he said to himself, *and poor Cecily stuck here too.*

He stood by a window and stared out at the rain. *By God,* he thought, *what a wretched night.*

"My lord," said a voice behind him, and Ashford turned with a start to see Cecily.

"Oh, I have startled you, sir," said Miss Camden.

"I fear I have been in a reflective mood. I did not hear you come in." Ashford looked at Cecily, who was now attired in a simple green dress and looked quite charming in the inn's unsteady light.

"That dress becomes you," he said matter-of-factly.

"Thank you, sir," replied Cecily, then rapidly changed the subject. "Is there anything to eat in this house? I fear I am famished."

Ashford laughed. "I have been assured by our host that we shall be feasting like the Prince himself, so if I may escort you to the table." He offered her his arm with exaggerated gallantry and led her to the table.

Cecily sat down and looked about the room. "My lord," she said in a whisper, "where is Mr. Landen?"

"Did you want to ask him to join us, ma'am?" whispered his lordship in return.

Cecily laughed. "You are being ridiculous. Although I am sure he is a most entertaining gentleman."

"Yes indeed, but I am sorry to report that entertaining gentleman has retired."

"A pity."

"Indeed."

They both laughed as the innkeeper brought a number of dishes to the table. Boiled mutton, steaming pudding, and bread and cheese were laid out and the two guests were both relieved to find the food quite palatable.

"I know it is unladylike," said Cecily, "but I am ravenous. I had not eaten since leaving Manchester."

"I hope you had a pleasant stay," said Ashford.

"It was very nice," replied Cecily. "Not at all dull."

For some reason Ashford heard this with disappointment. "Then you were not eager to leave?"

"No, not at all." Cecily thought she saw a trace of disappointment appear in Ashford's face, but his expression changed rapidly and Cecily decided that it was only her imagination.

"I heard that you were staying with your cousin. A Mr. Warren-Brewster, well-known by some odd coincidence by my nephew Reginald. Poor Mr. Warren-Brewster."

Cecily laughed. "Yes, my cousin Tom. He's a very sweet man. I think you would like him."

Ashford made no reply but doubted whether he would like that gentleman in the least.

"Of course, he's not in any way extraordinary and not at all fashionable or witty, but Aunt Sophie dotes on him."

"And what of Mrs. Warren-Brewster?" asked Ashford in feigned innocence.

"Oh, Cousin Tom is a bachelor and I fear shall remain one. He is three and forty and has no intention of marrying. I suppose you bachelors become terribly set in your ways."

Ashford laughed and found himself to be relieved that Cecily made no mention of intending to marry her cousin.

"Yes indeed, Miss Camden. But are you including me in this category of old bachelors?"

Cecily smiled mischievously. "Of course, you are perhaps a year or two my cousin's junior."

Ashford smiled. "Again we come to discussing my advanced age."

"Yes, my lord, for it is far more agreeable than discussing my advanced age."

Ashford laughed. "And you are always accusing me of being ridiculous. But tell me how you spent your time at Manchester. Did you ride?"

"Yes, a good deal, but I fear I spent most of my time gossiping with my aunt Sophie. A dangerous pastime."

"Indeed, and I imagine you had many stories to tell."

"After all, my lord, I had met you and Mr. Brummell and you must expect people to want to hear about you pillars of ton."

"Miss Camden!"

"But I didn't tell tell anything too dreadful, only dreadful enough to be entertaining."

"Miss Camden," repeated Ashford with an expression of mock dismay. "I shall never show my face in Manchester—although I do not find that such a horrible prospect."

Cecily laughed but turned suddenly serious. "And I also met your sister Arabella and her husband."

"I hope you found them well," Ashford replied.

"Yes indeed, and Lady Arabella is charming." Cecily watched Ashford curiously, and since her comments evoked no reaction she continued. "Lady Arabella looks very much like her son Reginald."

Ashford made no reply and Cecily decided to pursue the subject no further. "I do hope the rain will stop," she said.

This innocent remark caused the Marquis to burst into laughter and Cecily looked at him in surprise.

"Forgive me, Miss Camden," he said, "but you changed the subject so abruptly."

"I have never mastered the art of skillfully changing topics and I invariably begin talking about the weather," said Cecily awkwardly, "but I don't see why it is so amusing."

"Do forgive me, but I know you thought you had broached the rather delicate subject of my family and I was being very uncooperative. I really am not so sensitive. I fear I was just wondering whether you'd ask me why I never see my sister Arabella."

"My lord," said Cecily, "I was trying to be tactful and you have completely disconcerted me. I suppose I have no recourse now but to be tactless. All right, my lord, why do you never see your sister? I have been wanting to know that ever since I met her."

"That is better," he replied with a laugh, "but I'm afraid I have no good answer. You see, I was a mere boy when Arabella left and I had never really known her. It became something of a family tradition to disparage poor Ara and her husband. My mother never mentioned her and I resented the fact that my sister had hurt my mother very deeply.

"I never had any desire to see Arabella and make amends. I have really never even seen her these past twenty years, nor have I received any communication from her."

"But you have been helping Mr. Stonecipher, your nephew."

"And it is not out of kindness that I do so. My chief reason for sponsoring my nephew Reginald is to spite my sister Isabelle and that lout Chesterfield."

Cecily made no reply but looked at him intently.

"I must sound horrible but I fear I am devoid of family feeling. I cannot abide most of my relatives."

"I suppose it is very difficult to be in your position, sir," said Cecily thoughtfully. "I mean, I am sure your relatives are forever coming to you for favors. Since you are a man of position and wealth, of course. I have always been one of the poor relatives myself, petitioning my poor family for aid."

"Oh good heavens, Miss Camden," replied Ashford, "had I relations like yourself I would be a happy man." Cecily flushed. "And your relations must consider themselves lucky to have your company. Especially Throxton. I am grateful that coincidence and this abominable weather has brought you here, for I am enjoying myself immensely."

"You are too kind, sir," said Cecily, smiling, "but I will acknowledge that even my company is more agreeable than that of the gentleman in the chair over there."

Ashford laughed. "By the gods, this is a fine place. But tell me more about my sister. And what is her husband like? Is he indeed as rich as I have been told?"

"It would appear so," answered Cecily. "Indeed, I have never seen such a grand house. I was quite intimidated by it although I soon began to feel quite grand myself simply being there. Of course, it is a new house and without any history."

"I think I would gladly exchange some of the history of my house at Ashford for a way to reduce the drafts in the place."

"It is a very old house at Ashford?"

"The oldest part was built in the twelfth century. I must confess that I do love that house but seldom go there. But tell me more about my sister."

"She is really extremely nice and very beautiful. And Mr. Stonecipher is very affable. I liked them both. Mr. Stonecipher is a great friend of my cousin Tom's. And he is not at all like his son."

"That is a blessing!"

"My lord!"

Ashford laughed again. "I suppose I must one day go to Manchester to see this remarkable house and brother-in-law. One day I will."

"Oh, if you do, sir, I hope you will see my cousin Tom and aunt Sophie. My aunt is a dear and I already miss her dreadfully."

"I would indeed love to meet her," said Ashford.

"But we have talked too much about my visit. Do tell me of your plans. You said you were on the way to meet a friend."

"Yes, Lord Wingate. Thought I'd pay him a short visit before next week when I'm off to Throxton Hall."

Cecily's eyes met his. "It is good of you to go to Throxton Hall, my lord. I hope it won't be a terrible bore for you."

"No, I am looking forward to it," said Ashford, surprised that he was telling the truth. "Should be some dashed fine hunting."

At that moment the conversation was interrupted by the balding gentleman, who had awakened and stood up quickly, causing his chair to fall over backwards with a loud crash.

Cecily jumped at the unexpected noise and Ashford glared at his fellow guest. The gentleman stared about the room and awkwardly restored the chair to an upright position.

Noting Ashford and Cecily, he sauntered over and bowed to them.

"Beg your pardon, sir. Damned chair. And to your lady. Pardon, ma'am."

Cecily had a terrible urge to laugh and looked down at her plate.

Ashford looked at the balding man irritably and made no reply. "Allow me to introduce myself. Thadeus Baxter. Traveling to London I am with my partner, Mr. Landen."

"I have met your partner."

"You have, sir? Good man he is. And whom do I have the pleasure of addressing, sir?"

Ashford was reluctant to reply but the balding gentleman repeated himself. "I said whom do I have the honor of addressing?"

"I am Lord Ashford—" began his lordship.

"My lord Ashford," Mr. Baxter interrupted, "what an honor this is. How do, my lord. And your lovely lady. Honored, my lady."

By this time Cecily was trying her best to stifle her giggles and Ashford looked at Mr. Baxter with a disgusted expression.

Mr. Baxter turned to Cecily. "Lady Ashford," he said, "I hope you have not been too distressed at this weather."

"Not at all, sir," said Cecily, "but I am not Lady Ashford."

"I beg your pardon, ma'am," said Mr. Baxter. He looked back at Ashford and smiled at him. "I see," he said knowingly and winked at Ashford.

"Damn your impudence," cried his lordship, getting up from his chair and facing a very shocked Mr. Baxter.

"How dare you, sir?" said Ashford, his face white with rage.

"I beg your pardon, my lord," said Mr. Baxter, "and a

thousand apologies to the lady. I meant nothing. Please forgive me, my lord."

Ashford sat down again and looked coldly at the quaking Baxter. "Excuse me then, my lord," said Baxter and retreated hurriedly.

Cecily looked at Ashford's face and saw that he still was seething with indignation. She tried to maintain her composure but soon gave up and burst into laughter.

Ashford looked at her. "How can you laugh? The insolence of that boor."

"My lord," said Cecily, "it was funny, was it not? Pray admit it."

Ashford smiled and then joined in laughing. "But he was so damned impertinent."

"And so shocked. Did you see the look on his face when you stood up? My lord Ashford, your anger is indeed dreadful to behold. I feared for the poor man's life."

"The poor man? Good heavens, Miss Camden, the man is an idiot and you could not expect me to bear his insulting attitude."

Cecily smiled again. "Lord Ashford, I am touched that you are so eager to defend my honor. It is so medieval."

Ashford looked at her with an embarrassed expression. "It was silly, wasn't it?" Cecily nodded and the two of them laughed heartily for some time.

Cecily finally composed herself and said, "I fear it is time for me to retire, but I must first check on Becky."

"I do hope she's better." He signaled for the innkeeper, who appeared instantly. "The lady is concerned about her maid. Please take her to the girl."

"Yes, indeed, my lord," said the man with his usual subservience. "Follow me, ma'am."

Cecily rose from the table and offered Ashford her hand. "I don't think I ever had a more enjoyable dinner. Thank you."

"Nor have I, Miss Camden," said his lordship, holding her hand longer than convention dictated. "Sleep well."

Cecily could feel her face reddening as he pressed her

hand, and hoped desperately that he would not notice. "Good night, my lord," she managed to say and followed the innkeeper out of the room.

Cecily found Becky in a small servant's room. "Are you feeling better, Becky?" asked Miss Camden.

"Yes, thanks, miss," said the girl. "I think I'll be fine tomorrow."

Cecily smiled kindly. "You look much better but get your rest tonight, for I hope to leave here tomorrow."

"Yes, ma'am," said Becky, obediently closing her eyes as her mistress left the room and retired to her own bed.

Cecily was so exhausted that she went quickly to sleep, giving little thought to Lord Ashford. She awoke the next morning and was glad to see the sun streaming into the room.

Cecily got up and went to the window. The ground was covered with puddles from last night's rain but already the morning sun was helping to dry them up. *I suppose I will be able to leave today.* In spite of herself she felt a twinge of disappointment but she dressed and went downstairs.

The innkeeper spoke a respectful greeting as Cecily passed him and entered the large downstairs room. There, standing at the window, was Lord Ashford. Cecily noted that in spite of the absence of his valet, Ashford was impeccably dressed.

"Good day, my lord," said Miss Camden cheerily.

"Ah, Cecily," said his lordship and Miss Camden noted that he had used her Christian name for the first time. "Did you sleep well? You certainly look well."

Cecily smiled. "I fear I am getting used to these compliments. I shall grow terribly vain if you are not careful. But I do hope, sir, that you rested well."

"Tolerably well, Miss Camden, although Mr. Baxter's snoring was a bit annoying. But there is breakfast here for us and it looks quite adequate."

The breakfast was more than adequate and Cecily decided that in spite of the inn's shabby appearance its food was much above the average.

After they had breakfasted, Ashford and Cecily walked out into the inn's yard. The coachman was examining the post chaise and Ashford called over.

"We is in good form here, sir," said the coachman. "But the roads near the bridge is a bit bad. And the bridge is still impassable though I hear it will be ready by afternoon." He looked at Cecily. "So we should be able to leave, ma'am."

"Good," said Cecily without enthusiasm.

She and Ashford walked away from the inn. "I have a time to wait, sir," she said. "And I hate to detain you. I know you are eager to visit Lord Wingate. Do not stay on my account. I shall be fine."

"My dear Miss Camden. I have no desire to leave at this moment. Would you have me ride to Wingate House in this mud? Heavens, ma'am, my boots would be a sight."

Cecily laughed. "I just hate to have you stay about this boring place."

"Boring? Not with characters like Landen and Baxter roaming about."

They walked a little way further. "It's rather muddy," said Ashford. "Shall we go back?"

"No," said Cecily, looking down at the ground. "It isn't so bad and I need to be out. After all that rain it is so good to be able to be out here."

"And you aren't cold?" he asked in a solicitous voice.

"Not at all."

They continued to walk and Cecily looked out across the countryside. "It's beautiful country," she said, noting the green hills and autumn-tinged trees.

"Yes," he agreed, surveying the landscape. "But look over there." He pointed in the direction of a towerlike structure that stood tall and solitary across the expanse of green grass.

"I see it," said Cecily. "A church?"

"More like the ruin of a church," said Ashford. "Looks like that tower is the only thing standing."

"Let's go and see it," said Cecily, suddenly eager.

"But it's apt to be muddy," said Ashford, dubious.

"Is it your boots that are worrying you, my lord?" asked Cecily with a grin and Ashford grinned in return.

"All right, I shall risk my boots if you are willing to risk your shoes and dress. Let us go on fording rivers."

"And climbing mountains."

"And fighting hostile savages."

Cecily laughed. "I do hope we find no hostile savages," she said. "I have not had much experience with hostile savages."

"Nor have I," said Ashford solemnly, "so it would be best if we do not meet any."

Ashford and Cecily walked happily across the meadow and Ashford stopped to look down at his boots. "And I hope we don't meet any civilized people either."

The two of them continued and after nearly an hour of walking arrived at the ruin.

"It is beautiful," said Cecily, looking at the Gothic tower.

"I'm sure it was very beautiful indeed," said Ashford.

They sat down on a large stone and surveyed the site.

"We are near Hodgeson, are we not, my lord?" asked Cecily.

"Yes, not far."

"Then I am sure this must be the ruined abbey that Lord Higglesby-Smythe has spoken about."

"Is Higglesby-Smythe in the habit of giving lectures about ruined abbeys? I hardly thought that Lady Prunella would be much interested in such things."

Cecily laughed and ran her hand across the time-worn stone of the abbey foundation. "I'm afraid Pru isn't terribly interested but it is fascinating. This abbey was built in the time of Henry the Second. Thomas Becket had spent time here and it was destroyed by Henry Tudor. Lord Higglesby-Smythe is quite an expert on it."

Ashford got up and walked among the fallen stones. "It's sad, I suppose," he said. "These old stones are much like the oldest part of Ashford. Built about the same time. It must have been beautiful."

"Yes," agreed Cecily, staring at the ruin and conjuring up visions of monks filing silently through the abbey. "I am beginning to feel rather sad here," she said.

"I feel it, too," replied Ashford seriously. "I think we had better be getting back." He and Cecily left the ruin and began the return walk across the meadows. They were silent for some time, as a heavy mood had settled upon them both.

Finally, Ashford stopped and looked down at his boots, which were well-caked with mud. He said nothing but looked from his boots to Cecily's face and the two of them began laughing, breaking the abbey's ponderous spell.

They returned to the inn to find a handsome carriage newly arrived. As they approached, the crest of the Marquis of Ashford was visible on the carriage door and Ashford experienced an odd feeling of disappointment.

"Your carriage is here, my lord," said Cecily, herself disappointed. "The roads must be passable."

"Yes," said Ashford, "and there is Twilling." Twilling approached them and bowed respectfully.

"My lord," he said, "I am sorry that we were detained. I hope your lordship experienced no difficulty." The valet glanced down at his master's boots, but concealed the horror he felt at their mud-spattered condition. He also noted that the lady accompanying his master was quite mud-spattered and wondered what had possessed his lordship to wander through muddy terrain with a young lady at his side.

Ashford, knowing what his valet was thinking, laughed out loud. "Well, Twilling, I'm dashed glad to see you. Hope you have my other boots."

"Of course, my lord," replied the valet gravely, and Cecily looked at Ashford with an amused expression.

"I shall be with you shortly, Twilling," said his lordship, dismissing his servant.

Cecily looked at Ashford. "I do not think he approved," she said softly.

"Yes," said Ashford, laughing. "I hope I haven't upset him too much."

Cecily and Ashford entered the inn and Cecily stopped. "I believe we shall both be able to continue our journeys," she said. "I shall be at Throxton Hall in a few hours."

"Yes," said Ashford, "but I must say I'm not as happy to see old Twilling as I thought I'd be. I can't remember when I've had a more enjoyable time. Not often that I go tramping off exploring ruins."

"That is fortunate for your valet, sir."

Ashford laughed. "But Miss Camden, you are fine company. I am so glad that you will be at Throxton Hall next week."

Cecily did not have an opportunity to reply, for her maid, Becky, appeared in the room and made a deep curtsy.

"Oh, Becky," said Cecily, "I am glad to see you about."

"Thank you, ma'am," replied Becky. "I'm much better. I want to report, miss, that I have your things packed and ready and the coachman says he is ready to leave as soon as possible."

"Thank you," said Cecily. "Wait for me upstairs." Becky turned to leave and Cecily looked at Ashford. "Oh dear," she said. "I must hurry and change my dress."

"You must indeed," smiled Ashford. "Quite dangerous to keep coachmen waiting."

Cecily laughed, curtsied, and hurried off to her room.

The ride back to Throxton Hall passed quickly for Cecily. She was lost in a state of reverie and noticed very little the changing landscape and her maid's chatter.

She kept remembering the look on Ashford's face as she had made her farewell. He had seemed genuinely sorry to see her leave, and the memory of his parting words lingered in her mind. He had kissed her hand and helped her into the carriage. She had said nothing but had smiled at him as the carriage started on its way. Although she had tried to keep herself from doing so, Cecily turned and looked back at the inn as the carriage picked up speed, and Ashford had been still standing there watching the retreating carriage.

It's ridiculous, mused Cecily, *but I think he likes me a little. But I suppose that is little compared to my grand passion. And how can I bear to be at Throxton Hall with him.* Cecily smiled. *Of course, I don't know how I shall bear to be without him either. It's horrid that I should have to be so silly at my age.*

Cecily continued thinking of Ashford throughout the entire trip until the familiar grounds of Throxton Hall appeared through the carriage window.

Lady Prunella was overjoyed at her cousin's arrival at Throxton Hall, for she had been getting quite bored with the country. There was little for Prunella to do but sit and think about Reginald Stonecipher and count off the days until he would arrive with the other hunting party guests.

When Cecily arrived Prunella pounced on her eagerly and besieged her with questions. "How was Manchester, Cecily? You must tell me everything. It has been so unbearably dull here. But pray, tell me everything."

Mercifully, Lady Throxton intervened, admonishing her daughter to allow Cecily to rest from her journey, and Cecily was able to retire to her room. The next day Cecily was unable to avoid describing her visit to Manchester in minute detail to her aunt and cousin. Both of those ladies listened with rapt attention as Cecily described her cousin Tom's house and life at Manchester.

"Your cousin Thomas sounds like a very good man," said Lady Throxton, "and of course I know that your aunt Sophie is the dearest woman. But what of society? Did you meet any interesting people?"

Cecily hesitated. "I did meet Mr. Stonecipher and Lady Arabella, parents of Reginald Stonecipher."

"How marvelous," cried Prunella, clapping her hands together. "You must tell me everything. What is she like? Lady Arabella, I mean? Oh, tell me everything."

Lady Throxton also looked at Cecily with great interest. "I am eager to hear of the Stoneciphers."

"They are quite nice," began Cecily. "I only met them once, of course, but Lady Arabella was quite charming. And very beautiful."

"Does she look like her son?" asked Prunella.

"Yes, very much like him."

"And what sort of man is this Stonecipher?" asked Lady Throxton. "I have heard he is of the vulgar sort, engaged in trade as he is."

"Indeed not, ma'am," said Cecily. "He seemed quite a gentleman. Perhaps not as polished as some but certainly not vulgar."

Cecily tactfully refrained from mentioning Maggie Skruggs and continued to describe the Stoneciphers' house.

Cecily's aunt seemed relieved to hear her niece confirm reports of Stonecipher's wealth, for Lady Throxton was somewhat worried about her daughter's obvious infatuation with young Reginald. Although Lady Throxton hoped her daughter would come to her senses and marry Lord Higglesby-Smythe, she was glad to hear that Reginald was heir to a considerable fortune.

The three ladies talked for some time and Lady Throxton left the two young ladies alone.

"Cecily, I am so glad you are here," said Prunella, "and your news of Reginald's family is wonderful. Mama can have no objection to Reginald now."

Cecily said nothing but deeply regretted that she had furthered Reginald's cause. "But Pru, have you seen Lord Higglesby-Smythe?"

"Oh, Gerald, of course. But Cecily, why must you talk of Gerald? I am only glad that soon I shall be seeing Reginald again. These weeks have been agony without him." Prunella sighed melodramatically. "Time has been moving so slowly but I shall see him soon. Oh, Cecily, I don't think I can bear it."

Cecily tried to appear sympathetic. "It is but a few days more that you shall have to wait."

"Yes," said Prunella. "I am sure I could not exist any longer without him."

Cecily smiled and thought, *As silly as you are, Prunella, you are no more silly than I with my schoolgirl's feelings for Ashford.*

Prunella began to chatter about the approaching hunting party, and Cecily was soon lost in her thoughts about the Marquis of Ashford.

CHAPTER 11

There was much commotion at Throxton Hall the day that the hunting party guests were to arrive. Lady Throxton had spent the morning making a last-minute check to see that her orders had been carried out properly. When Cecily found her aunt in the parlor, she was alarmed by Lady Throxton's harried expression.

"Is something wrong, ma'am?" asked Cecily.

"Oh no, my dear," replied Lady Throxton calmly. "I have just been checking the preparations and am happy to say that everything is going smoothly." Her ladyship gave a short sigh of relief. "The hunting party this year should be quite a success!"

Cecily, although not as optimistic as her aunt, doubted it could be as tedious as the last season at Throxton Hall. She felt the presence of the Marquis of Ashford guaranteed that.

While she and Lady Throxton were talking, Lady Prunella hurried into the room. "Mama, Cecily, some carriages are driving up through the gate. Come, Cecily, let's go meet the guests," urged Prunella.

"All right, Cousin," said Cecily as she got up and smoothed her dress. Lady Throxton, also eager to welcome her guests, scurried ahead of them. Lord Throxton was already outside, shouting a greeting to the approaching carriages.

As the first carriage neared them, Prunella frowned in disappointment. "Oh, it's only Gerald."

The carriage pulled up and the stout figure of Lord Higglesby-Smythe alighted from it.

Lord Throxton shouted, "Gerald, how capital to see you." He grasped the young lord's hand and pumped it enthusiastically. Lord Higglesby-Smythe smiled and glanced shyly toward the ladies.

Lady Throxton advanced toward him and said warmly, "Gerald, it's always wonderful to see you. Prunella has been so looking forward to your visit." Higglesby-Smythe blushed a furious red and Prunella gave her mother an indignant stare.

"How are you, Prunella?" stammered his lordship.

"I'm fine, Gerald," said Prunella in an indifferent voice as she glanced to see if any other carriages were approaching.

"Lovely weather, don't you think?" asked Lord Higglesby-Smythe, vainly trying to summon up a conversation.

"What?" asked Prunella impatiently, but before Higglesby-Smythe could reply, Prunella noticed another carriage approaching. "It must be Lord Ashford's party!" she shouted happily, ignoring Higglesby-Smythe.

Prunella seemed so eager that Miss Camden was afraid for a moment that she would run to meet the carriage. However, her cousin was able to confine her excitement to a few incoherent exclamations.

As the vehicle drew up before them, Lord Throxton bounded over to it. "Ashford!" he shouted, grabbing the Marquis from the carriage. He patted him roughly on the shoulder. "God, but you do remind me of your papa," Throxton said in a gruffly sentimental voice.

Ashford smiled at him and extended his hand.

"It is good to see you again, sir. I am glad to find you in such excellent health."

Throxton chuckled. "I tell you, my lad, I wouldn't let anything stop me from this hunt. Even this blasted gouty leg!" He gave the leg a gleeful slap.

Reginald and Jeeters had followed Ashford out of the carriage and were immediately greeted by a rapturous Prunella.

"Oh my, but you two are handsome!" she gazed admiringly at Reginald, who mumbled how wonderful it was to see her.

Mr. Crimpson, thinking it a rather poor effort on his friend's part, leaned over to Prunella and whispered, "Lady Pru, I think you've made another conquest. I've never seen Reg in such a distracted state."

"Really?" gasped Prunella.

Jeeters shook his head in confirmation. "I say, I know it's improper for me to ask you this but Reg is a dear friend of mine . . ."

"Oh, pray what is it?" whispered Prunella.

Jeeters's face took on a tragic expression. "Well, I just wonder if—I mean I don't know what your feelings are for Reg and it certainly ain't none of my business either. But I'm worried about him." He seemed embarrassed and continued haltingly, "If . . . if you snubbed him I don't know what he'd do." He looked at her grimly. "I'm afraid it might be something drastic."

"Oh no!" cried Prunella. Jeeters almost laughed at seeing the shocked but nonetheless pleased look in Prunella's eyes. She suddenly smiled at him. "You don't have anything to fear on that score, I assure you, Mr. Crimpson." She blushed and Jeeters grasped her hand and uttered his profuse gratitude.

While Jeeters and Lady Prunella were having their whispered conversation, Reginald had observed Lord Higglesby-Smythe standing near his uncle and Lord Throxton. He smiled a greeting and strode over to him.

Lord Higglesby-Smythe took an involuntary step backward as Reginald approached him. He had no inkling that his childhood tormentors were going to be among the hunting party. At the sight of them stepping out of Ashford's carriage, Higglesby-Smythe emitted an unhappy groan. He became even more dismayed when he viewed Prunella's evident partiality toward Reginald.

As that gentleman advanced, Higglesby-Smythe grimaced. He was beginning to feel ill and wished he were back home.

"Why, Higglesby-Smythe!" exclaimed Reginald, slapping him on the shoulder. "How famous that you should be here. We'll be sure to have a deuce of a good time now."

Higglesby-Smythe shuddered at that ominous statement and forced a smile. Reginald continued talking and Higglesby-Smythe just stood watching him nervously.

Miss Camden had been observing the arrival of Ashford's party with considerable interest. She was somewhat disturbed at finding how glad she was to see Ashford's familiar form. *I must be sensible,* she told herself sternly. However, her resolve was shaken when Ashford, conversing with Lord and Lady Throxton, glanced over at her. His face had been a mask of civility but when he saw her a genuine smile appeared. She returned his smile, pleased that he was apparently glad to see her.

After a few moments Lord Ashford strolled over toward Cecily. He smiled and took her hand. Miss Camden was making an effort not to betray her emotions and said lightly, "Well, my lord, I see you have survived the journey here."

Ashford looked meaningfully over to where Jeeters was conversing with Prunella and then returned his gaze to Cecily. "Miss Camden," he said wryly, "you don't know how close a thing it was."

Miss Camden laughed. She turned to see Higglesby-Smythe approach them. He had escaped from Reginald and was seeking more congenial company.

"Higglesby-Smythe," said Ashford. "I am glad to see you among the guests."

"How are you, sir?" said Higglesby-Smythe.

Ashford noticed that the Baron seemed a bit uncomfortable. "I am glad to see you," he said, "for I had heard that you may be able to provide me with some information."

"I, sir!" replied Higglesby-Smythe.

"Yes," continued Ashford. "I was traveling near Hodgeson last week and came upon the most remarkable ruins. I thought of you, for I had been told that you have studied such things."

Lord Higglesby-Smythe flushed with pleasure. "I am no expert, sir," said the Baron, "but I am quite familiar with those ruins."

"Yes, Lord Higglesby-Smythe," said Cecily innocently, "were you not telling Prunella and me about those ruins? Pray tell his lordship."

"Yes, I should be very much interested," said the Marquis. "It was a church, was it not?"

Higglesby-Smythe smiled. "An abbey, to be exact. Built in 1152. A center of learning at that time." Higglesby-Smythe continued in an animated fashion, and Ashford was amazed to see that as he talked about the ruined abbey he became quite eloquent.

"And I hope I ain't boring you, sir," said Higglesby-Smythe after describing the abbey's history in some detail.

"No, indeed not," said Ashford, realizing that he had actually been quite interested. "Perhaps you could accompany me there some day and serve as a guide."

The young man beamed. "I'd be honored to, sir," he said.

"Then we shall go." Ashford smiled at Miss Camden. "Perhaps you would like to see it too, ma'am."

"I should love to," said Cecily, returning his smile.

At that moment Lord Ashford looked up and saw Lord Throxton motioning toward them. "I believe our host wants to see you, Higglesby-Smythe."

"Oh yes," said Higglesby-Smythe with a grin. "Pray excuse me, and I am glad to see you here, sir. Excuse me, Miss Camden."

After he had gone Cecily looked at Ashford in admiration. "You have again done wonders for poor Lord

Higglesby-Smythe. I do hope you weren't bored. He is terribly interested in Hodgeson Abbey."

"It is amazing, I know," said his lordship, "but I was not bored in the least. I have a great fondness for that abbey."

Cecily smiled. "And a fondness for a certain inn nearby?"

Ashford laughed. "That was a wretched place, was it not? But I must say, Miss Camden, that after you arrived I did not even notice." Cecily blushed and Ashford continued, "But did you have a good journey back to Throxton Hall?"

"Yes, it was fine. I arrived here quite early."

"And I hope you are enjoying your stay. It's a fine place, Throxton Hall. I haven't been here for several years. But I hope you are well. Are you looking forward to the hunt?"

"Indeed, sir," replied Cecily. "My uncle has talked of nothing else for days."

"I am happy to be here," said Ashford. "Or at least I was," he added as he noticed the approach of Mr. James Crimpson.

"Miss Camden," said Jeeters eagerly. "So wonderful to see you. Forgive me for not being able to talk to you sooner."

"That is quite all right, sir," said Cecily.

"It is wonderful to be here, Miss Camden," continued Jeeters, "and may I say that you are looking quite lovely." Cecily had her usual impulse to laugh but managed to thank the young man civilly.

Ashford stared at Jeeters grimly and had his usual impulse to do bodily injury to that young gentleman.

"Lord Ashford was terribly kind to allow Reginald and me to come with him. Dashed nice of you, my lord. And we shall have a wonderful time, I know, for it is a dashed fine place and dashed fine country."

Luckily Mr. Crimpson was cut short when Lord Throxton shouted for everyone to come inside. Jeeters quickly offered Cecily his arm and she took it reluctantly, casting an amused look at Ashford. The Marquis looked at Mr.

Crimpson with irritation, but when he met Cecily's glance he softened and smiled and the Throxtons and their guests entered the manor house.

Miss Cecily Camden was appalled at the seating arrangement for the evening's dinner party. It was a small affair, only fourteen at table, and that understandably increased the odds of finding oneself next to someone like Sir Chesterfield Willoughby or Mr. James Crimpson.

However, Cecily was extremely unfortunate to be placed between these two gentlemen, and therefore looked forward to a most unpleasant evening as the guests were seated at the table and the dinner began.

Seated diagonally across the table from Miss Camden was the Marquis of Ashford. This was small consolation, however, for Lady Throxton was very strict about talking across table. Ashford did smile encouragingly at her and Miss Camden steeled herself for Mr. Crimpson's conversation.

Lord Ashford had not fared much better in terms of dinner companions. Seated on his right was his sister Isabelle and on his left was Prunella Throckmorton. Directly across the table was Sir Chesterfield Willoughby, and Ashford eyed him with revulsion.

Fortunately for the Marquis, Lady Prunella was in a quiet mood and was content to cast longing glances down the table at Mr. Reginald Stonecipher.

That young gentleman returned these glances with an expression of passionate love that sickened Ashford. Reginald Stonecipher had been well satisfied with his position at the dinner table. Being so far from Lady Prunella, he did not have to listen to her tedious conversation, but could simply direct longing glances at her at intervals.

Between glances he talked amiably to Lady Throxton and Mrs. Constance Bagby, who were seated on either side of him. Mrs. Bagby was a comely widow and the elder sister of Miss Helena Chatham. Miss Chatham and her parents were also in attendance and seemed to be enjoying themselves immensely. This was due chiefly to the excellence of the celery soup and deviled kidneys, but also to the fact that Lady Chatham was finding Lord Throxton's accounts of various hunts quite fascinating.

"And wasn't it the coldest day you can recall that year, Lady Chatham?" said the Earl of Throxton, leaning toward her.

"Indeed," replied Lady Chatham. "November of '93 it was, and I recall it so well as that was the year Sweet Bess was foaled."

"The devil!" exclaimed Lord Throxton. "Sweet Bess. Aye, there was a bang-up piece of bone and blood if ever I've seen one. When Harold rode Sweet Bess, she cleared the pond gate as easy as a bird."

"Yes, it was splendid," said Lady Chatham. "And His Royal Highness was there. Oh, he was handsome in those days. And so impressed with Sweet Bess."

This conversation continued enthusiastically and Lord Ashford listened to it with a bored expression. His sister Isabelle, who was sitting between her brother and Lord Throxton, was quite intent on the conversation.

"I daresay," said Lady Willoughby, "tomorrow's hunt will surely prove as fine as anything we have been privileged to see."

"I am hopeful of that," said Lord Throxton, thrusting a portion of deviled kidney into his mouth.

"We've got some damned fine riders and bang-up horses. Your brother Ashford, for instance. I've heard much of him. Even better than his father, they say, and remembering old Ashford, that's a mighty fine compliment. And I've seen that chestnut stallion he's brought. Dashed fine animal."

"Oh yes, indeed," said Lady Willoughby. "And my own son Chesterfield will be riding that horse."

"What?" exclaimed Ashford, nearly choking on his dinner and looking at his sister in amazement. "Whatever do you mean?"

"Oh heavens, Geoffrey," returned Isabelle. "Chesterfield has reminded me that you promised him he could ride the chestnut."

Ashford looked across the table at his nephew Chesterfield, who was grinning broadly at him.

"Damned generous of you, Ashford," said Lord Throxton doubtfully. "If that were my horse I'd want to ride him myself. Damned good-looking animal."

Miss Camden was also listening to this conversation, although pretending to listen to Jeeters. Luckily, Mr. Crimpson's attention was also taken up by Mrs. Bagby, who was seated on his right and was discoursing eloquently on the Prince Regent's whereabouts for the past six months.

Ashford glared at Chesterfield and said, "I fear there is some mistake, Isabelle, I never said Chesterfield could ride the chestnut. He can ride one of the others, but I was going to ride the chestnut myself."

Lady Willoughby turned to her brother. "Really, Geoffrey, if you are going back on your word I suppose there is nothing I can do about it."

"I never promised him in the first place."

Chesterfield had been listening to this with his usual dull expression, but he turned to Lady Chatham and said quietly, "He did, you know, he promised me last month."

Ashford looked at his nephew incredulously. His good breeding prevented him from making a scene, but he would dearly have loved to take a whip to his oafish nephew.

"A shame to spoil your hunt," said Lady Chatham sympathetically to Chesterfield.

"Oh, I shall get over it after a while," said Chesterfield dismally.

"Of course, I did hear Geoffrey promise the boy myself," said Lady Willoughby, "but I will certainly not press my dear brother. I am far too dependent upon my brother's generosity."

Isabelle said these words very convincingly, and Ashford could see that Lord Throxton and Lady Chatham were eyeing him with disapproval. He was forced into the position of ogre, having in their eyes called his sister a liar and gone back on his word to poor Sir Chesterfield.

"All right," said Ashford in desperation. "There is some mistake, I assure you, but he may ride the blasted animal."

"Oh, Geoffrey," gushed Isabelle, "how sweet of you."

"Damned generous of you. So much like your father," said the Earl.

Ashford scowled as Lord Throxton returned to his reminiscences. Cecily had watched the Marquis with some trepidation. Although she knew that he was a gentleman and terribly well-mannered, she had been frightened by the look he had given his nephew.

Poor Ashford, thought Cecily after the Marquis had agreed to Chesterfield's absurd request. *Chesterfield Willoughby is the most unbearable man I have ever met.*

Mr. Crimpson then said something to her, and Cecily wondered if perhaps Sir Chesterfield were only the second most unbearable man she had ever met.

Mr. Crimpson had been talking to Mrs. Bagby and was unaware of the unpleasant conversation at the other end of the table. "And how are you enjoying your dinner, Miss Camden?" said Jeeters.

"Oh, very much, sir," said Cecily without much conviction.

"And I'll wager you are excited about tomorrow's hunt."

"Yes indeed."

"Reginald and I are quite excited although we are quite used to hunts of this kind."

"Indeed?"

"Oh yes, we hunt at Reggie's home all the time."

"I do hope it is good sport."

"Oh yes, not so good though as when we were at Devonshire, of course. The Duke of Clarence was there, too."

"Indeed?" said Miss Camden, stifling an urge to laugh. "And did you see much of the Royal Duke?"

"Oh yes, charming fellow, Clarence."

Fortunately, Mrs. Bagby said something to Jeeters and

Cecily was spared any more of his fabulous tales of his meetings with royal dukes.

Although Cecily Camden and the Marquis of Ashford were having quite unpleasant times that evening, the most miserable of all the dinner guests was undoubtedly Lord Higglesby-Smythe.

The Baron had been strategically placed beside his beloved Prunella, but instead of making him happy, this circumstance plunged him into misery. Lady Prunella refused to talk to him, and spent the entire evening staring down the table at Reginald Stonecipher. Higglesby-Smythe was crushed to have to watch this display and found that he had lost his appetite. Usually a great eater, the Baron picked listlessly at his food and played absently with his fork.

To make matters worse, Miss Helena Chatham was seated on the other side of Lord Higglesby-Smythe and persisted in attempting to engage his lordship in conversation. She was quite unsuccessful in this, but continued to plague him by commenting on how well Reginald Stonecipher looked and how well Prunella and he were suited.

So the dinner went on and some of the guests thought that it would never end. Cecily was glad when the last course appeared and gladder still when the ladies were able to retire to the parlor.

Cecily talked briefly to Helena Chatham and Lady Chatham and then found herself facing Lady Isabelle Willoughby. Cecily found this lady somewhat intimidating, but smiled cheerfully at her.

"Miss Camden," said Lady Willoughby, "I trust you are having a pleasant evening."

"Indeed, my lady," replied Cecily. "Dinner was excellent."

"Yes indeed," replied Isabelle. "Of course, I was not impressed with the beef."

Although Lady Willoughby seemed to expect a reply to this announcement, Cecily remained silent.

"And I fear my brother Geoffrey did little to aid my appetite."

Miss Camden could think of nothing to say to this and Lady Willoughby continued. "My brother is a difficult man."

"But I have found the Marquis to be quite charming, ma'am," said Cecily, feeling obliged to defend Lord Ashford.

"Indeed? Well, my dear Miss Camden, I fear you have been taken in by my brother's superficial charm."

Miss Camden blushed and Isabelle continued, "Yes, I see you have been. But you are one of many, my dear, and I must warn you about him."

"Really, ma'am," said Cecily. "There is no need for you to warn me."

"But there is. You are young although not awfully young, and I know how young ladies on the road to spinsterhood sometimes get romantic notions."

"Really, ma'am," said Cecily indignantly, but Lady Willoughby continued.

"He is not a man to be trusted, my brother the Marquis. He's rich and tolerably good looking and he's left a great number of young innocent females regretting that they ever laid eyes on him."

"Lady Willoughby, I thank you for your concern, but I assure you that you may have no worry on my account. Pray excuse me."

Cecily left Lady Willoughby and hurriedly informed her aunt that she had a dreadful headache and would retire. She left the parlor but, instead of going directly to her bedchamber, went outside and walked over to the stone bench near the old Tudor fountain that stood near the garden.

What a gorgon that Lady Willoughby is, thought Cecily angrily, but after a while her anger subsided and she found herself smiling. *A veritable dragon, that Lady Willoughby. Poor Ashford.*

She had no sooner sat down on the bench when another person exited the house and began to pace up and down. Through the dim moonlight Cecily could see that it was none other than the Marquis of Ashford. Cecily remained still, hoping he would not see her. However, the moon caught the pale ivory of her dress and Ashford came closer to see who it was.

"Why, Miss Camden," he said in surprise. "What are you doing out in the night air? And it is freezing out here." The Marquis quickly took off his coat and wrapped it around her shoulders. "You must come in immediately."

"Thank you, my lord, but I needed some air. It was unbearably hot inside. I see now it is cold out here. It's silly, but I really didn't notice at first.

Ashford escorted her back inside and they stood in the side entry hall. Cecily took off his lordship's coat and handed it back to him. He started to put it on, but had some difficulty.

"These blasted coats," he said, smiling. "They're made so it's nearly impossible to get them on without the aid of a valet and six or seven footmen."

Cecily laughed and helped him into his coat.

"There," he said. "Without your assistance I could never have accomplished this feat."

Cecily smiled and suddenly thought of Lady Willoughby's words. *He's not at all like that,* she thought. *If he is anything, it is honest.*

"And now, Miss Camden," said his lordship, "what has possessed you to go out into the wintery air?"

"But I might ask you that same question, sir," replied Cecily. "I fear the night air must hold some attraction for both of us."

"I fear you are right. I was getting a dreadful headache."

"And I was, too."

"I hope this does not mean we have not been enjoying ourselves this evening."

Cecily laughed. "I know that dinner was quite trying for you, sir."

"Oh yes," said his lordship thoughtfully. "You heard my conversation with my sister and charming nephew."

"Yes, and I thought it was dreadful. I have heard about Sir Chesterfield's skill with horses."

Ashford laughed. "Has his fame spread so far?"

"I fear it has, my lord."

"Well, I must make the best of it, but I hope I can bear to watch that idiot tomorrow. I shall probably do something quite rash." Ashford paused a moment. "But if I recall, Miss Camden, you were not at a loss for charming dinner conversation. Seated as you were between my nephew Chesterfield and that charming Mr. Crimpson."

"Indeed, my lord. Mr. Crimpson was enchanting. He told me many good stories of his experience with his good friend Clarence."

"Clarence?"

"Yes, His Royal Highness the Duke of Clarence."

"God, no!" exclaimed Ashford. "He told you that?"

"Yes, and I'm sure he would have had even better stories had not Mrs. Bagby commanded his attention."

Ashford laughed. "How unspeakably rude of Mrs. Bagby. But you had at least the solace of Sir Chesterfield Willoughby's witty conversation."

"Alas no, my lord," said Cecily with feigned sadness, "for that gentleman was far too intent on his deviled kidneys and roast beef to pay me much attention."

"My poor Miss Camden. But was the after-dinner conversation with the ladies no better?"

"I fear not."

"Then you must have been talking to my sister Isabelle." Ashford smiled but when Cecily made no reply, he continued, "You were talking to her, were you not?"

"Yes, I was, my lord, but not for very long. I had a headache and left."

"How very understandable. My sister, as you so well know, is not a very tactful or endearing creature."

"She has definite opinions," said Cecily.

"Such a skillful way of putting it," said Ashford. "But I should like to box her ears." The picture of the Marquis so treating his formidable elder sister was so ludicrous that Cecily laughed.

"That's better," said Ashford.

"But I see that you did not find the gentlemen's company very agreeable, my lord."

"I found myself talking to Mr. Crimpson, if you must know. Had he told me any details of his intimate friendship with the Duke of Clarence, I should have undoubtedly found it much more agreeable."

Cecily laughed again. "Pray excuse me, my lord. I must retire before anyone notices that I have not done so. I have enjoyed talking to you, sir."

"And I enjoyed talking to you," said Ashford, taking Miss Camden's hand. "I find that the evening has not been a complete loss. Good night."

Cecily blushed and curtsied and hurried up the stairs to her room. As her maid helped her undress, Cecily stared silently into space. *I must control myself,* she thought. *As ridiculous as it is, I am in love with him.* She thought of Lady Isabelle Willoughby's warning and smiled. *I must be on my guard,* she thought with amusement as her maid left the room. She lay back and soon fell into a heavy, dreamless sleep.

CHAPTER 12

The day of the hunt proved to be a clear fall day, which Lord Throxton proclaimed to be without equal in his memory. His lordship was in fine spirits as the ladies and gentlemen gathered in the yard dressed for the hunt and mounted on their well-bred hunters. All signs pointed to a remarkable day of sport and all the hunt's participants seemed in a rare state of excitement. The horses and riders alike seemed to share a feeling of eager expectation, and the hounds sniffed the morning air, eager to be off.

Lady Prunella watched this high-spirited gathering with little joy from her seat in her father's carriage. An indifferent horsewoman, Lady Prunella did not hunt, and in fact was little interested in the sport. Prunella gazed at the hunters with a bored expression and patted the two spaniels that were snuggled in her lap. At intervals she would nod her head in acknowledgment of a remark made by her mother or Lady Willoughby, who were seated with her in the carriage.

At the appearance of Reginald Stonecipher Lady Prunella's face broke into an animated grin. "Oh dear me," she cried. "Mama, look at Mr. Stonecipher. Don't he cut a dashing figure?"

Mr. Stonecipher did indeed create a sensational appearance. His hunting coat was of a splendid cut although perhaps too flamboyant for the taste of that paragon of fashion, Mr. Brummell. Reginald's boots gleamed black in the sunlight and contrasted sharply with the white boot tops.

Mr. James Crimpson appeared with his friend and he, too, was dressed strikingly. He also wore the white boot tops that Mr. Brummell had introduced into fashion and every so often would glance down at them to see if any spot of mud had dared to mar their unblemished whiteness.

It was the white boot tops that had been responsible for the Messrs. Stonecipher and Crimpson's late arrival. While they were dressing, Jeeters Crimpson had suddenly thought of a frightening possibility. "Ye gods," he had cried in alarm. "How in heaven are we to keep these damn white boot tops clean? Good God, Reggie. There ain't a chance the mud won't spatter them."

"Oh no," Reginald had cried in alarm. "There must be a way, Jeeters. God, Brummell does it."

At that point the valet, Hacker, respectfully coughed. "If I may comment on that, sir, but Mr. Brummell don't hunt."

This communication filled Jeeters with a terrible fear, and it had taken Reginald a great amount of coaxing to convince his friend that there was no way to avoid the hunt and that to miss it would be ridiculous. And since Mr. Crimpson's love of hunting was nearly as great as his love of fashion, he was finally reconciled to the unfortunate prospect of mud-spattered boots.

So the two young gentlemen joined the rest of the party. They were well-mounted on two of Lord Ashford's hunters and both felt that their splendid equestrian figures could not be equaled even among the nobs of the Carlton House set.

In contrast to the modish appearance of the Messrs. Stonecipher and Crimpson, Sir Chesterfield Willoughby presented a careless, untidy picture. His cravat was loosely tied and his coat was of undistinguished cut. His boots were dull and mud-spattered and his long black hair fell in untidy ringlets about his face. Although Sir Chesterfield's appearance was quite dowdy, he was seated on the most striking horse at the entire hunt. It was Ashford's prize hunter, a well-made chestnut who pranced eagerly under Sir Chesterfield's inexpert hand.

Lord Ashford scowled at his nephew Chesterfield and his rage mounted as he watched his nephew's inept handling of his horse. His lordship turned his own mount in disgust and found himself facing Miss Cecily Camden.

"Good day, my lord," said Miss Camden cheerfully.

"Good day," said his lordship politely but in a preoccupied tone.

"Oh dear," said Miss Camden, "I fear you don't wish to be bothered. Pray excuse me."

Lord Ashford looked at Cecily in some embarrassment and smiled. "I daresay, ma'am, I fear I'm in a devil of a mood. It's that ass Chesterfield."

Miss Camden looked in Sir Chesterfield's direction. "I see," she said. "To see such a rider so mounted. It's abominable."

Lord Ashford smiled at the seriousness of her voice and was able for the first time to take his mind off his nephew. He gazed down at the extraordinary creature Miss Camden was riding and replied, "And it seems to me, ma'am, that it is quite abominable to see such a rider as yourself so mounted. Heavens, Miss Camden, couldn't your uncle find you a better mount than that?"

Miss Camden looked at his lordship with a hurt expression. She patted her horse's back and said with some indignation, "You are referring to my own Ajax. He may not be beautiful, but he can outjump half of the horses here."

Lord Ashford's eyebrows arched in amusement as he looked from Miss Camden's indignant face to her ungainly mount. Her Ajax was a large blue roan gelding, too long of limb to Ashford's trained eye, with a large head that gave him an awkward appearance.

"I beg your pardon," said Ashford. He continued with mock solemnity. "And my dear Ajax, I crave your pardon and beg you to intercede on my behalf with your mistress."

Ajax replied to his lordship's plea with a most uncivil snort and shook his head back and forth.

Ashford broke into laughter and Miss Camden joined him.

"You see, my lord," said Cecily, "Ajax is a remarkable animal and you will soon see that he is a fine jumper. I know I tend to ignore his faults." Miss Camden looked at Ashford's bay stallion, with its finely bred lines and delicate head. "And he's certainly not pretty like that fine one of yours, my lord, but I raised him from a foal and he's about the only thing I have now that is really mine."

Lord Ashford's eyes met Cecily's and a subtle communication passed between them. "I can see how you can be attached to the brute, ma'am, and I'm sure we will all be following on your heels," said Ashford lightly.

Cecily smiled in reply. At that moment there came a signal from the field. "They've spotted the fox!" cried Cecily excitedly. Soon the sound of the horn carried the signal for the riders to be off.

"Tally ho!" cried Lord Higglesby-Smythe from across the group of horsemen. Miss Camden smiled over at Ashford and tapped Ajax slightly with her whip. That noble animal was off with a remarkably fast start and Lord Ashford soon saw that Cecily's Ajax was far from the ungainly hack he had first thought him to be. The gelding cantered evenly alongside Ashford's bay stallion and broke easily into a gallop, leaving Ashford behind. Cecily smiled back at Ashford and he urged his horse to increase his speed.

Lord Ashford noted with approval that Miss Camden was an accomplished horsewoman who seemed in perfect harmony with her unusual mount. Ashford's bay soon matched Ajax's stride and they galloped neck and neck across the field toward a stone wall that would be the first jump. The hunt had gotten off to a good start and all the riders seemed in good form.

However, Sir Chesterfield Willoughby was having some difficulty in controlling his high-spirited mount. "Damn you," cried Chesterfield as the horse hesitated to obey him. He jerked the reins brutally and the chestnut lurched in pain.

"You bastard!" screamed Sir Chesterfield, applying the whip vigorously to the horse's flanks. The chestnut reared angrily and Chesterfield jerked again at the horse's sensitive mouth. The now terrified stallion plunged forward and broke into a frenzied gallop that caught Sir Chesterfield off guard. "What the . . . ?" cried Chesterfield, nearly losing his balance as the horse increased his speed and approached the field.

Ashford turned his head and saw his nephew's frenzied progress. "God!" he shouted at Miss Camden. "Damn that fool Chesterfield! His horse has bolted!"

Miss Camden turned as Chesterfield, with a terrified expression, went racing past her own horse and then past the master. The chestnut's hooves thundered across the field and soon the panic-stricken animal had left the other hunt participants far behind.

Chesterfield clung to the horse in terror as he approached the stone fence. Fear gripped him as the horse raced toward the barrier. Upon reaching the jump, the chestnut leaped over the top and Chesterfield was thrown headfirst to the ground.

The rest of the party had watched Sir Chesterfield's progress in horror. Lord Throxton urged his gray mare on and muttered under his breath, "I hope the damned fool breaks his neck."

Never had there been such an escapade at Throxton Hall, and afterward Lord Throxton spent much time trying to recollect if he had ever before witnessed a greater exhibition of stupidity and incompetence.

Ashford and Cecily arrived first at the scene and his lordship pulled his horse up before the jump and leaped off.

"Good God," he said as he saw his nephew's inert form on the other side of the wall, and for a moment he feared that the young fool had killed himself. Cecily watched his lordship's expression turn from rage to fear and she dismounted quickly. The other ladies and gentlemen were soon there and they all waited silently for word of Chesterfield's condition.

Ashford pressed his ear against his nephew's chest and felt relieved to hear a steady heartbeat. He slapped Chesterfield's face cautiously and his nephew's eyes opened.

"What?" said Chesterfield in confusion as he opened his eyes and looked groggily up at his uncle.

"You damned imbecile!" said Ashford angrily, but not without relief. The thought of facing his sister Isabelle with news of her son's untimely death had passed through his lordship's mind, and as much as he despised Chesterfield, Ashford had prayed that he might survive.

"Thank God," said Cecily, kneeling beside Lord Ashford. "I had feared the worst. It was a bad fall."

"Yes," said his lordship, "but I am afraid my dear nephew will recover to ruin even more of my best hunters."

They were joined by Lord Throxton and some of the other gentlemen. "Is the young fool all right?" asked Sir Harold Chatham, the master of the hunt. After being assured that Chesterfield had sustained a broken leg but was otherwise all right, Sir Harold muttered, "He's damn well ruined what could have been a fine hunt."

Lord Throxton nodded and turned to Ashford. "And what of the horse, sir?" asked the Earl. "That was a real smart one and I say, sir, if this young blockhead has ruined him, I'd have his head for sure."

"That I will have in any case," said Lord Ashford. "But we'd best get him back to the hall and send for a surgeon."

Ashford looked in disgust at his sister Isabelle as she arrived at her son's side. Lady Willoughby cried hysterically and clutched Chesterfield's hand.

"I don't think I can bear any more of this," said Ashford as a number of the gentlemen carried Chesterfield over to the Throxton carriage. "This must be my punishment for trying to spite my dear sister."

"Did you say something, my lord?" asked Miss Camden, who was still standing next to Ashford.

"Oh no, dear lady," replied his lordship. "I was merely talking to myself. I fear my oafish nephew has made a mess of this hunt. Sir Harold is in a decidedly bad mood, it seems."

"Well, Sir Harold lives for his hunts, you know," said Cecily with a smile. "In time he will feel sympathy for poor Sir Chesterfield."

Ashford laughed. "I shall have a great deal less respect for him if he does." However, his lordship's good humor was cut short by the appearance of his nephew Reginald and Mr. Crimpson.

"Heavens, Uncle," said Mr. Stonecipher. "A deuced bad fall, that, sir."

"Yes," contributed Mr. Crimpson. "I was sure Reginald's cousin was in for a bad one. By Jove, that's a fast horse you have there, my lord," continued Jeeters enthusiastically. "And how he took that jump! He might have been flying. A regular flyer, that one. God, it was a beautiful jump, and I see one of Sir Harold's men has brought him back. Lucky thing, my lord. He seems unharmed. Damned lucky. It would have been a dashed sorry thing had any harm come to that horse. A real fine one, indeed."

"Mr. Crimpson," said Cecily with mock severity, "I do not see how you can talk about a horse at a time like this. His lordship's nephew has nearly been killed."

"Oh," said Mr. Crimpson, blushing hotly at this rebuke. "That's so, my lord. It must have been a real shock for you, knowing how you are so fond of your nephews and all."

Reginald glared at his friend, but Jeeters continued. "It was indeed lucky that Sir Chesterfield didn't break his neck. Reginald was terribly worried, of course."

Ashford studied the ludicrous pair and replied solemnly, "Yes, Mr. Crimpson. It was a great shock. Certainly, we must thank providence for sparing dear Chesterfield. It was so fortunate that he escaped without greater injury. Now, if you gentlemen will excuse me, I must escort Miss Camden back to her horse."

The gentlemen bowed and stood aside as Lord Ashford led Cecily back to Ajax and helped her up into the saddle. Cecily smiled down at him and said, "I do not see how you can say such things and keep such a solemn expression on your face. I feared I would let out a most unladylike whoop at any moment."

Lord Ashford grinned up at her. "I am glad you were able to maintain the proper decorum in this situation. It would have been most distressing to me to have heard someone laughing uncontrollably when I am worrying so about my beloved nephew."

Cecily laughed and, turning Ajax, started back to the house.

Lady Throxton shook her head nervously. "I fear, Cecily, that my plans are not going as well as expected."

Miss Camden looked sympathetically at her aunt. "My dear aunt," she said, "you must not blame yourself for any of the misfortunes that have beset us."

"I know," replied Lady Throxton, "but I know that the dinner party did not go very well and then Lord Higglesby-Smythe began to feel ill and then today at the hunt . . ." Her ladyship threw her hands up in dismay. "I fear Sir Harold Chatham was in a dreadful rage over it. I daresay that Sir Harold will be reluctant to lend his hounds to our hunts again."

"Goodness, ma'am," replied Cecily. "Sir Harold is not such a fool as to blame my uncle for Sir Chesterfield Willoughby's folly."

"Perhaps so," said her aunt thoughtfully, "but now we have to care for Isabelle's son. I never did like that boy, but it is dreadful to think of him lying up in his bed in agony."

"I am sure he is probably resting peacefully, ma'am," said Miss Camden, "and we should be glad that his injury was not more severe."

"You are very right," said Lady Throxton. "It would have been most disagreeable to have had him die on our hands. I suppose we are lucky."

Lady Throxton got up from her chair in her sitting room and Cecily rose with her. "I suppose we must go down," said her ladyship, smoothing her dress. "I only hope that the card party will not be ruined by any further calamity. Now where is Prunella?"

At the mention of her name Lady Prunella appeared at the doorway. "Aren't you ready to go down, Mama?" she asked. "I'm sure the guests are waiting for you."

The three ladies descended the stairs and entered the drawing room, where most of the guests had gathered.

Miss Camden gazed upon the party wearily. Unlike her aunt, Miss Camden had no fear of some calamity upsetting her aunt's party. *Indeed,* thought Miss Camden, *I might prefer some calamity to this dull evening.*

To her dismay Miss Camden observed Mr. James Crimpson among the company, and to her greater dismay he saw her enter and rushed to her side.

Miss Camden also noted with a great deal of disappointment that the Marquis of Ashford had not yet made his appearance. *Don't be a goose,* she told herself. *It is nothing to you whether Lord Ashford is here or not. Why should you care at all?*

However, as Mr. Crimpson addressed her, Miss Camden wished desperately that she could somehow make him vanish and Lord Ashford stand in his place.

"Goodness, Miss Camden," grinned Jeeters Crimpson. "You're looking splendid. That blue dress is really the thing, you know. Brings out the color in your hair."

In spite of herself Miss Camden smiled. "I never thought, sir," she replied, "that my hair was of a color that needed bringing out."

Jeeters laughed. "Truly, Miss Camden," he said, "I have always thought my red hair one of the unfortunate tricks of nature, which I was obliged to tolerate, but I swear, ma'am, if your hair ain't absolutely smashing."

"Thank you," replied Miss Camden, laughing. "And I must say, sir, that I have always thought red-haired men most distinguished. Although," she added mischievously, "perhaps that is a somewhat prejudiced viewpoint."

The Marquis of Ashford entered the drawing room and was surprised to see Miss Cecily Camden talking pleasantly to Mr. Crimpson. The sight irritated his lordship and further blackened his mood.

He had a completely wretched day. His nephew's bungling had caused him great embarrassment and his sister's whinings had enraged him. His best hunter had nearly been lamed and now he faced a tedious evening of cards with some of the most frightful bores he had ever met. And to make it even worse he had entered the room to find the only person worth talking to engaged in animated conversation with a young fop.

Ashford scowled and felt a sudden urge to turn around and leave the room. However, at that moment Miss Camden saw him and smiled. He saw that she was glad to see him and his mood softened to some degree. Ashford returned her greeting and reflected that she had a most charming smile. There was nothing of the coquette in her and he found her lack of guile refreshing.

Jeeters was delighted that Miss Camden was being so agreeable. "I do hope, Miss Camden," said Mr. Crimpson, "that you will join Mr. Stonecipher and myself at the card table. Lady Prunella has graciously consented to join us and we are hoping you will make a fourth."

Cecily hesitated for a moment, but could find no suitable reason to refuse. "Why yes, Mr. Crimpson," replied Cecily reluctantly and allowed the young gentleman to escort her to the table.

The play began in a desultory fashion, the players with the exception of Miss Camden lacking skill and imagination. Lady Prunella maintained a puzzled expression throughout, and Miss Camden watched her cousin's perplexed face with some amusement.

Jeeters Crimpson chattered constantly and Miss Camden soon found her mind wandering. Mr. Stonecipher remained silent and every so often cast incredulous looks at Lady

Prunella as she played her cards with alarming ineptitude.

As the time passed, Cecily found herself stifling yawns and looking about the room. Most of the guests seemed engrossed in their cards, but Lord Higglesby-Smythe kept staring over at Miss Camden's table. Miss Camden knew that the objects of Lord Higglesby-Smythe's interest were her cousin and Reginald Stonecipher, and she noted his obvious disapproval.

Miss Camden stole another glance at Lord Higglesby-Smythe's table and saw that Lord Ashford was listening to Lord Throxton with well-bred politeness. Lord Throxton was enjoying himself immensely, undoubtedly regaling his guests with tales of his youth.

Miss Camden returned to her cards but as her attention wavered, she looked again at the Marquis of Ashford. He had been looking in her direction and met her gaze with a light smile.

"Oh dear," cried Prunella, returning Cecily's attention to the game. "I fear I am a chucklehead."

This remark provoked little controversy, but Mr. Stonecipher said gallantly, "I say, Lady Prunella, you must not worry about this silly game."

Lady Prunella smiled and looked adoringly at Reginald. "You are too kind, sir," she said.

The evening of cards had been an interminable bore for Miss Camden. She was thankful when it was finally time for her to retire to bed, and had entered her bedchamber wearily.

She fell asleep immediately, but awoke at dawn the next day. She lay in bed staring up at the canopy over her head.

To her irritation, the image of Lord Ashford kept appearing in her mind. *I can't believe this silly infatuation of mine,* she thought, pushing away the bedclothes and getting out of bed. She sat down at her dressing table and began to brush her red hair. She paused and stared into the mirror. "Perhaps, if I were beautiful," she said dejectedly to her reflection. "Oh, stop being such a goose," she told herself impatiently. She rose and took her riding dress from the closet.

Miss Camden dressed quickly and noiselessly left her room, descended the great stairs, and left the house. She entered the stables and requested one of the grooms to saddle Ajax. This was done with alacrity and the groom led Ajax over to his mistress.

"And would you be wanting me to go with you, miss?" asked the groom.

"Certainly not, Jack," replied Miss Camden. "I am certainly old enough to go riding by myself. Or don't you think I can be trusted to handle Ajax?"

The groom laughed good-naturedly. "If there's any lady what can be trusted with any horse in the stables, that's you, miss," he admitted. He helped her up and she carefully placed her feet into the stirrups of the sidesaddle and was off.

Ajax seemed happy to be out in the early morning air. He trotted joyfully down the old road that led toward the pasture gate. Cecily eased him into a canter at the gate and continued on toward the village. It was a lovely morning. The air was cool and fresh and the newly risen sun caused the dew-laden grass to sparkle.

Cecily turned her horse from the road onto the path that led to the mill pond. *It's so lovely*, she reflected and approached the pond. She signaled to Ajax to reduce his speed and continued at a walk around the pond, noting how beautiful it looked in the early morning sun.

As Miss Camden neared the far side, she was surprised to see a horse tied to a tree near the edge of the pond. She commanded Ajax to stop and inspected the riderless animal for a moment. *It's Ashford's bay*, she thought. *Whatever could he be doing here?*

The question was immediately answered as his lordship appeared. "Miss Camden," called his lordship, waving to her. "I thought I heard someone." He approached her horse and patted Ajax. "And the noble Ajax." Ajax snorted in reply and Miss Camden smiled.

"Good morning, my lord," said Miss Camden. "You are certainly out early. Is something amiss with your horse?"

"No," replied Lord Ashford. "Jasper is in fine form. But I am surprised to see you here so early, ma'am. You had such an exciting time last night and retired so late that I expected you ladies to rise no earlier than noon."

"Indeed, sir?" answered Cecily. "When I left last night's festive gathering you were still listening to my uncle's enthralling conversation. You astound me, my lord, that you have the energy to be riding this early after such a night."

Ashford laughed. "I felt a great need to get away from Throxton Hall this morning. I am afraid you have discovered me in one of my rare reflective moods. Pondering the beauty of nature and that sort of thing."

"Well, I am sorry to have disturbed you, sir," said Cecily, "but I, too, found it necessary to get away this morning. But I will bother you no longer."

"Heavens, ma'am," said his lordship. "You are not bothering me. Indeed I am glad to see you. You have saved me from sinking into a state of melancholy."

"In that case, sir, I am glad to have come and disturbed your ponderous mood."

"Yes," agreed Ashford. "Your arrival is most fortuitous. However, I fear you may now discover my dark secret, the reason that brings me to this sylvan glade."

"Oh, my lord," said Cecily with a twinkle. "How ominous you sound. Have you murdered someone this morning? Pray, do not expect me to assist you in your dastardly schemes."

"Certainly not!" exclaimed Ashford. "I have never allowed a lady to involve herself in any of my murders. But I have murdered no one this morning, although I have a few likely victims in mind, including my nephews and a certain young redheaded gentleman."

"My lord," laughed Cecily. "You are a dreadful man. I beg you to spare your nephew, although I can find no sympathy for a certain red-haired gentleman."

"Indeed, ma'am," said Ashford in mock surprise. "But I

was sure that Mr. Crimpson had captured your heart. Last night you seemed enchanted by his conversation."

Cecily laughed again.

"May I help you down, Miss Camden? I am afraid I will have no recourse but to reveal to you my secret." Ashford assisted Cecily down from her horse and, offering her his arm, escorted her toward the pond.

"There it is," said his lordship, pointing at the water. "My secret."

Cecily looked at the pond and saw several ducks swimming near the shore. "Ducks?" she asked.

"I am afraid so," replied Ashford, sheepishly extracting a piece of bread from his coat. "I've been feeding them. I know it's ridiculous, but yesterday I passed by here and saw the ducks and remembered how I used to spend hours as a boy feeding them. I felt an odd compulsion to bring them something. I trust, Miss Camden, that you will not betray this confidence, for my reputation will be ruined. Imagine what Lord Alvanley would say if he saw me here."

"Your dark secret is safe with me," said Cecily, looking closely at his lordship. "I suppose you will find this silly," she continued, suddenly becoming serious. "But it's hard for me to imagine you as a little boy standing by a pond."

"Perhaps you had thought I sprang full-grown from the head of Zeus."

Cecily laughed. "No, I am being serious. I suppose that it's because you are so . . . so respected, I suppose. Everyone looks up to you. And it's not only your position. It's more than that. All the young men try to copy everything you do. And it's hard to think of you as a boy running through mud puddles and being scolded."

"I assure you, Miss Camden," replied Ashford, smiling, "that I was once a small boy and a terrible brat."

"You a terrible brat? I cannot believe that."

"Then you must talk to Edwards, my old nurse, and to Carter, the grounds keeper at Ashford. They could tell you stories that would amaze you."

Cecily smiled and watched the Marquis as he absently

tossed a pebble into the pond. "Do you spend much time at Ashford?"

"Oh, not so much. I stay in London a good deal and also spend time at my house in Riddleshire. But I think I shall spend Christmas at Ashford. I am suddenly feeling quite nostalgic about my old boyhood haunts."

"I should love to spend Christmas in my childhood home. It wasn't a grand house. But very comfortable, and I miss it."

"You don't ever go back?"

"Oh no, my lord, for the house was sold after my father died. I'm afraid Papa was not very good with money. And, of course, he never had a great deal of it to begin with. But I fear the conversation is getting so melancholy. I must think of the present and look forward to spending my first Christmas at Throxton Hall."

"My dear Miss Camden," returned his lordship, "Christmas at Throxton Hall is certainly the most melancholy thought I have heard today."

Cecily laughed and Ashford continued, "However, it is not as melancholy as the thought of Christmas at Oakland with my sister Isabelle and her son." They both laughed and Cecily directed her attention to the pond and the noisy quacking of a number of ducks.

"Oh my," said Cecily. "Perhaps you should feed them something."

They approached the water's edge and Ashford extended his hand to Miss Camden as she stepped on a large rock at the edge of the water.

"It will never do to have you tumbling into the water, Miss Camden," said his lordship as she took his hand.

"No indeed, my lord," returned Cecily with a smile. "Not at this hour of the morning in any case."

They stood watching the ducks for a moment and Cecily turned and looked at Ashford.

"You know, you are quite different from the way people describe you," she said.

"Indeed?" replied Ashford in mock indignation.

Cecily laughed. "Oh, you know, my lord. You are known as one of those unfeeling men of fashion who do everything with style, always maintaining that cool indifference to everyone and breaking the hearts of scores of women."

"My dear Miss Camden," replied Ashford, "you would be surprised to learn how many women have been immune to my charm."

Cecily looked at him seriously. "Indeed I would, sir," she replied.

The seriousness of her reply caught him off guard, but he answered lightly. "Come now, Miss Camden, to accuse me of breaking hearts when you are so heartlessly playing with the affections of a sensitive young man like Crimpson. I say, ma'am, I wouldn't have thought it of you."

Miss Camden laughed again. "May I toss some bread to the ducks? There is a creature over there who looks quite hungry. I am afraid that if we do not provide it with some food, it will come from the water and attack us!"

"Never fear," said Ashford. "I will protect you from the feathered threat, but do toss the creature a few crumbs so we may avoid a confrontation."

Cecily broke the bread and tossed pieces of it into the water. They both laughed to see the ducks rush madly for the morsels. When the bread was gone, Cecily took Ashford's arm.

"If you please, my lord," she said with a smile, "will you take me to my horse? I am anxious to get to safety. Now that the bread is gone, these fearsome ducks may get angry."

"Of course, ma'am," he said gallantly and they returned to the horses. Ashford lifted Cecily up onto Ajax's back and then mounted his bay stallion. "I hope you will allow me to accompany you," he said.

"I'd be honored, sir," said Cecily.

They rode together in silence. Ashford's bay seemed restless and strived to pass Ajax. Ashford held him back but called to Cecily, "Miss Camden, Jasper is anxious to run.

Would you care to run a bit?" Cecily nodded and Ashford was off. Cecily followed behind, restraining Ajax to some degree.

Cecily concentrated on Ashford's back. *I hope he never realized that I am so much in love with him,* thought Cecily. *Of course, he is a gentleman, and I'm sure he would let me down lightly if he knew. He has probably had considerable practice.* She smiled ruefully and gave Ajax his head. Ajax accepted this new freedom eagerly and soon outdistanced Ashford's bay.

"By God," cried Ashford as Cecily's horse passed him. He watched Cecily with admiration. *Quite an equestrienne,* he thought as he encouraged his mount to lengthen his stride. *And a damned fine woman.* He realized that he liked Miss Camden possibly better than any woman he had ever known. *The kind of woman I'd want for a wife,* he realized in some surprise. "By God," he repeated aloud, "the kind of woman I'd want for a wife." He urged his stallion on and reduced the distance between them.

Reginald Stonecipher yawned listlessly as he surveyed his appearance in the mirror. "I don't know why I bother," he said as he completed his toilette. "That silly moon calf Prunella is certainly not worth my best efforts."

There was a knock at his door and before he could answer his friend Jeeters Crimpson entered the room. Reginald looked at his friend's reflection and noted with dismay that Jeeters was carrying a small liver-and-white animal.

"God!" cried Reginald, jumping up and turning toward his friend. "Why the devil did you bring that bastardy dog in here!"

The dog growled and Jeeters laughed. "I can't believe that you haven't developed some affection for Rex here."

"Rex?" replied Reginald. "I thought his name was Spot."

"Whoever cares, dear boy?"

"Good God. Now get rid of him."

"Indeed not," said Jeeters. "For if you would be so good as to peer out that window."

Reginald scowled but turned to the window. Beneath him in the garden strolled Lady Prunella with her two pet dogs.

"Not this again," cried Reginald. "Oh Lord, Jeeters. What are you trying to do to me?"

"Make you rich, Reggie, and you are very close to it now. How that Prunella is mooning over you. Why it's damnable. But you mustn't rest on your laurels. I see Higglesby-Smythe has just joined the fair Lady Pru and I am afraid that Old Higgy is doing his best to snatch your prize from you."

"Oh, don't be absurd."

"See for yourself."

Reginald returned to the window and watched Lord Higglesby-Smythe greet Lady Prunella.

"And although Higgy don't have your charm, old chap," said Jeeters with a grin, "he does have a title and a tidy fortune and Prunella's parents are encouraging his suit."

"And you think Prunella cares about her parents' wishes?"

"No," replied Jeeters, "but as addlebrained as Prunella is, I fear she has a soft spot for Higgy. We must never underestimate the power of old childhood attachments."

"Oh rot!"

"We must take your darling pet down to the garden and you must continue to charm Lady Prunella."

"Oh God, no," cried Reginald, glaring at the little spaniel in Mr. Crimpson's arms. Reginald glanced down again at Prunella and Lord Higglesby-Smythe, who were talking amiably together.

"Well, I will go," said Reginald finally, "but I insist that you handle the little monster."

"But of course," said Jeeters and the two friends left the room.

As they entered the garden Lord Higglesby-Smythe looked at them blackly.

"Why, Gerald," cried Lady Prunella, "it's Mr. Stonecipher and Mr. Crimpson and they've brought Blackie. How sweet." Lady Prunella rushed toward the two newcomers and Lord Higglesby-Smythe stared sullenly at his feet.

"Good morning, Lady Prunella," said Reginald in his most charming manner. "And to you too, Lord Higglesby-Smythe."

"Humph," mumbled Lord Higglesby-Smythe in acknowledgment of this unwelcome greeting.

Jeeters smiled broadly and placed the dog on the ground. "We thought dear Spot needed a bit of exercise." The little dog broke away from Jeeters and ran eagerly to Lord Higglesby-Smythe.

"Humph," said his lordship, bending down to pat the dog. Spot wagged his tail happily.

"Oh my," cried Prunella, "he likes you, Gerald. Isn't it sweet?"

Jeeters viewed Spot's display of affection glumly. *Damned if Higgy don't get on with the mutt,* thought Jeeters. *I'd better get the cur away from him.*

"Yes," said Mr. Crimpson, "Spot seems to like you, Higglesby-Smythe. And he don't take to many people. I don't want him to bother you though. Come on back here, my nice little fellow."

Jeeters moved toward the dog. "Come here, Spot old boy." Spot looked at Jeeters and barked.

"Why don't you go and get dear Spot, Mr. Stonecipher?"

"Oh yes," said Reginald with some hesitation. He stepped toward the dog and Spot began barking furiously.

"It's a game they play," explained Jeeters.

"How sweet," cooed Lady Prunella.

Reginald moved toward Spot and the dog leaped away and began running in the opposite direction.

"Oh dear," cried Lady Prunella, "what an amusing little game."

"Oh yes, indeed," said Reginald.

"But you must catch him, Mr. Stonecipher," continued Lady Prunella. "He may come to harm if he runs into the road."

Reginald looked blackly at Jeeters and took off after the retreating spaniel.

"Come back, you," shouted Reginald as the dog ran toward the grove of trees. Jeeters joined his friend and ran toward the trees too, hoping to cut the animal off at the grove. The dog saw him and swerved toward the road.

At that moment Miss Cecily Camden was nearing Throxton Hall at a gallop with Ashford many lengths behind. As she reached the bend in the road, a small dog rushed out from behind a clump of bushes, barking furiously.

Ajax saw the dog and, terrified, reared up wildly, nearly throwing Miss Camden from the saddle. It took all of Miss Camden's skill to stay on and she clutched Ajax's neck, trying to calm him. The horse reared again, lashing out at the dog with his forelegs. The animal dodged the hooves and ran back into the bushes.

Ashford had watched this scene in horror. He whipped his bay horse up to Cecily, jumped off, and grabbed at Ajax's head, grasping the bridle firmly. The horse calmed down to some degree and Ashford rushed to its side and reached up to help Cecily down.

"Thank you," said Cecily, clutching his lordship's arms and shaking involuntarily.

"Are you all right, Cecily?" asked Lord Ashford, his eyes grave with concern.

"Yes, I'm fine," said Cecily, smiling weakly at him. "I've had such a fright though. Ajax isn't usually a skittish horse. I'll be all right in a moment."

Ashford held her gently in his arms. "If you weren't such a damned fine horsewoman, Cecily," he said, "you'd have probably ended up with a broken neck. And if I get hold of that infernal dog I will wring its neck," he said savagely.

Cecily looked up at him in surprise, marveling at the anger in his voice.

"I say, are you all right?" called a voice. Ashford turned his head to see his nephew Reginald. He was followed by

Jeeters Crimpson, who had recaptured the wayward Spot and was holding him tightly in his arms.

Lord Ashford looked grimly at his nephew and then at Mr. Crimpson. "I might have known," said his lordship in a soft but terrible voice, "that you two young idiots were involved. I suggest you two young fools leave my sight before I lose control over myself and pound you into dust." Ashford's face had grown white with rage and his nephew gazed at him in horror.

"I'm sorry, sir," he stammered, "but the dog got away." By this time Lady Prunella and Lord Higglesby-Smythe had arrived on the scene, and Reginald cut off his words as he saw the murderous glint in his uncle's eye.

"We'd better go," whispered Jeeters, tugging at his friend's sleeve.

"Oh, goodness," cried Lady Prunella, "are you all right?"

"Yes, Pru," said Cecily, still somewhat shaken.

Prunella's dogs had followed close at her heels and Ajax shied nervously.

"I will have to ask you to take your dogs elsewhere, Lady Prunella," said Ashford. "Miss Camden's horse has had a severe scare and your damned dogs aren't helping."

Lady Prunella looked at Ashford in horror. "How dare you, sir," she cried.

"I suggest you take them and leave," said Ashford, "or I will not be responsible for my actions."

Lady Prunella turned abruptly and walked off, followed by the three gentlemen and her two pets.

"Ashford," said Cecily, still clutching his sleeve, "thank you but I fear you may have offended Prunella."

Ashford laughed. "I swear I don't know how you abide that cousin of yours and I care little whether I've offended her or not. But are you all right now?"

"Yes," said Cecily, releasing her hold of his lordship's arm and turning toward Ajax. "I'm quite all right." She reached up and patted Ajax's neck. "And I believe that

Ajax has also recovered. So if you will help me up, my lord."

"Are you sure that you wouldn't prefer to walk?"

Cecily laughed. "I am no shrinking damsel, my lord," she said, "and surely you would not think much of me if I were unable to mount my own horse after a silly little mishap. I will be fine." She paused and looked at him. "But I do appreciate your concern."

Ashford helped her up and mounted his own horse and they proceeded toward the stables at a walk. They arrived there shortly and Ashford instructed the grooms to take care of the horses. He then escorted Miss Camden to the main house.

There they were met by Lady Throxton, who, in a most solicitous way, insisted that Cecily retire to her bedchamber for some rest.

"And please don't argue, miss," said Lady Throxton. "Prunella has told me all about your narrow escape. Goodness, child. And I was all worried, and then to see you riding toward the stable as if nothing had happened."

"Miss Camden is a remarkable lady," said Ashford.

"Indeed she is, my dear Ashford, but pray excuse us, sir. I must insist that Cecily get some rest now."

Cecily sighed in resignation. "I fear I must consent to being treated like some poor delicate creature. I suppose an attack of the vapors would be appropriate." Her aunt looked at her disapprovingly. "Yes, Aunt, I will retire to my room. Pray excuse me, my lord." Cecily looked at his lordship. "And thank you," she said softly and then followed her aunt to her room.

After assuring her aunt numerous times that she was quite well, Cecily was finally left alone. She lay on her bed gazing reflectively at the window.

"Oh, there you are," said a voice, interrupting Cecily's musings. Miss Camden looked up to see her cousin enter the room.

"Oh, hello, Prunella," said Cecily without much enthusiasm.

"I hope you can explain Lord Ashford's rudeness. I think that that man is insufferable."

"Come now, Prunella, Lord Ashford was upset because he had been riding with me and was upset at my near fall. I suppose he felt he would have been responsible if something had happened."

"But nothing happened, did it?" replied Lady Prunella. "And I am very glad of that, but he had no call to use such language."

"I'm sure he will apologize after he has thought it over."

"I hope so," said Prunella. She stopped and looked curiously at her cousin. "And what were you doing out with Ashford anyway, Cecily? I don't know if it's really the thing to go off with a man like that."

"Whatever can you mean?" said Cecily indignantly.

"Well, Cecily, I fear I must be blunt. Everyone knows about Ashford. He's one of the Carlton House set and you know what that means."

"No, I do not. Pray, enlighten me, Cousin."

Prunella continued in a whisper. "Oh, you know. Running in fast company and gaming and . . ." Prunella hesitated. "And those women."

Cecily stared at her cousin angrily. "I am astonished that you are so well acquainted with Lord Ashford's personal life."

"Of course, I am not well acquainted with him," replied Prunella, "but since he is Mr. Stonecipher's uncle, I have taken some pains to find out things about him. Fortunately Mr. Stonecipher has not been under Lord Ashford's influence for very long."

Cecily looked incredulously at her cousin and broke into laughter.

"I see nothing amusing in all of this, Cecily. I am saying this to you for your own good."

"My own good?"

"Yes, of course. I don't want to hurt you, Cousin, but I must warn you to be on your guard. Ashford's attentions toward you may not be strictly honorable. I mean that, and please do not be offended, but you are not exactly the type of woman a man like Ashford would intend to marry."

"Indeed?"

"Your birth is fine enough, Cecily, but your consequence is another matter and I'm sure Ashford has known many beautiful women."

"Cousin Prunella," said Cecily icily, "I do not need or want your advice and I do not need you to remind me that I have neither beauty nor consequence. And have no fear that I will not guard my honor faithfully. Do not fear that any scandal will mar the tranquility of dear Throxton Hall."

"Good," said Prunella, oblivious to the irony in her cousin's voice. "I am sorry that I have to be so blunt, but I felt it was my duty. I will leave you now, Cecily."

As her cousin departed, Cecily shook her head angrily. "The nerve of that gudgeon. And to have to put up with her insults."

Cecily threw herself onto her bed and began to cry. *And the most horrid part of it is that she is probably right about Ashford,* she thought bitterly. *He must be frightfully bored out here in the country and I am the only female here who is a likely candidate for his gallantry.* Cecily got up from the bed and wiped her eyes.

You are a great goose, she told herself, and vowed to avoid Lord Ashford as much as she could during the rest of his stay at Throxton Hall.

After returning Cecily to her aunt, the Marquis of Ashford was ensnared in several hours of dreary conversation with Lord Throxton. This was followed by an unexceptional luncheon, which was made more miserable by the fact that Miss Camden did not appear.

The afternoon was even more disastrous as his lordship found himself obliged to accompany his host, the Messrs. Stonecipher and Crimpson, and Lord Higglesby-Smythe on a tour of the Throxton properties.

Ashford's nephew and Jeeters Crimpson seemed to enjoy

the little journey immeasurably, as did Lord Throxton. However, Lord Higglesby-Smythe seemed rather uncomfortable and rode the entire trip in stony silence until Ashford dropped back to talk to him.

"I fear you look rather out of sorts, Higglesby-Smythe," said Ashford. "And I daresay that I am not in the best of moods myself. It is not a good day."

"Yes," answered Lord Higglesby-Smythe. "But it is dashed lucky that Miss Camden was not injured."

"Yes," replied Ashford thoughtfully, and Higglesby-Smythe studied him curiously. Although the Baron did not appear to be a very quick-witted gentleman, he was not in the least dull and he had observed Ashford and Cecily throughout the visit at Throxton Hall with the same studious concentration with which he scrutinized his Latin textbooks.

After watching the Marquis and Miss Camden, he had concluded that Ashford was in love with her and that Cecily reciprocated this feeling. In fact, Higglesby-Smythe was the only person at Throxton Hall to note this interesting development, which had he been indiscreet enough to divulge, would have astonished the other guests.

"I think that Miss Camden is a fine lady and a good companion for Prunella. I have great respect for Miss Camden, sir."

Ashford looked at Higglesby-Smythe in surprise, for he had never heard the Baron speak so many words on his own initiative. "And if only Prunella could be a bit more like Miss Camden I should be happier I suppose," continued Higglesby-Smythe with a sigh.

"You amaze me, sir," said Ashford with a smile, "for I thought that you held Lady Prunella in great esteem."

"But I do, sir," said Higglesby-Smythe quickly. "I do not mean I would want her to change her character to resemble Miss Camden's, but I wish that she could feel the same affection for me that Miss Camden feels for you." As soon as he said these words, the Baron blushed with embarrassment.

The Marquis stared at him intently. "My dear Higglesby-Smythe. You do amaze me indeed. I am at a loss for words, for it seems that the lady has confided much more to you than she has to me."

"Forgive me, sir," stammered the Baron awkwardly. "I don't mean that Miss Camden has told me anything. I have just observed you two and everyone believes me to be a slow top but I do see things sometimes."

Lord Ashford laughed. "Dear Higglesby-Smythe, I have never thought you a slow top and I see my confidence in you has been justified. I have not tried to hide my affection for Miss Camden, and had hoped she would return this feeling."

Higglesby-Smythe looked at Ashford with an amazed expression. "You mean, sir, that you did not know she returned your affection? Oh God, I am the greatest fool. I hope you will forgive me."

Ashford smiled kindly at the younger man. "Pray do not be disturbed. There is nothing to be forgiven. And do not despair over Lady Prunella. She shall surely come around to seeing that you are a fine fellow."

"I don't know, sir," replied Higglesby-Smythe. "I fear Prunella has developed a great fondness for Mr. Stonecipher."

"My nephew? Heavens, sir, have more faith in Lady Prunella. She shall soon realize that Reginald is not the man for her."

"I hope you are right, sir."

"I am invariably right," said Ashford with a grin, and the two gentlemen continued the ride in silence. Both were reflecting upon the conversation. Higglesby-Smythe was hoping that Ashford was right about Prunella and Ashford was hoping that Higglesby-Smythe's indiscreet remarks had some basis in fact.

Ashford stared thoughtfully ahead as his horse walked toward the manor house. *I am in love,* he mused and realized that he had never before been able to make that admission, and that his lack of passionate affairs was a source of great discussion among his modish friends. Ashford smiled thoughtfully and rode the rest of the way in silence.

Upon returning to Throxton Hall, Ashford was greeted by his sister Isabelle. "Good day, Geoffrey," began Lady Willoughby.

"I am not so sure of that," said his lordship affably. "I hope you are well, Isabelle, and how is that son of yours? Mending, I hope."

"That is gracious of you to inquire after your nephew," said Lady Willoughby. "But I cannot understand why you do not go up to his room and see him."

"See him, Isabelle?" said Ashford in surprise. "Good God, Isabelle, I have seen enough of that young idiot to last me a lifetime. You cannot expect me to rush to his bedside, can you? You may have forgotten but your darling son has caused me untold embarrassment and has nearly ruined one of my best horses."

"There it is," cried Isabelle in disgust. "You care more about your horses than your own sister's child."

Ashford did not deny this remark but smiled at his sister.

"And you continue to favor Arabella's son and disdain my own."

"I do not favor Arabella's son, but disdain is certainly what I feel for yours."

Lady Willoughby quaked with rage. "I will not stay in the same house with you. I am moving Chesterfield back to Oakland immediately."

"Are you sure that's wise, Sister?" said Ashford. "The boy's leg has not had too much time to mend."

"Oh, I am sure you care for that," shouted Isabelle. "We are leaving!" Lady Willoughby turned angrily and walked off.

Lady Isabelle Willoughby's announcement that she was leaving Throxton Hall drew cries of protest from Lord Throxton. However, Lady Willoughby was adamant and directed her servants to make ready for their removal from Throxton Hall. Since the Willoughby estate, Oakland, was scarcely four miles away, Isabelle had no hesitation in starting for her home in the late afternoon.

Lady Willoughby arrived at her home early that evening, causing great surprise among the servants, who had to scurry about to make ready for their mistress's unexpected appearance.

After seeing her son off to bed, Lady Willoughby returned to her drawing room and sat impatiently looking about the room.

"I can't believe the gall of my brother," exclaimed Isabelle. "I despise him."

"Excuse me, my lady," said the Willoughbys' butler, who had noiselessly entered the room. "There is a lady to see you."

"What?" said her ladyship in surprise. "At this hour? It is most unconventional."

"It appears, my lady, to be a most unconventional lady."

"Indeed?" said Lady Willoughby with increased interest. "Then show her in." The butler bowed and left, returning moments later with the caller.

Lady Willoughby gaped in bewilderment at the visitor.

"How do you do, Lady Willoughby," said the caller, undaunted by her ladyship's look of surprise. "Pray forgive the lateness of this call, but I was aiming to leave early tomorrow. Mr. Skruggs insisted I be home on that day and I must obey him."

Isabelle studied the visitor intently. She was wearing a shocking lavender and yellow striped pelisse over a violet dress. The dress was covered with yards of velvet ribbon. Her enormous hat was also adorned with shocking yellow ostrich plumes.

"I am, of course, Mrs. Skruggs, my lady," continued the remarkable caller. "I heard that you had returned tonight. You see, I am visiting my cousin Mary Potts."

"Oh yes," replied her ladyship, realizing that Mary Potts was the plump and stonyfaced wife of the village innkeeper.

"And I wanted to see you, feeling like I do that it's my duty."

"Whatever do you mean?" asked her ladyship.

"I mean it's about your sister, Lady Arabella."

"My sister?"

"Yes, indeed, my lady. She's far too fine and proud a lady to go asking her relatives for help—especially," Mrs. Skruggs paused, "them that scorned her."

"I don't know what you are talking about," said Lady Willoughby impatiently. "How do you know my sister?"

"I am proud to be Lady Arabella's sister-in-law. Her husband Albert Stonecipher being my brother, I am proud to say."

"Oh," gasped Isabelle in astonishment.

"And your sister is a fine lady and now that she's in trouble, I thought you might perhaps help her out."

"Help her in what way?"

Mrs. Skruggs looked carefully about the room. "You see, my lady, my brother Albert's business ain't been doing especially good, you see. I'm afraid poor Albert may lose most of his fortune."

"How do you know this?" demanded her ladyship.

"Why, my own Mr. Skruggs, my lady. He is a good man and works for Albert and he's one to know, he is."

"Indeed! And what does he know?"

"Well, my lady. The blacking business has taken a bad turn and Stonecipher bootblacking is in a sorry state. I'm worried. Especially for Arabella and her poor boy. If Albert's business goes down what will become of them? That's why I thought you could help. If you could reconcile yourself with Lady Arabella, it might go easier for her. I don't know what dear Arabella will do. And that poor, sweet Reginald. Although a boy of his charm could marry an heiress, I'll bet."

Isabelle looked at Mrs. Skruggs. "Marry an heiress," she repeated and was struck by an astonishing revelation. *An heiress,* she thought, *of course.*

"My good woman," said Lady Willoughby, rising and ushering Mrs. Skruggs quickly from the room, "I do appreciate your concern for my sister. I will contact her, I assure you."

"Oh, that's so wonderful, my lady," exclaimed Mrs. Skruggs.

CHAPTER 13

Isabelle Willoughby's absence at dinner that evening at Throxton Hall was not commented upon. All the guests were aware of the situation and tactfully avoided mentioning it.

Ashford found his sister's absence quite a relief, and this opinion was shared by most of the guests. Even Lady Throxton found that her dear friend's absence was not too difficult to bear, and unknown to her ladyship, the departure of the Willoughbys had caused great joy in the servants' hall.

Conversation at dinner was quite dull and although Miss Camden was present, she was seated too far from Lord Ashford for him to talk to her. After dinner the ladies retired to the drawing room and Ashford was again faced with the company of his host, his nephew, Mr. Crimpson, and Lord Higglesby-Smythe.

After some moments of desultory conversation Lord Ashford begged to be excused. He retired to his bedchamber with a headache and, after dismissing his valet, sat in his dressing gown in a chair and stared into the fire.

I swear, he thought miserably, *I have never spent such a day in my life. And to think that Cecily has to live here every day. It's unthinkable.* He got up from the chair and took a book from a shelf. "*The Mysterious Count*," he said, looking at the book's title. "Good God, am I reduced to finding amusement in some harebrained novel?" However, finding no more suitable reading material, Lord Ashford returned to his chair and opened the book.

While his lordship sat reading, Lord Throxton and his young guests were engaged in conversation. After some time Lord Throxton excused himself.

"I fear I am a most inhospitable host," he said, "but I beg you gentlemen to excuse me. This infernal gout has begun to plague me and I must retire to my bedchamber. The ladies have already retired but I pray you young gentlemen stay as long as you want. I know you young ones have a bit more stamina than we old dodderers."

"Oh no," said Lord Higglesby-Smythe. "That ain't so, Lord Throxton. I find myself a bit weary and if these two gentlemen will excuse me. . . ."

"Oh, you can't leave so soon, Higglesby-Smythe," protested Jeeters. "It's early."

"Mr. Crimpson is right, Gerald," said Lord Throxton. "I am counting on you to entertain these gentlemen for me."

"Yes, of course," stammered Lord Higglesby-Smythe, looking distrustfully at his two young companions.

Lord Throxton left the room and the three young gentlemen sat down at the table.

"Well, old man," said Jeeters, patting Higglesby-Smythe on the shoulder. "I thought we three could sit here and talk about the old school days."

Higglesby-Smythe looked at Mr. Crimpson nervously.

"Yes indeed," continued Jeeters. "Remember old stony-faced Crabbtree? God, there was a strange one."

Higglesby-Smythe relaxed, glad that the object of Mr. Crimpson's reminiscence was not himself, but the learned pedagogue who had taught Latin to the less than enthusiastic young gentlemen.

"Have some wine, Higglesby-Smythe," said Jeeters amiably, filling his lordship's glass. Jeeters looked over at Reginald and winked. Mr. Stonecipher seemed to understand this communication and joined in the conversation.

"Yes, old Crabbtree. Remember the time when Adolphus Atherton put a turtle on Crabbtree's chair and he came in and nearly sat down on it?"

"Lord!" chortled Jeeters. "And the expression on his face when he saw it."

"And how he held it up by the tail and said, 'Who has dared put this reptile on my chair?' " offered Higglesby-Smythe, who had now entered into the spirit of the conversation after downing another glass of wine.

"Oh, it was famous," laughed Jeeters, refilling Higglesby-Smythe's glass.

"And remember how the headmaster used to walk across the yard?" said Reginald, getting up from his chair and imitating the headmaster's distinctive gait.

"Oh yes," laughed Lord Higglesby-Smythe, who was now losing his inhibitions and for the first time seeing the Messrs. Crimpson and Stonecipher as agreeable companions.

These nostalgic reminiscences continued for several hours and throughout the scores of amusing anecdotes. Reginald and Jeeters encouraged Higglesby-Smythe to drink more and more.

Lord Throxton's butler watched the young gentlemen with disapproval, conscious of the quantity of wine that was disappearing from his master's cellars. However, there was little he could do but keep supplying the gentlemen with wine, although as the night progressed the butler was able to substitute his lordship's best with an indifferent wine without fear that the young gentlemen would notice.

As it got late, Lord Higglesby-Smythe descended into a state of near stupor and rested his head on the table.

"God," said Jeeters to his friend. "He's drunk, by God!"

Mr. Stonecipher was not far removed from that condition himself and roared with laughter. "Look at old Higgy-Piggy there," he said, pointing to his lordship's inert form.

"Don't it remind you of when we put the snake in his bed when he was sleeping like a baby?"

"Oh Lord, yes!" cried Jeeters. "But it looks like we better take old Higgy off to bed."

At this moment Lord Throxton's butler stepped in, suggesting that some of the servants might take his lordship to bed.

"Good heavens, no, man," cried Reginald. "Don't call a soul. Mr. Crimpson and I will see his lordship safely to bed."

"And you may leave us, my good man," said Jeeters. The butler made no move to go and Jeeters threw the contents of his wine glass at him. "I said leave us!" shouted Jeeters and the butler retreated hastily.

"And now, Reggie, old man, let's get Higgy to bed."

"Whose bed?" asked Reginald and both of them burst into whoops of laughter.

"That's a good one, Reggie," said Jeeters. "Whose bed?" he repeated. "That's a good one!"

Lord Higglesby-Smythe lifted his head groggily.

"Come on, Higgy," said Reginald. "You are going to bed."

"Right," said Jeeters and the two friends lifted Lord Higglesby-Smythe to his feet. "We'll get you to bed, old Higgy," said Jeeters.

"Thanks awfully," replied his lordship, walking shakily but supported by his two companions. They assisted him up the stairs and down the hallway.

"Here it is, Higgy," whispered Jeeters, stopping in front of Prunella Throckmorton's door. "Go on in."

Reginald looked at his friend in admiration and grinned. Jeeters put an index finger to his lips, motioning Reginald to remain silent. He patted Higglesby-Smythe on the shoulder, turned the knob on the door, and directed his lordship inside. The two friends then retreated hastily to their rooms.

Lord Higglesby-Smythe entered the darkened room and

stumbled toward an object he dimly perceived as his bed. "Johnson," he said, uttering the name of his valet. "Johnson! Where are you?"

"What is it?" cried a high-pitched feminine voice. "Who's there?"

"Johnson?" said his lordship in confusion and tottered toward the voice.

A scream penetrated the room and Higglesby-Smythe stopped cold. "What?" he said. "What?"

The screams were first heard by Miss Camden, who occupied an adjoining room, and Lord Ashford, who was sitting up reading. Both of them rushed into the hallway, carrying candles.

"What is it?" called Cecily, seeing Lord Ashford.

"I don't know," said Ashford, joining her. Another scream echoed from down the hall.

"It's Prunella!" cried Cecily and they hurried to Lady Prunella's room. Ashford kicked open the door and rushed in to the room. In the dim candlelight he could see the silhouette of a large man poised over Prunella's bed.

"Good God," cried Ashford, leaping toward the man and grasping him from behind in a firm grip.

Cecily ran behind him and in the flickering candlelight saw that the looming form was that of Lord Higglesby-Smythe.

"Ashford!" cried Cecily. "It's Higglesby-Smythe!"

Ashford gaped in amazement as he saw for the first time the face of Prunella's supposed assailant.

"Good God!" shouted Ashford, releasing Higglesby-Smythe, who dropped heavily to the floor. "What in God's name? Have you lost your mind, sir?"

Cecily rushed to her cousin's side, for Prunella was sobbing hysterically in fright. "Calm yourself," said Cecily gently as Prunella threw her arms tightly around her neck. "You're all right."

Higglesby-Smythe looked at Ashford with tears in his eyes. "What's this?" he said quickly. "Where's Johnson?"

"What the deuce!" said Ashford, now well aware of Lord Higglesby-Smythe's inebriated condition. "You're drunk, man."

He helped Higglesby-Smythe to his feet. By this time Lord and Lady Throxton had joined them.

"What is happening?" said Lord Throxton, a ludicrous sight in his nightshirt and cap.

"Nothing to worry about, sir," said Lord Ashford. "It seems Higglesby-Smythe had a bit too much to drink and mistook Lady Prunella's room for his own. Caused your daughter a good deal of fright, I'm afraid."

"Why, I shouldn't wonder," exclaimed Lord Throxton. Lady Throxton joined Cecily in trying to comfort Prunella, and Lord Higglesby-Smythe stared stupidly around the room.

"Jim," called Lord Throxton to a servant who was waiting in the hallway. "Take Lord Higglesby-Smythe to his room and find his valet."

"Yes, my lord," replied the servant, entering the room and propelling Lord Higglesby-Smythe out of the door.

"Damned awkward business," said his lordship. "I never knew Gerald to be one for acting so foolish, drunk or otherwise."

"Well, sir," said Ashford, "Higglesby-Smythe is young. I'm sure he had no idea what he was doing. I hope you'll forgive him."

"Oh, that I will, sir," said Lord Throxton, "but I wonder if Pru will. Well, we may leave. I suppose the ladies can handle things." Ashford looked over at Cecily and their eyes met. He thought he could detect a trace of a smile in them and he turned and left the room with Lord Throxton.

Cecily Camden woke up late the next morning and the first thing she thought of was the previous night's adventure with Lord Higglesby-Smythe.

"Good heavens," said Cecily aloud, "was that a dream?" After considering this possibility for some time, Cecily decided that the unfortunate incident had indeed occurred, and she giggled as she remembered the look on Higglesby-Smythe's face.

And when Ashford saw who it was, she thought, smiling—but her smile soon vanished as her thoughts turned to Lord Ashford.

Her maid entered the room and interrupted her musings. "Good morning, Becky," said Miss Camden.

"Good morning, miss," said the maid.

"I think I'm going riding this morning. Please set out my riding clothes." Becky nodded and set about her work.

Once attired in her riding clothes, Miss Camden hurried down the stairs, hoping to leave unobserved.

She succeeded and was soon at the stables. As she entered the building she glanced at the stall where Ashford's bay had been stabled. "Oh," said Cecily to one of the stablemen. "Has Lord Ashford gone riding?"

"Yes, miss," replied the stableman, a young lad of sixteen. "His lordship was out early, miss."

I hope I will not see him, thought Cecily, resolving to take a different path on her morning ride. *He's probably at the duck pond,* she said with a wry smile.

"Would you be wanting the big blue roan, miss?" asked the lad.

"Yes, but I would like to take a look at him first," said Cecily, walking over to Ajax's stall.

Ajax whinnied in recognition as his mistress approached.

"Good morning, old boy," said Cecily, affectionately patting the horse's nose. Cecily rubbed Ajax's head and patted his neck.

"You seem to be well recovered, Ajax," she said, and was startled to hear a voice behind her reply, "But have you recovered from last night's exertions, Miss Camden?"

Cecily started and turned to face Lord Ashford. "Oh," she cried. "Lord Ashford. You gave me such a start."

"Pray forgive me, ma'am," said his lordship with genuine concern.

"I thought you had gone riding, sir," said Miss Camden. "I did not hear a rider approach."

Ashford smiled. "That is because I did not ride. My horse picked up a stone and I was obliged to walk him the rest of the way."

"Oh, I do hope it was not far, my lord."

"Only as far as the duck pond."

In spite of herself Cecily began to laugh. "And how are the little creatures?" asked Cecily.

"I am sorry to report that I did not see them, for after Jasper was inconsiderate enough to pick up that blasted stone, I decided to start back immediately."

"I am sure they were disappointed, sir," said Cecily with a grin.

"No more so than I," said his lordship, who then turned his attention to the admirable Ajax.

"I see that the noble Ajax is in fine form, but I am afraid that I am covered with dust. Forgive this appearance."

Cecily looked at his lordship's impeccably cut riding dress and considered that a bit of dust did little to tarnish his dapper appearance.

Cecily smiled. "My lord," she said, "you need not apologize. You look splendid as ever."

Ashford laughed. "And you, Miss Camden, look as lovely as this fall morning."

Miss Camden flushed at this compliment and was abruptly reminded of her conversation with Prunella. He was flirting with her, she decided. He must truly be bored.

"My lord," she said, "you are being ridiculous."

Ashford smiled. "I am being truthful," he said.

Cecily found the conversation taking a dangerous turn and changed it quickly. "I hope you were able to rest, my lord," she said, "after that unfortunate incident."

Ashford laughed. "Oh God, ma'am," he said, shaking his head. "The things that happen at Throxton Hall. I swear, Miss Camden, I have never seen such foolery in my life. It seems that every day something happens that proves false my feeling that nothing more ridiculous could ever happen."

"Poor Higglesby-Smythe," said Cecily sympathetically. "I fear Prunella will never consider his suit now."

"Oh, that is a pity, my dear Miss Camden," said Lord Ashford, "for I have never seen two persons more suited."

Cecily laughed. "They are, aren't they? And they would be happy together, I know."

"Well, I wish them happiness," said his lordship, looking closely at Cecily, "but I am more concerned about my own happiness."

Cecily looked into his eyes and felt dizzy. *Control yourself,* she thought desperately. At that second Ajax shifted in his stall, nudging his mistress against Lord Ashford.

"Oh!" cried Cecily as she was thrown against his lordship.

"Cecily!" cried Ashford, catching her in his arms, and before she could say a word she found herself locked in his lordship's firm embrace, his lips pressed against hers in a long, passionate kiss. Cecily found herself clutching him tightly and returning his kiss with a fervor that matched his own.

"Ashford!" cried a voice from across the stable. "Are you in here, my boy?" The unwelcome voice of Lord Throxton boomed across the stable and Ashford released Cecily with an exasperated "Damn!"

Cecily stepped back and blushed deeply as Lord Throxton spied Ashford and hurried toward him.

Of all the times for our host to appear, thought Ashford blackly. Lord Throxton was unaware of the black and dangerous thoughts his appearance had provoked in Ashford's mind. He ignored the icy look on Ashford's face and Cecily's look of embarrassment.

"Oh there you are, old chap," said Lord Throxton breathlessly. "I heard your horse had a bit of trouble. Damned unfortunate. And Cecily, are you out to do some riding?"

"Yes," said Cecily uncertainly.

"Well, you go ahead, my dear. I have got to show Ashford a new brood mare that Sir Harold Chatham sold me.

Arrived this morning. Irish stock. Good lines. Sire was Allenby Red out of Gallant Lady, a damned fine Irish mare. Any colt of hers ought to be a rare one, eh, sir?"

Ashford was finding it difficult to be civil and nodded coolly. "If you will excuse me, Uncle," said Miss Camden in an unsteady voice. "I have decided against riding. Pray excuse me." She looked down at the ground and hurried off.

Ashford watched her go with a worried expression and turned to stare grimly at his host. Lord Throxton did not notice Ashford's mood but continued to enumerate the fine qualities of his newly acquired mare.

As Throxton continued to babble on about the horse, Ashford cursed the ill luck that had brought Throxton to interrupt him and Cecily.

Lord Ashford had set off on that ride that morning hoping to sort through his thoughts about Cecily. Throughout the time he was at Throxton Hall she was never out of his mind.

He had liked her from the first. He appreciated her sense of humor and her honesty. He admired her horsemanship and good sense. He approved of her manner of dressing with elegant simplicity and had even grown fond of her unruly red hair. Indeed, Lord Ashford had early strived in vain to find any quality in Miss Camden that he disliked.

However, Lord Ashford had not realized that he loved Cecily until her near fall the day before. When he had watched her horse rear up, he had been filled with terror. The thought of losing her was unbearable. And that afternoon talking to Higglesby-Smythe had made him realize more clearly that he loved her and wanted to marry her. When he had seen her in the hallway the night before in her nightdress holding a candle, he had wanted to take her in his arms. Yes, he loved her desperately.

Throxton droned on for a time and then took Ashford's arm and propelled him out of the stable.

"Come sir," he said. "Wait till you see her. She is a beauty. Upon my word she is."

Summoning all his self-control, Ashford replied, "I beg your leave, Lord Throxton, but I must hold off seeing your wonderful mare. I must find Miss Camden."

"What?" said Lord Throxton. "Whatever for? Was the girl sick?"

"I can't explain now, sir," said Ashford, "but I must see her at once. Excuse me." Ashford rushed off hurriedly, leaving Lord Throxton standing in front of the stables with a puzzled and slightly insulted expression on his face.

"What the?" said Lord Throxton as Ashford walked briskly toward the house. "What's gotten into that one?" Lord Throxton shrugged and began walking slowly toward the house.

Ashford entered the hall to find Lady Throxton standing in the hall with an angry look on her face.

"What is wrong, ma'am?" asked Ashford, noting her ladyship's outraged expression.

"I am shocked," began Lady Throxton, "that you would have part in such a scheme."

"Good heavens, Lady Throxton," exclaimed Ashford in surprise, "whatever can you mean?"

"I mean this," cried Lady Throxton, waving a piece of paper in her hand. "I received this letter this morning by a messenger from your sister Isabelle. I can't believe it."

"By God, ma'am," said Ashford, "I demand to know what you are talking about."

Lord Throxton then appeared, slightly out of breath from his walk from the stable. "What is happening?" he asked in alarm. "Elizabeth, what is the matter?"

Lady Throxton handed her husband the paper. As Throxton read it Lady Throxton gazed indignantly at Ashford.

"That letter," began her ladyship, "says that you, sir, have been plotting to marry your nephew Reginald Stonecipher to Prunella. That you have been contriving ways to throw them together, to do everything in your power to encourage that alliance."

"You can't believe that," said Ashford in shock. "Why would I do such a thing?"

Lord Throxton looked up from the letter. "I say, sir, I find this hard to believe after knowing your father, but Lady Isabelle says here, 'It is a shock but true, nevertheless.' Damnation, Ashford, I wouldn't have thought it of you."

"By God, sir," exclaimed Ashford in frustration. "Isabelle has accused me of trying to make a match between your daughter and Reginald? Why it's absurd. And even if it were true I can't understand this reaction."

"Indeed, sir!" said Lady Throxton. "You attempt to foist a penniless fortune hunter on my daughter and find it hard to understand our reaction?"

Ashford stared at her incredulously. "Penniless? My God, ma'am, Stonecipher's fortune puts yours to shame."

"Huh!" replied Lord Throxton. "Fortune? Why, your sister says he hasn't a fortune left. Lost it all. And that rascally nephew is out to snare a rich bride."

Ashford looked at him with a stunned expression. "By my honor, sir," said Ashford, "I had no idea and I am highly insulted that you could believe me capable of taking part in some . . . some plot? And where, pray tell, is my fortune-hunting nephew?"

"He and Mr. Crimpson have taken your carriage to the village, I am told."

"Well, they shall plague you no more. I shall meet them there and inform them that they shall not be returning to Throxton Hall. My servants will pack our things and meet us. I will stay here no longer and bear these insults. I only request that you allow me to see Miss Camden."

Lord Throxton shook his head. "I am afraid that I cannot permit you to see any of my family. You will please leave my house."

"I will first see Miss Camden," said Ashford firmly.

"And I say no. I will not allow it," said Throxton, striking a menacing pose and looking quite ludicrous.

"As you wish," said Ashford. "Be so good as to instruct my servants to meet me at Parson's Gate." Ashford turned and walked angrily toward the stables.

"I can't believe it," said Lord Throxton as he watched Ashford go.

"It must be true," returned his lady. "And we must be thankful to have learned of his true nature in time."

Lord Ashford's anger was little abated when he arrived in the village. He had ridden the five miles in a seething rage and the presence on the village road of several slow-moving rustic carts blocking his passage did little to soothe his lordship's temper.

He arrived at the village inn and dismounted. An awkward youth scrambled up to take his horse and was rewarded with one of his lordship's most disdainful looks.

Brushing the dust from his coat and cursing his ill luck for the hundredth time, Ashford entered the inn. He glared about the room as the innkeeper hastened to his side. This worthy man had scrutinized his lordship's attire and, deciding that he was a gentleman of consequence, was eager to be of service.

"Good day, your honor," said the innkeeper with an obsequious bow. "What may we do for your honor?"

Ashford scowled. "I am looking for two young gentlemen. One has a head of damnable red hair."

"Of course, sir," replied the innkeeper. "The two young gentlemen are there, sir, in the corner."

The man motioned toward the far corner of the room. Ashford looked in that direction and saw the two gentlemen seated at a table with tankards of ale in hand.

They were laughing merrily and their joviality incensed his lordship even more. "Thank you," said his lordship to the innkeeper. "I will call you when I need you."

Reginald and Jeeters had been having a merry time at

the inn. The chief cause of this merriment was a discussion of the events of the previous evening.

"Lord," said Jeeters, "and Higgy was so drunk he walked right into Pru's room."

Reginald chortled in return, "And Ashford goes in to rescue the fair Prunella. It was too perfect, Jeeters."

This discussion had been continuing for nearly an hour when Reginald's joy was cut short by the appearance of his uncle.

"Oh my God," cried Reginald, clutching his friend's arm. "It's my uncle."

Jeeters nearly choked on his ale and looked up to see Lord Ashford approach. His lordship's normally swarthy countenance took on an even more formidable appearance, and Reginald readily perceived his uncle to be in a dangerous temper.

The two young gentlemen rose quickly to their feet as the Marquis approached. "Good day, Uncle," said Reginald bravely.

Ashford replied curtly, "Sit down."

The two friends obeyed with alacrity and Ashford continued in an ominous tone.

"I do not wish to cause a scene in this rustic establishment, and I shall do my best to restrain myself from giving the both of you a good beating."

"My lord!" cried Jeeters, looking up at Ashford's enraged face. "Surely you cannot be angry about yesterday. It was an accident that the dog ran out in front of Miss Camden's horse. You must know, sir, that I hold Miss Camden in the highest regard."

Ashford's furious look silenced Mr. Crimpson, and his lordship replied with some difficulty, "I warn you, sir, I never want to hear you mention that lady's name."

Jeeters looked at him in surprise and was about to mutter some indignant reply but his friend's hand on his shoulder restrained him.

Ashford continued, "This has nothing to do with that blasted dog."

"Oh," said Reginald. "Then it is because we didn't keep Lord Higglesby-Smythe from getting drunk. I say, Uncle, we tried but Higglesby-Smythe is a bad one where wine is concerned."

Jeeters nodded in confirmation of this statement.

"So you two were responsible for that," said Lord Ashford. "I might have known. Is there no end to your stupidity?"

Reginald looked at his uncle in surprise. "But my lord," he said, "if you didn't know about Higglesby-Smythe what is it we have done to enrage you so?"

"You have deceived me and dishonored me. You have implicated me in your damned schemes to find a rich wife. Perhaps I deserve it for being such a fool. Believing your father to be rich as Croesus. I never thought your pursuit of Prunella Throckmorton anything more than a childish prank."

"Oh God," said Reginald.

"And now, sir, I know the truth. You are penniless and have been using me to ingratiate yourself into the Throckmorton family. Well, sir, your plans have not worked, for I have been thrown ignominiously from the Throxton establishment. Lady Throxton received a letter that revealed the true state of your father's fortune, and you two jackanapes are no longer welcome at Throxton Hall. Indeed should you appear there I believe Lord Throxton would feel no compunction in having you flogged."

"Oh no," gulped Reginald.

"Your baggage will be returned to you in London," continued his lordship in an icy tone. "You may take my carriage, since you have evidently taken to thinking of it as your own." His lordship looked at them with derision and tossed a heavily laden purse on the table.

"That is for your journey home," he said scornfully. "You need look for no more rich wives until you return to London."

The Marquis turned to leave but stopped and looked back at them. "And I advise you to never let me catch sight of either of you again." With that warning his lordship left the inn, mounted his horse, and continued his journey.

The two young gentlemen sat in shock for a few moments.

"Oh my God!" cried Reginald, covering his eyes with his hand. "This is too abominable."

"Bear up, old man," said his friend bravely. "His lordship will come round some day. He's just a might upset is all."

Reginald looked at his friend angrily. "Upset? Damnation, Jeeters, I thought he would murder me. Now what are we to do?"

Jeeters picked up the purse that Ashford had left on the table. "At least he's generous when he's in a rage. There's enough here for us to live a month."

"And then what?"

"I'm sure I don't know. The fates is hard, old boy," said Jeeters philosophically. "Just yesterday you was nearly betrothed to sweet Lady Pru. Your fortune was nearly made and mine too, since I know you ain't one to forget old friends."

The two friends sat in dismal silence for a while until Jeeters suddenly sat up and pounded the table excitedly with his fist.

"What in the devil?" exclaimed Reginald.

"Buck up, Reg," cried Jeeters. "We ain't through yet!"

"What do you mean?"

"Prunella loves you, right?"

"Of course."

"Madly?"

"With every ounce of her limited brain."

"And the news that you ain't rich ain't going to change that, is it?"

Reginald's face suddenly lit up in a flash of understanding. "Of course not. Why, she'll love me even more if I'm a pauper."

"That's the spirit, Reginald."

"But what will that get me?"

"Oh, Reginald, have you no imagination? You must spirit the lady off to Gretna Green."

"An elopement?"

"Of course!"

"But you can't be serious, Jeeters. Why, Throxton would disown her."

"Oh, you know how he dotes on her. Do you actually believe he'd disown her?"

Reginald thought a minute. "I believe you're right, Jeeters, but an elopement with Prunella? I'm not sure I could bear it."

"Of course you could. One can stand anything when one has to. And let's face it, Reggie, we're in pretty desperate straits."

Reginald nodded. "All right, Jeeters, but how can I contrive to see Prunella?"

"Oh, you won't have to see her, old man," said Jeeters. "A note will do it. I'll write it. Where's that blasted innkeeper? He must bring us some paper."

After obtaining some paper and ink and a pen, the two sat down to their task, their good humor nearly restored.

CHAPTER 14

Cecily Camden was in a state of great confusion after meeting Lord Ashford in the stables. His behavior had disconcerted her and plunged her into gloomy reflection.

Prunella was right, she thought bitterly. *He is simply in the mood for a country flirtation.* However, the memory of his kiss lingered and seemed to hint that his feelings ran deeper than a casual flirtation. *Nonsense,* she told herself. *Don't imagine him in love with you.* She shook her head. *And why must I pick the Marquis of Ashford to fall in love with? Had it been Mr. Forbes or the Honorable Mr. Dinsdale there would have been some logic to it. Oh well,* she sighed, *why am I trying to find logic in love anyway? I fear I must remain misty-eyed and miserable.* She smiled weakly. *I will have to reread* The Mysterious Count *to get the proper spirit of tragedy.*

Thus regaining her composure, Miss Camden left her room and went downstairs to join her aunt and uncle. When she arrived downstairs she was greeted by the sight of her aunt and uncle in mournful poses and her cousin Prunella sobbing miserably.

"Gracious," cried Cecily, "whatever is the matter?"

Her aunt looked at her sadly. "My dear," began Lady Throxton. "I fear we have had a viper in our midst!"

"What do you mean?"

"Lord Ashford."

"Lord Ashford a viper!" gasped Cecily. "Come now, ma'am, you cannot be serious!"

Lady Throxton sniffed into her handkerchief before continuing. "I know it is difficult to believe but we have just learned that Ashford has been aiding his nephew in a plot to ensnare Prunella in marriage."

"Mama," cried Prunella, "Reginald was forced into it by that Ashford. He's a wicked man like Baron Diablo in *The Mysterious Count.*"

"What is going on?" cried Cecily. "What plot? And how can you accuse Ashford?"

Lord Throxton shrugged. "You see, Cecily," he said, "we just received a letter from Isabelle Willoughby that says she has discovered from a reliable source that Reginald Stonecipher's father has lost his fortune. Young Stonecipher was trying to marry Prunella and Ashford was aiding him."

"Oh heavens, Uncle," cried Cecily, "you can't believe that of Ashford. He's a gentleman. You knew his father."

"I did indeed," replied Lord Throxton, "and that is what hurts me even more."

"I cannot believe it, sir," said Cecily. "Perhaps Reginald Stonecipher, but you can expect nothing dishonorable from Ashford!"

"Oh yes!" shouted Prunella at this remark. "Your precious Ashford can do no wrong. You will find, Cecily, that he is a villain and poor Reginald is under his power."

"Stop that ridiculous babble, Prunella," cried Lady Throxton. "I want you to return to your room. You are not to mention Mr. Stonecipher's name again."

Prunella gave her mother a rebellious look and ran from the room.

"My dear Aunt," said Cecily, "can there be some mistake? Perhaps Lord Ashford was unaware of the state of the Stonecipher fortune?"

"I wish I could believe it, Cecily, but I fear I must believe the worst."

"But where is Lord Ashford?"

"He has left. Gone back to London I should think," said Lord Throxton. "We are well rid of him."

Cecily excused herself and went dejectedly to her room. Unfortunately, she could hear Prunella's dismal sobbing Just as Cecily was about to retreat from her cousin's wailing, Prunella became suddenly silent.

Puzzled, Cecily went to her cousin's room and found Prunella sitting on her bed gazing at a piece of paper with a rapt expression on her face. As Cecily entered, Prunella quickly thrust the missive down the front of her dress and returned a pitiful expression to her face.

"Hello, Cousin," said Prunella.

"Hello, Prunella," said Cecily, regarding her cousin suspiciously. "You seem to be somewhat recovered."

"Yes," said Prunella, wiping a tear from her face. "I must live with my sadness, I suppose."

Cecily gave her cousin an amused glance. "That is terribly mature of you, Pru."

Prunella smiled. "I know. I only hope you forget your dear Ashford. The only good thing about this whole tragic affair is that it has exposed Ashford's true character."

"Don't be absurd, Cousin."

"One day you will see," said Prunella finally.

"Perhaps," replied her cousin, leaving the room.

As Cecily reached the doorway she turned to look again at her cousin, who was once more smiling raptly at the window.

Poor Cecily, thought Prunella as her cousin left her room. She retrieved her note and looked at it lovingly.

"It is all too wonderful!" exclaimed Prunella, clasping the letter to her breast. "He loves me and we are to be wed. Oh, he is so very romantic," she exclaimed, rereading a portion out loud. " 'I cannot live without you. I cannot endure being separated from you, my heart's darling, my angel love. You must marry me, my sweet. I could not bear it if you refuse me. You must meet me tomorrow at Potter's Crossing at three o'clock. We will fly together to Gretna Green and wedded bliss. No power on earth can stop our love. My life begins when I behold your beautiful face again. Adieu, my fondest love. Yours, Reginald.' "

Tears of joy streamed down Lady Prunella's plump face. " 'No power on earth can stop our love,' " she said dreamily and kissed the letter. "I don't think I can bear it until tomorrow." However, Lady Prunella finally reconciled herself to the unbearable wait and began looking through her closet for clothes suitable for an elopement.

Cecily returned to her room and sat down at her dressing table. She stared bleakly into the mirror.

They're wrong about Ashford, she thought. *How could they say such things about him?* She stared at her reflection for some time. *I suppose I will never see him again, and I suppose it is for the best. And I don't know why I keep thinking about him. I'm sure he has forgotten about me by this time, and I shall simply have to forget him.* But even as she said this Cecily realized that it was quite absurd and that forgetting the only man she had ever loved would be no easy task.

Cecily suddenly felt an urge to get out into the air. "Perhaps I shall go walking," she said, leaving her room and walking down the hall toward the staircase. At that moment Lord Higglesby-Smythe appeared at the door of his room. He was about to make his first appearance downstairs and had a very dismal expression on his face. He also had a tremendous headache and what was worse than that, the dim memory of the previous night's events. As he saw Miss Camden he seemed somewhat relieved.

"Oh, Miss Camden," he said weakly, joining her in the hallway. "I am so glad to see you. My man tells me that the household is in a great uproar this morning, and I do not feel that I can face anyone, especially Prunella. After last night they have good reason to be upset. I must have been awfully drunk." His lordship winced and put his hand to his head. "Oh, I've got the worst headache."

Cecily looked at him for a moment in some confusion. She had been so concerned with the problem of Lord Ashford that she had quite forgotten Higglesby-Smythe's unfortunate display of the previous night.

"Oh, Lord Higglesby-Smythe," said Cecily gently, "the household is in an uproar this morning but it has nothing to do with you."

"But last night. I can't remember very well what happened but my man tells me that I went to Prunella's room last night. She will never speak to me again. I must have frightened her terribly." The Baron shook his head miserably.

"My dear Higglesby-Smythe," said Cecily, "I have seen Prunella this morning and she has quite recovered. It was quite frightening for her last night but I know she will certainly forgive you. After all, you simply made a mistake. And my aunt and uncle have already forgotten the entire affair."

"Oh, Miss Camden. They surely have not forgotten."

"But I assure you, sir, they have."

"But my man said that Lord Throxton was quite agitated."

"He is indeed but he is upset over something entirely different. It is really quite ridiculous. You see, my aunt received a note from Lady Isabelle Willoughby that said that Reginald Stonecipher is a penniless fortune hunter."

"What?" cried Higglesby-Smythe, forgetting his headache for a moment.

"And I don't know if that is true, but Lady Willoughby has also informed my aunt that Lord Ashford is in league with his nephew and they have been plotting to have Reginald marry Prunella."

"Oh, that is nonsense. I know Stonecipher wants to marry Prunella but Lord Ashford is a gentleman. I don't even believe he likes his nephew."

Cecily smiled. "I am unable to believe the Marquis is capable of anything dishonorable. I fear that Lady Willoughby has made a mistake."

"She must have indeed. Why, Ashford's a fine man and has been dashed kind to me and I don't think it was only politeness either. But I would believe anything of Reginald Stonecipher." Higglesby-Smythe continued in a low voice, "I know he acts like we were friends at school but it ain't so. I tell you, ma'am, I never could abide him or Crimpson. And Edmond Thornridge did not like them either."

Cecily pretended to be surprised. "Indeed, sir? Well, I myself share your opinion of those gentlemen."

"If only Prunella did too."

"Yes," agreed Cecily, "but pray remember that Prunella is a young girl and prone to romantic fantasizing."

"Yes," said Higglesby-Smythe sadly. "But where is Lord Ashford?"

"He has left for London, I am told. I do not expect we shall see him again."

"Oh, he shall surely return to see you, Miss Camden."

Cecily looked at Higglesby-Smythe in amazement.

"I mean since he is so very fond of you."

"Lord Higglesby-Smythe, I am sure I do not know what you are talking about."

The Baron realized that he had been indiscreet and blushed. "I mean he is very fond of you and I do not mean to embarrass you but I am not mistaken and he will be back. I am not a betting man but I would wager a substantial amount of money on this."

Cecily gaped at him and then burst out laughing. "Heavens, sir, if you are willing to risk money I fear I must take you very seriously." Cecily then took the Baron's arm. "But you must believe me when I assure you that no one is upset with you. We shall go downstairs and I shall prove it."

"All right," said the Baron with a slight smile, "but I shall not allow Lord and Lady Throxton to slander the Marquis. He is a fine man in spite of Stonecipher. A man cannot be responsible for his relations."

Cecily looked gratefully at the Baron. "Come, sir, let us join the others," she said and they descended the great staircase together.

* * *

When Lord Ashford returned to his London house, his servants were astonished to see him but even more astonished to see him in such a black mood. Their master was usually an even-tempered man whose rare displays of temper were usually justified. His butler reflected that his lordship had never been so downcast and wondered what had occurred at Throxton Hall to cause this depression.

The morning after his arrival in London, Ashford was sitting in his library drearily attempting to write a letter to Miss Camden that would adequately express his feelings. He was having little success and crumpled up the paper and tossed it into the fire.

"Excuse me, my lord." The voice of his butler brought Ashford out of his melancholy musings.

"What is it, Smithson?"

"There is a lady and gentleman to see you," said Smithson with a tinge of excitement in his voice.

"Who the devil is it?"

"It is Mr. Albert Stonecipher and Lady Arabella Stonecipher, my lord," said the butler, watching his master closely to see the reaction this announcement caused.

To Smithson's disappointment the Marquis received the news with calm reservation. "I will be in to see them," he said.

Ashford entered the drawing room and surveyed the visitors. Mr. Stonecipher was a stocky, gruff-looking individual who bore no resemblance to his son. Lady Arabella, his lordship's older sister, looked quite beautiful. She appeared quite youthful and was attired in a most becoming and fashionable blue dress, which set off her gold curls to perfection.

"Arabella," said his lordship.

"Geoffrey," replied her ladyship coolly.

"And Mr. Stonecipher."

"Lord Ashford," replied Stonecipher, gruffly shaking the hand that Ashford had extended to him.

"My lord," began Stonecipher, "I know it's damned

awkward for us coming here like this, you never giving us leave and all. But I have come about our son."

"Indeed," said Ashford curiously.

"We have heard that he had taken up with you." Stonecipher looked shrewdly at his lordship. "And I find it damned odd."

"Albert," said Lady Arabella.

"Yes, I do," continued Mr. Stonecipher, undeterred by his wife's warning. "After all, sir, I know Reginald and he ain't the sort a man like you would want to associate with."

"Albert!" cried his wife.

"Damn it," continued Mr. Stonecipher, "it's true. He's a young fool and a man of his lordship's cut don't seem likely to put up with that sort."

Lord Ashford looked at Stonecipher with amusement and found that he was beginning to like the man. He made no reply and Stonecipher continued.

"Arabella told me that Reginald was going to try and meet you and I found that likely, you being his uncle, but when I heard you were sponsoring him in high society I began to get suspicious." Mr. Stonecipher paused and looked at Ashford. "I could only conclude, my lord, that there was more to this than meets the eye. I never told Arabella this 'cause she's still your sister and she never would have agreed to us coming if she knew what I was going to say to you."

"And what, my good sir, did you conclude?" said Ashford curiously.

"That you was trying to get on Reginald's good side so as to hit him for some money."

"What?" said Ashford incredulously.

"I know you nobs got your high expenses, and although Arabella insists you've got plenty I know how you high ones can go through the blunt."

Ashford stared unbelievingly at his visitor. "You believe that I am paying attention to your son to get money from you?"

"I can think of no other reason."

Ashford laughed. "I can't believe this, sir," he said. "Is there no end to the insults I must endure? And I must tell you that I know the true state of your fortune. Why should I try to get money from a man who is financially ruined?"

"What!" cried Stonecipher. "What do you mean?"

"I have been informed that your factories have been losing money and that you face ruin."

"Oh God!" exclaimed Mr. Stonecipher, guffawing loudly. "Ruin! Why, you must have mighty inferior sources of information, my lord. Ruined? Good God, sir, I am one of the richest men in England."

"Albert," cried Lady Arabella, who had been listening to this conversation in amazement. "Is that true, Albert?" asked Lady Arabella. "But what about Bingham's Blacking? Maggie told me Stonecipher's was being cut out of the market."

"Good heavens!" cried Stonecipher. "You mean to say you thought I was facing financial ruin? By my soul, Ara, I can't believe it. Why, the business has never been better. I bought up Bingham's three months ago. Kept it quiet though. Didn't even tell Skruggs, since I knew Maggie would blather the news about."

"But why were you so upset when Reginald lost the money gaming?" asked his wife.

"By God, ma'am," cried Stonecipher. "You expect me to coolly stand by while your son turns into a damned gamester?"

Ashford watched the two of them with considerable interest. "I hate to interrupt you two," he said finally, "but am I to understand that you are even richer now than before?"

"I am indeed, my lord."

"Then I wonder why a number of people, including your own son, believe you to be a mere step away from debtors' prison."

Stonecipher looked at his wife with a bewildered expression and Lady Arabella looked at the floor in embarrassment.

"Good God, Arabella, you mean you actually believed me on the brink of financial disaster?"

"Oh, Albert," cried his wife, bursting into tears. "I am the greatest simpleton. Maggie said you were in trouble and I know that you will never discuss the business with me, and I fear I told Reginald what Maggie said."

Stonecipher patted his wife sympathetically. "Don't cry, my sweet," he said. "No harm done."

Stonecipher turned to Ashford. "You thought I was a pauper, sir?"

"I was unaware of your alleged poverty until yesterday. But don't worry that I was scheming to take poor Reginald's fortune. In spite of my profligate ways, I have somehow managed to hang on to some of my fortune. If you would care to go over my accounts, sir, I will have my man show them to you."

"That won't be necessary, my lord," said Stonecipher. "But if you would tell me where I might find Reginald."

"I have not the slightest idea, sir," returned his lordship. "He was to return to London, but thus far has not returned or at least has not returned my carriage."

"What?"

"Nothing, sir. I loaned him my carriage and he will return it to me when he arrives."

"Well, if your lordship will excuse us," said Mr. Stonecipher, "we will be going."

"Are you staying in London?"

"Yes. I will have to see that son of mine."

"Then, Mr. Stonecipher," said his lordship, "and Arabella." He extended his hand to his sister. "You will stay here with me."

Arabella looked at her brother in surprise. "You want us to stay here?"

"Yes, I do," replied Ashford. "It is time to end this silly feud. Had I ever met your admirable husband, Arabella, I would have insisted on reconciliation immediately. After all, I was only a boy when you were married. I suppose I accepted your estrangement from the family as a long-standing tradition."

Mr. Stonecipher looked at Ashford. "If you ain't a right one, my lord," he said in admiration.

"Nonsense," replied Ashford, clapping him on the shoulder. "I would be a fool to reject a brother-in-law who was one of the richest men in England. And please, sir, you must call me Ashford."

After making sure that his guests were well taken care of, Ashford retired to the library to make another attempt at writing Miss Camden. He began writing, stopped, and crumpled up his paper in disgust. He started again but his second letter met a similar fate.

"God," cried his lordship, "I will soon deplete my supply of writing paper at this rate." Lord Ashford rose from his desk and began to pace back and forth. *Damn,* he thought, *I was an ass for leaving that accursed Throxton Hall without Cecily.*

He continued pacing but stopped suddenly as an idea occurred to him. "Throxton or no, I am going back for Cecily," he said. "I'll not have her living at that madhouse with that half-witted cousin of hers." He rang for his butler, who appeared instantly.

"My lord," said the butler.

"Smithson, I am leaving for Throxton Hall immediately. Inform the grooms. I'll want the carriage, the new one. And Cooper can drive me. And Bigelow. Tell them to be ready or I'll have their heads."

"Yes, my lord," answered Smithson in some surprise. His master had been behaving strangely but this was strangest of all. To return early from a country visit in the blackest of moods and suddenly insist upon returning to what must have been a disagreeable place was most peculiar.

Smithson sighed softly and left to convey his lordship's instructions to the grooms.

Ashford quickly wrote a letter of explanation for the

Stoneciphers and retired to his bedchamber, where he instructed his valet to arrange for his journey. Twilling received the news without any noticeable reaction and went busily about his work.

Soon Ashford was on the road to Throxton Hall. He gazed impatiently at the passing scenery. *I should be at Throxton Hall by late afternoon,* he said to himself and smiled as he thought of being reunited with his beloved Cecily.

CHAPTER 15

Jeeters Crimpson was as cheerful as ever as he helped his friend prepare for his rendezvous with Lady Prunella Throckmorton. In contrast, Reginald was in one of his blackest tempers. Hacker, who had endured the worst of his young master's tantrums, couldn't recall any to equal the foul mood Mr. Stonecipher was presently in. Reginald's black mood didn't appear to affect Jeeters at all. He gaily hummed a tune as he watched his friend finish dressing.

"Come on, Reg, hurry, won't you? You don't want to keep the fair Prunella waiting, do you?"

Reginald picked up his boot and waved it menacingly at his friend. "Damnation, Jeeters, if you don't stop it I swear you will feel my boot!"

"Why, Reggie!" said Jeeters in a shocked voice, "how can you talk to your old chum that way?"

Reginald put down the boot and growled. "Some friend. I'm facing the firing squad and you're acting as happy as a hog in a wallow."

Jeeters chuckled. "Of course I'm happy. You've fought hard and won the prize."

"The prize? Prunella?" said Reginald with distaste.

"Well, she ain't a fairy princess," said Jeeters philosophically, "but at least you'll get to live like a prince off the Throckmorton purse."

Reginald muttered nervously, "But what if old Lord Throxton decides to boot us out after all?"

"Dash it, Reggie, you know he wouldn't cut off his darling Prunella. Besides, once the old boy gets used to the idea I'll bet he'll think of you just like a son. And wait until you see how he dotes on his grandchildren."

"Oh God, his grandchildren," said Reginald, repulsed.

Jeeters took his watch from his pocket, glanced at it, and frowned. "Reg, you really must move quickly. The carriage I hired to drive you and Prunella to Scotland should be arriving in a few moments."

His friend sighed deeply. "Oh, all right. There's no way out now."

As Jeeters had predicted, a few minutes later there was a knock on the door. Hacker answered it and came back to announce that the person with the carriage had arrived for Mr. Stonecipher. Reginald grimaced and yelled at the valet to take his things to the vehicle.

Hacker carried the huge portmanteau out the door and Reginald turned gloomily to Jeeters. "Well, I guess this is it, Jeeters." He stuck out his hand and smiled bravely.

Jeeters grabbed the hand and squeezed it. "Bear up, old boy, it will all be over before you know it." He patted Reginald on the back and pushed him toward the door.

"Oh, wait a minute," Jeeters suddenly cried. He ran into the other room and returned with Reginald's furry adversary, the liver-and-white spaniel.

"What the deuce did you get that blasted thing for?" shouted Reginald. The dog, seeing Reginald, immediately started yapping at him.

"Why, Reg, Prunella would think you hardhearted if you left behind your beloved Blackie."

Reginald scowled at his friend and grabbed up the noisy bundle. "I swear, Jeeters, if I live through this you had better beware!" With that threat he abruptly walked out the door, with Blackie protesting loudly in his arms.

* * *

The carriage stopped at the appointed meeting place at Potter's Crossing and Reginald was dismayed to find Prunella waiting there already. When she saw Reginald her face lit up in a blissful smile. "Oh, Reginald!" she gushed, running to him.

Reginald took her hand and kissed it. He felt as though he were living out some dreadful joke. "Prunella, my dear!" he choked. His beloved, thinking him overcome with emotion, flushed happily.

"Oh, we must hurry. I don't know what Papa should do if he should find us."

"What?" said Reginald, alarmed. "Does your father know you're gone?"

"Of course not!" giggled Prunella. "I was very clever in making my escape." Reginald looked at her somewhat dubiously.

"Well, my sweet," he said, "we had better fly."

"Yes, Reginald darling," she said. "I will just get my little darlings and we can be off."

Reginald looked at Prunella, dumbfounded. "Your what?"

"Why, my Tutti and FruFru," said Prunella as she stepped over to her luggage. Stooping behind a bag, she picked up the two plump spaniels.

"Oh God, no," muttered Reginald.

"What?" asked Prunella, looking over at him.

"Er, I just said how sweet," said Reginald quickly. "I brought my little Blackie along too."

"Wonderful!" cried Prunella as she hugged the two dogs to her. Tutti and FruFru, irritated at being disturbed from their rest, began barking. Blackie jumped up to the carriage window and joined in the din.

Reginald cursed to himself and glanced around apprehensively. "Come, Prunella, we must go right away or we'll be found out."

Prunella hugged the dogs again and hurried over to the carriage. Reginald helped her into the vehicle with some effort. *By God, what a load,* he thought. He shouted at the driver to get the lady's bag. The driver, a rough-looking man with a grizzled face, muttered something and jumped down from his seat. Reginald watched him somewhat anxiously as he dragged the bag over to the carriage.

Wonder where Jeeters found that fellow, he thought. *He looks like he makes a living of slitting throats.*

"Are you ready, sir?" sneered the driver after he had lifted the bag onto the coach. Reginald detected the contempt in the man's tone and for the first time felt intimidated by an inferior.

"Yes, we're ready," he replied with as much authority as he could muster.

Reginald climbed into the carriage next to Prunella. The dogs continued barking and jumping around the now moving carriage.

"Quiet," said Reginald to the dogs, attempting to remain calm. However, when the dogs continued their yapping he lost his temper and shouted, "Damn it, be quiet!"

Prunella gasped. "Reginald, how could you?" Her eyes were wide with shock.

"I'm sorry, dearest," he said, patting her hand. "I'm just anxious about our getting away safely."

Prunella grasped his arm. "I understand, Reginald." She leaned her head on his shoulder and smiled happily. Reginald sat silently muttering oaths to himself.

At least the blasted dogs have quit yelping for a time, he thought as he glanced over at them. They appeared to be worn out from all their exertions.

Reginald was also relieved that Prunella was quiet. He didn't think he could endure her brainless chatter during the entire journey. However, after some distance he began to grow uncomfortable with Prunella's head leaning heavily on his shoulder. He suddenly shifted his position, causing Prunella's head to jerk off his shoulder. She gave an exclamation of surprise and looked at him.

"Is something wrong, dearest?"

"No, nothing at all," Reginald answered brusquely.

Prunella, thinking she knew the cause for the troubled look on her beloved's face, squeezed his arm reassuringly.

"Don't worry about Papa, dearest. He'll never find us!" She gazed dreamily at Reginald. "I don't believe this is happening to me. It's so romantic!" she squeaked. Prunella reached over the seat for FruFru.

"Darling, isn't your Papa wonderful?" she said in a babyish voice, pulling the dog's fluffy ears. FruFru immediately started barking again. The other two spaniels, not wanting to be outdone, also started yelping. Blackie leaped over to Prunella's lap and began jumping all over her.

"Oh, but you're a playful one," giggled Prunella. She caught Blackie up in her arms and put him on Reginald's lap. "Now you talk to your Papa for a while."

The dog began growling and then started clawing at Reginald's pantaloons, causing the would-be bridegroom to finally lose control. He picked up the dog and flung it over to the other side of the carriage.

"Blast these dogs! I'm sick to death of them!" he shouted angrily.

Prunella drew back from him in horror. "Reginald! How could you?" She burst into tears, hugging FruFru close to her bosom.

"Will you quit that infernal wailing?" yelled Reginald. His outburst caused Prunella to sob even louder.

Blackie and Tutti were growling from the other side of the carriage at Reginald and appeared ready to lunge for his throat. He glanced at them threateningly. "Just try it, you bastards!"

"I'm going to faint!" shrieked Prunella.

"Thank God!" said Reginald. "Then I won't have to listen to your caterwauling."

However, her ladyship did not faint. She continued sobbing loudly, gulping every few seconds for air.

She dabbed her crumpled handkerchief at the tears rolling down her cheeks and said falteringly, "You are horrid. I shan't marry you. Take me back to my papa."

Reginald burst out laughing. "It's too late now, Lady

Pru. You've been compromised by running off with me and the only way out is to become my wife."

Prunella shrieked again and this time all three dogs went into action and leaped on Reginald.

"Damnation!" shouted Reginald, fending off the dogs. He grabbed Blackie by the scruff of the neck and tossed him out of the carriage window.

"No!" screamed Prunella. She began pummelling Reginald's shoulder with her fists.

The coach driver began to wonder what all the commotion was about inside the carriage. He turned around and saw the dog come flying out the window. "What the devil! What's going on back there?" he shouted.

While his attention was diverted from the road he failed to see a large rock in the path of the carriage. One of the carriage wheels hit the rock and there was a loud crunch as one of the spokes snapped.

"Damn blast it!" bellowed the driver as he quickly pulled up the horses. He jumped down from the carriage and surveyed the wheel, muttering darkly to himself.

Reginald was eager to escape from Prunella and the dogs and quickly climbed out of the carriage. "What in God's name has happened?" he said crossly as he walked over to the driver. He was met by a murderous look and retreated a few steps from the towering form of the driver. "Oh, I mean, have we had a little mishap?" he asked politely.

"By God!" fumed the driver. "If it weren't for all that commotion you was kickin' up back there, I would've noticed the accursed rock." He leered at Reginald unpleasantly. "When your friend hired me he said this would be an elopement . . . not a kidnaping."

"Kidnaping?" gulped Reginald.

The coachman eyed him contemptuously a few moments and then guffawed. "I don't care what you call it. It's just that I ain't putting up with some kicking, screaming female for the rest of this trip, not to mention this blasted wheel, without something extra to make it worth the trouble . . . if you know what I mean," he added with a grin.

Oh Lord, thought Reginald fearfully, *Jeeters has hired me a bloody highwayman!*

Reginald eyed the driver warily as Prunella scrambled out of the carriage. She ran blindly over to the driver and grabbed his arm. "You must help me escape from this madman!" she cried.

The driver looked down at her in amazement. She was clutching his arm and watching Reginald with a terrified expression on her tear-stained face.

"If this ain't rich!" chortled the coachman. Prunella let go of his arm and stared at him in alarm.

The scene was suddenly interrupted by furious barking. Blackie had survived his fall from the carriage and was seeking revenge. The small dog ran over to Reginald and sank his teeth into his finely polished boot.

"Blast it, you mutt, get away from me!" cried his victim, attempting to shake the dog loose. The coachman was highly amused as he watched Reginald fight off the dog. Prunella viewed the scene in horror.

To Reginald's relief a stern voice called out a command and Blackie finally let go of his boot. Reginald looked up and was shocked to see his uncle, Lord Ashford. Reginald had been so involved in his struggle with the spaniel that he had failed to notice Ashford's carriage drive up.

The Marquis had been quite as shocked as Reginald when his carriage approached the outrageous scene. "What the deuce?" he uttered out loud as he saw the waylaid carriage and his nephew being attacked by the small dog. He observed Prunella and realized that he had happened upon an elopement. *Why am I cursed with such idiot nephews?* he thought as he jumped down from his carriage.

Reginald flushed under his uncle's icy stare. "Uncle Geoffrey, I—that is—we—" he stammered.

Unlike Reginald, Prunella had no difficulty finding any words. She flew over to Ashford and began the long tragic tale of her ill treatment. Ashford listened to her calmly for a while and then cut her off, saying, "That will do for now, ma'am. I've heard quite enough about my nephew's infamous behavior. Reginald," he continued in a cool voice, "I wish to speak to you privately."

Reginald grimly followed his uncle away from the carriage.

"You young fool," said Ashford angrily. "What business is this, running off with the Throckmorton girl? By God, you're worse than Chesterfield."

"You don't understand," said Reginald indignantly. "It was the only thing I could do."

"Yes, I do understand," replied Ashford. "You thought your father's fortune was collapsing and so you schemed to marry an heiress. Unfortunately, I was dragged into your scheme. And so, it appears, was Lady Prunella," he said, casting an ironical glance at the lady.

The Marquis looked back at Reginald. "Why did you throw away the game when you were so close to victory?"

Reginald gave a half shrug. "Oh Lord, I don't know. I was never much for the idea anyway, but Jeeters said . . ."

"Ah, I thought that fellow might have something to do with it," observed Ashford.

"Well, anyway, I guess what with Prunella and those blasted dogs I decided I might be better off a begger after all."

Ashford laughed. "You are foolish, Nephew, but also damned lucky. You're not a begger. Your father is richer today than he ever was."

"What!" exclaimed Reginald incredulously. "But the business . . . Bingham's bootblack . . ."

"Your father owns Bingham's," said Ashford. "That story you heard was poppycock."

"It was!" cried Reginald excitedly. He suddenly looked puzzled. "But how do you know all this, sir?"

"Your parents came to visit me. It seems your father thought I was trying to put the touch on you."

"Oh God, no!" said Reginald, mortified. "Will the old boy never stop humiliating me?" he muttered.

"Your father is a fine man," said Ashford angrily. "God

knows why he had to be saddled with such a coxcomb for a son!"

Reginald stuck out his lip in a pout. Ashford looked at him and shook his head. "Damned if I can't see a resemblance to Chesterfield." He turned his glance back toward Prunella. "I suppose we better see to the business at hand. I'll take Lady Pru back to Throxton Hall and you better be on your way back to town as fast as you can."

His nephew smiled a bit nervously. "Don't worry. I can't wait to get away from here." Ashford walked back over to Prunella and the coachman.

"I'll take you back to Throxton Hall now, Lady Prunella," said Ashford.

"Oh thank you, my lord," cried Prunella. Ashford helped her into his carriage and she began chattering. "I'm afraid I was very stupid about everything. I thought your nephew was such a gentleman. Imagine being married to such a beast!"

"Yes," replied Ashford gravely, "you've made a narrow escape."

Prunella looked at him and giggled. "Do you know, my lord, I thought you were the villainous one. But you are not at all like the wicked Baron Diablo."

"I am truly relieved to hear that," he replied, smiling.

"Cecily was right about you. In fact," she sighed, "my cousin was right about everything."

A look of amusement came into Ashford's eyes. "Your cousin is indeed remarkable."

Prunella nodded and settled back in the carriage. Ashford told her he would be back directly and began walking toward Reginald. Before he got a few feet a frantic voice called to him.

"Oh, my lord, my dogs!" cried Prunella. "I must have my Tutti and FruFru. They are in the other carriage."

Ashford turned and replied in mock gravity, "Have no fear, ma'am. I will rescue your dogs from the clutches of my nephew."

Reginald heard the exchange and as his uncle approached he said, "Tell Lady Pru she can have my mutt, too. God, I never want to see one of those blasted pug faces again."

Ashford looked at him critically. "Nephew, I wish I could feel that you've learned something from this episode but I fear it is too much to hope." Reginald stared at him in unrepentant silence. Ashford shrugged. "I advise you to follow a straighter course when you return to London."

Reginald still looked unrepentant but replied hastily, "I shall do so, Uncle."

"See that you do," replied the Marquis, who then returned to his carriage and Lady Prunella and drove off.

Reginald watched his uncle's carriage travel down the road and suddenly remembered that he was still stranded on a country road. The coachman stood near the disabled carriage and Reginald turned to him. "Well, my good man, see to finding me a way back to the village." The coachman made no reply but twisted his mouth into a sinister grin.

Jeeters Crimpson had found some very jovial company at the inn after sending off his dear friend Reginald on his romantic adventure. Mr. Crimpson was in exceptionally high spirits as he sat downing pints of ale and trading anecdotes with some young gentlemen who had recently arrived at the inn.

The time was passing very agreeably and Jeeters was filled with a sense of well-being that could be attributed to the quantity of ale he had consumed and the knowledge that his dearest friend was on his way to Scotland with an heiress. "Good old Reggie," mumbled Jeeters in a slightly inebriated state. "And not one to forget his oldest and dearest friend."

But just as Jeeters was uttering these sentiments, the door of the inn was flung open and in strode the object of Mr. Crimpson's sentimental reflections.

"Good lord, Reggie!" cried Jeeters in astonishment, and

his drinking companions looked questionably at the now rather disheveled-looking young man who had just entered. "What in God's name has happened?" continued Jeeters, getting up from the table with some difficulty and walking over to his friend.

Reginald scowled at him and sank exhaustedly into the nearest chair.

"In God's name, Reg," cried Jeeters. "What has happened? Not highwaymen? And where is Lady Pru?"

Reginald looked darkly at his friend and replied, "Yes, it was a highwayman, the one you hired to drive the damned coach."

A look of horror came to Jeeters's face as he surveyed his friend's appearance. Reginald's coat was torn and his neckcloth hung in ragged disarray. His boots were covered with mud and his handsome face was marred with a very nasty purple and black bruise beneath his eye.

"But how was I to know, Reginald? You can't blame me. Surely not. Although he did look to be a nasty brute, but God, Reg, these fellows always look to be nasty brutes. But Lady Prunella. What the devil happened to her? I don't want to think of this and we are so near Throxton Hall. His lordship will have our heads."

"Dash it, Jeeters. It is I who will have your head. Precious Prunella is in good hands. She went off with my beloved uncle."

Jeeters was thunderstruck. "Reginald, you must have suffered head injuries. Prunella off with Lord Ashford? Come come, old man, pull yourself together."

"Damn it," replied Reginald harshly. "Of course she ain't run off with him. He's taken her back to her father. And he left me there with the bloody highwayman. A miracle I'm alive. Oh God, I ache all over. And after the rogue beats me and takes every last penny I have, I have to walk all the way back here. Must have been nigh on six miles and here you are sitting warm and cozy. Lucky for you, Jeeters, I'm too damned tired to kill you."

Jeeters was so relieved to find that Lady Prunella had

not fallen victim to the highwayman that he listened to the rest of his friend's talk without much concern.

"Come now, Reggie," said Jeeters, patting him on the shoulder and ignoring the glowering looks that greeted his sympathetic gesture. "It ain't so bad. He didn't kill you, now did he? And when I think of the fellow I suppose it is a miracle. But you can't blame me after all."

"I can and do," shouted Reginald. "It was you who put me up to this business in the first place. Forcing me to marry Prunella. Oh God! At least I am not tied to that scatterbrain. I shudder to think of it."

"But what happened and where did Ashford come in? I swear that fellow is always around at the most inopportune times."

Reginald glumly began to relate the experience and as he described Prunella and her dogs and the broken wheel, Jeeters's face suddenly broke into a grin and he burst into laughter.

"Jeeters," cried his friend, "I swear I shall kill you!" But he, too, found himself breaking into laughter.

"There, you see, old chap," cried Jeeters merrily. "There's my old Reggie. A damned funny business it was. And I knew you couldn't be angry at your dearest friend, who's only concerned for your welfare."

"Damn it, Jeeters," laughed Reginald. "You've been concerned about your own welfare and you know it and a cheeky bastard you are, but damned if I won't forgive you."

"That's the spirit, Reginald! And I've got a bit of your uncle's blunt left. You'll feel better after a bit of ale. And who cares if we're paupers? There's other rich young ladies who'll fall for your charm."

Reginald laughed. "No more talk of that. I swear I'll cut out your liver and feed it to the crows if I hear that again. And I shouldn't tell you this but I'm damned if I ain't rich, or will be."

"What's that?" asked Jeeters.

"This business of my father's fortune. Damned if it

weren't a lot of loose talk. My dear papa remains rich to a somewhat vulgar degree. And none other than the Marquis of Ashford has told me, so you can be sure it's true. So now, my dear Jeeters, it's you we find the rich wife for!"

Jeeters broke into hearty laughter, slapped his now jovial friend on the back, and called for some ale and dinner to celebrate.

When Prunella's elopement was discovered, the entire Throxton household was thrown into an uproar. Prunella had left a very melodramatic note for her parents, and the Countess of Throxton had an attack of the vapors upon reading it. The Earl shouted about honor and vengeance, causing Lord Higglesby-Smythe and Cecily to come running to see what was the matter.

"Please, sir," said Higglesby-Smythe, "what is wrong? Is it Prunella?"

Lord Throxton nodded and handed Higglesby-Smythe the missive.

"God," sputtered his young lordship. "This is infamous! We must save Prunella!"

"Yes, we will," said Lord Throxton, patting his wife's hand. "Never fear, Elizabeth. They couldn't have gone far."

"No, Uncle," contributed Cecily. "I saw Prunella not more than two hours ago."

"Then we can catch them," said Lord Throxton eagerly. "I will get some of my men. If I could ride I could catch 'em myself! A plague on this infernal gout."

"Never fear, sir," cried Lord Higglesby-Smythe. "I'm off myself and I'll catch them. That dastardly villain Stonecipher will pay. By my honor, he will pay!" Before Lord Throxton could reply, Lord Higglesby-Smythe dashed out of the house as fast as his rotund form would allow him and over to the stables, where he called a groom to saddle the fastest horse. The grooms were amazed to see Lord Higglesby-Smythe so animated and rushed to make ready a horse.

Higglesby-Smythe leaped onto the unsuspecting animal, whipped it savagely into a gallop, and raced toward the road. The grooms watched in amazement and then were treated to the sight of Lord Throxton limping from the house, waving his hands and shouting.

Higglesby-Smythe had gotten only a few hundred yards when he spied a carriage approaching. As the vehicle neared him, Lord Higglesby-Smythe slowed his mount and moved over from the road. The carriage slowed too and as it passed him, Higglesby-Smythe saw Prunella's face in the window.

"Prunella!" cried Higglesby-Smythe, turning his horse and shouting.

Prunella looked out the window. "It's Gerald," she cried. "Lord Ashford, stop." Ashford peered out the window and saw Higglesby-Smythe racing after them. "Stop!" he called to his driver, and the man obediently pulled up the horses.

Higglesby-Smythe rushed up to the carriage, dismounted, and ran over to the carriage door. He flung the door open and cried "Stonecipher, you villain, get out, you despicable viper. I am calling you out."

"My dear Higglesby-Smythe," said Lord Ashford, emerging from the carriage. "I fear my nephew Reginald cannot oblige you. He is not here."

Higglesby-Smythe stared at Ashford. "What?" he said. "What is the meaning of this, sir?"

Ashford helped Prunella out of the carriage.

"Prunella!" cried Higglesby-Smythe in an enraged voice. "You had better explain this."

"Oh, Gerald!" cried Prunella, rushing up to Higglesby-Smythe and throwing her arms around his neck. "Forgive me, Gerald."

Lord Higglesby-Smythe accepted this embrace with an astonished look on his face. He placed his arms around Prunella protectively and said, "You silly goose, Prunella. I was off to find you. Where is that damned Stonecipher and what is Ashford doing here?"

"Oh, Gerald!" exclaimed Prunella, her face buried in Lord Higglesby-Smythe's ample chest. "You were going to rescue me?"

"I was indeed," said Lord Higglesby-Smythe, "and I demand to know what you are doing with Lord Ashford."

"Oh, Gerald," said Prunella, looking up into Higglesby-Smythe's eyes. "Lord Ashford saved me. He happened by just as I had realized the true nature of Reginald Stonecipher. Oh, Gerald, he is such a beast. If Lord Ashford had not come along Mr. Stonecipher would have forced me into marriage."

"The blackguard," said Lord Higglesby-Smythe. He looked at Ashford. "I see I am in your debt, sir."

"I assure you, sir," replied the Marquis, smiling graciously, "I was most happy to aid a lady in distress. I regret that Reginald Stonecipher is my nephew but, unfortunately, there is no way to alter that. However, I would be obliged to you, sir, if you do not seek vengeance upon him. You see, my dear Lord Higglesby-Smythe, if you were to demand satisfaction and kill my nephew I would have a difficult time of it with my sister Arabella. And since I have only just been reconciled with her, it would be a pity to offend her. So I hope you will leave my wretched nephew's punishment to the fates."

Lord Higglesby-Smythe thought this over for a few minutes. He looked questioningly down at Prunella.

"Oh please, Gerald, I owe Lord Ashford so much. You must spare his nephew."

"Well," said Higglesby-Smythe slowly, "I will do as you ask, sir, but I warn you that if I see that man again I may not be able to control my temper."

"That is very generous of you, sir," said Ashford. "And now if you will allow Lady Prunella to return to the carriage." Prunella continued to grip Higglesby-Smythe tightly. Ashford noted this and continued, "And I insist that Lord Higglesby-Smythe accompany you, Lady Prunella. I shall follow on the horse."

Higglesby-Smythe and Prunella found this arrangement most agreeable and without another comment entered the carriage.

Ashford mounted Higglesby-Smythe's horse and set off. "Go ahead," he said to his driver and the carriage continued on to Throxton Hall.

Lord Throxton was outside rushing frantically back and forth. He watched the carriage approach and recognized Ashford as the rider following the carriage.

"By God," shouted Lord Throxton. "What the . . . ?" The carriage stopped in front of Lord Throxton, and Ashford's groom jumped down and opened the carriage door.

Lord Throxton watched in surprise as Higglesby-Smythe and his daughter Prunella emerged. "By Jove!" cried Throxton as Prunella raced into his arms.

"Papa," she cried.

"I daresay, Higglesby-Smythe," said Lord Throxton, "you do act quickly when you act!"

"Well, sir," said Lord Higglesby-Smythe, "I must say it was Ashford's doing. He rescued Pru from his infamous nephew Stonecipher. He was bringing her back when I caught up with them."

Ashford had by this time dismounted and Lord Throxton looked at him in embarrassment. "I daresay, Ashford," said Lord Throxton, "I am damned grateful to you. But I feel the fool. I should have known you to be a man of honor. I hope you can accept my humble apology, sir."

"With pleasure," said Ashford, smiling and extending his hand. Throxton grasped it warmly.

"Prunella!" cried a voice from the house as Lady Throxton rushed out.

"Mama," cried Prunella, disengaging herself from her father and embracing her mother. "Mama, Ashford saved me from that dastardly Stonecipher. I am such a great ninny." Prunella burst into tears.

"Oh, dearest," said her mother soothingly. "I am so glad you have returned. I have never been so happy."

Lord Higglesby-Smythe cleared his throat and began speaking in a halting voice. "Lord Throxton," he said, "I hope you will grant me the favor of your daughter's hand in marriage."

"What?" said Lord Throxton in surprise.

"What is this?" asked her ladyship, equally astonished.

"Oh yes," cried Prunella, leaving her mother and rushing to Higglesby-Smythe's side. "It is Gerald that I truly love and wish to marry."

"Oh, this is marvelous," cried Lady Throxton, raising her eyes gratefully to the heavens.

"It is indeed," said Throxton enthusiastically, patting his future son-in-law on the back. "I say, Gerald, there is no one else I had ever hoped to have my dear Pru's hand in marriage. You have my blessing."

Lord Ashford had had little interest in the scene. He had seen Miss Camden follow Lady Throxton from the house and his attention was focused on her.

"Felicitations," said the Marquis absently to Higglesby-Smythe, and since the happy couple and the Throxtons were paying little attention to him, he turned to Cecily.

"My lord," said Miss Camden, "I see you are a hero of some kind. But I never thought to see you again."

"Cecily," said his lordship, taking her hands in his. "Since I have left this abominable house I could think of nothing but returning."

"Returning?" asked Cecily in some surprise.

"Yes, for you," replied the Marquis softly.

"Oh, Ashford," said Cecily, trembling, "can you mean it?"

"My darling," said Ashford, raising her hands to his lips and kissing them gently. "I love you so very much. I want you desperately. I hope that you will consent to be my wife."

Cecily flung her arms around his neck and hugged him tightly. He put one hand under her chin and raised her face to his, kissing her tenderly and passionately.

"Dearest," he murmured, "does this mean that you will marry me?" She laughed and kissed him again.

"I love you so much," she whispered. "I never thought it possible to love someone like this."

His lordship made no reply but embraced Cecily tightly.

At that moment Lady Throxton glanced over and saw her niece locked in Ashford's embrace. "Oh my heavens," cried Lady Throxton to her husband. "Do something."

"By Jove," said her husband. "Looks like another wedding in the family."

"Ashford," whispered Cecily, finally noticing her aunt's disapproving stare, "I fear we are being observed."

Ashford looked in Lady Throxton's direction. "Never fear, my darling," he said. "Nothing can shock Lady Throxton after the exploits of Lady Pru."

Cecily laughed and, ignoring her aunt, joyfully kissed the smiling Marquis.